SAVED BY TWO

L.S. PULLEN

Copyright © 2023 by L.S. Pullen

Saved by Two

Text copyright © 2023 L. S. Pullen

All Rights Reserved

Published by: L.S. Pullen

Edited by: Cassie Sharp

Proofread by: Crystal Blanton

Formatted by: L.S. Pullen

Cover: Licensed Stock Designed by L.S. Pullen

The right of L.S. Pullen to be identified as the author of the work has been asserted by her in accordance with the copyright, Designs and patents act 1988

No part of this book may be reproduced in any form or by any electronic or mechanical means, including information storage and retrieval systems, without written permission from the author, except for the use of brief quotations in a book review.

All characters in this publication are fictional and any resemblance to real persons, living or dead, is purely coincidental.

To all the OG authors who paved the way to show us it can be done and continue to keep up the good fight. And to authors, both new and old, who continue to inspire me daily.

Author's Note

Due to adult content, all my books are recommended for readers 18 years and over.

For detailed CW/TW, please visit my Website
Thank you, and happy reading!

Chapter One

Jessica

I wrap my arms across my chest but can't stop the shivers that rattle through my body. The rain isn't helping, pelting me like sharp drops of stinging ice. And this oversized hoodie is doing nothing to keep my extremities warm.

There was no time to think of what to wear as I stuffed a bag full of essentials; my purse, a toiletry bag, sentimental items, a change of clothes and some underwear. That's all I have in my possession.

I blow out a breath, causing a cloud of mist and immediately wish I hadn't. The pain in my ribs hurts with every exhale and inhale.

Of course, the first place I tried was my brother, but I've not heard from him in months, which is worrying, and when I told Curtis I was worried, he told me to stop bitching.

I left countless voicemails and sent text messages, but they're all left on read.

He's the only family I have, well, the only family that matters, and I have no idea where he is or if he's all right.

And now I'm hiding in some bushes, scoping out the row of

beautiful townhouses to see if I can remember which house belongs to his friends, Caleb and Noah.

I've only met them once when they arranged a surprise party for him. He told me he trusted them explicitly and that if I ever needed anything, I could go to them. He always sang their praises, which coming from Mason, means a lot if he holds someone in such high esteem.

So here I am.

One of my eyes is now swollen shut, my head is pounding, and there's a heavy pulsing in my ears. Bile rises in my throat, but I force myself to swallow it back down. The thought of throwing up with how my ribs already hurt makes my breathing harsh as I tremble even more.

It's now or never.

I'm sure it's the one with the old-fashioned streetlight directly across from the townhouse, with the iron-wrought fence and those iconic stone pillars.

I take a slow step and look both ways before crossing the street, but I have to grab the railing for support to make my way up the small steps.

Pressing the doorbell, I shift uncomfortably on my feet. I can't even feel my toes. Staring down, it's only now I realise why. I'm still wearing my slippers. Not that anyone noticed, or if they did, I was too busy and desperate to get away to pay attention, but in somewhere like London, it's easy to disappear in the shadows and throngs of people on nights out. It's late and dark, which also seems to be in my favour.

I was only wearing a thin cotton t-shirt and bed shorts right before he lost his shit…

The door opens, and I'm temporarily shrouded in light before a dark shadow forms a silhouette in the entryway.

"That was quick," says a deep voice with an Irish lilt, and I know without even seeing his face that it's Caleb. He steps forward as I look up through the hood surrounding my face.

"Sorry, I thought you were the delivery guy," he says, but the smile on his face falls, and if I look as bad as I feel, there's no surprise as to why.

Swaying on my feet, I feel lightheaded, like I might pass out, but he grabs the top of my arm, causing me to flinch and simultaneously let out a strangled cry.

"What the actual fuck? Are you okay?"

I try to answer, but I'm running on empty. Everything around me spins, making me nauseous and dizzy—black spots clouding my vision.

"Need help." My words sound cracked and croaky, slurred even, my windpipe hurting from the hands I once trusted holding my throat in a chokehold.

And then I'm falling, my entire body tense, expecting to connect with the concrete tiles beneath my feet, but then I'm floating, spinning, suddenly as light as air. It takes me a few moments before I realise Caleb caught me. His strong arms picked me up and are now cradling me to his solid chest.

"Shit, Noah," he booms.

I try to pry my good eye open or lift my hand, try anything, but my body is refusing to work; it's finally had enough, shutting down. Any energy reserves I might have had are well and truly diminished.

"What the hell?" another male voice says. I know it must be Noah. His voice reminds me so much of Tom Hardy. "Fuck, is that Mason's sister, Jessica?"

I feel a cool hand against my cheek, a whimper escapes me, and I know I flinch, my body's natural reaction to physical contact, even now.

"Sorry, sweetheart, can you hear me?"

I take in a deep breath. One I need in preparation to try to form an answer, but the action causes my ribs to groan in protest like heavy splinters.

"Squeeze my hand if you can't speak."

A warm, calloused palm gently takes my hand, and I listen to his instruction, using his coaxing voice as a guide. I give it a slight squeeze.

"Fuck, we need to call an ambulance or get her to the hospital."

My heart begins to accelerate at the thought, and I tremble, my entire body shaking uncontrollably. Fuck, is this shock? Am I going into shock?

"No, please," I rasp between my chattering teeth. "Not safe."

The sounds of murmurs breeze above me. Full-blown panic sets in again, unable to decide between flight or fight—in this moment, I know I have neither. I wonder if I ever did.

I make a poor attempt at trying to get him to release me, but my body feels weighted and entirely out of my control.

And then Caleb's moving as he holds me bridal style.

"Sssh, I'm just taking you to the guest bedroom, okay?"

The metallic smell dulls slightly as a masculine scent overrides it. For reasons I cannot even fathom, it makes me feel safe, makes it a little easier to breathe. I'm gently shifted out of those arms and onto fresh, crisp linen and a soft mattress, causing me to groan.

"Mitchell said he can be here in twenty."

The bed dips next to me. I feel the brush of fingertips against my temple, my hair matted to my face.

"Jessica, can you hear me?"

I force my good eye open and wait until Caleb comes into focus.

His eyes are dark as he takes in my face, his jaw chiselled like an ice sculpture.

"Who the fuck hurt you?" His question makes me tense, my breathing more erratic, wishing I could disappear.

Noah leans over and whispers something to Caleb. I watch as he grinds his jaw, his nostrils flaring. He inhales deeply and lets it out before taking my hand and speaking again.

"Sorry, Jessica, can you tell us what happened?" His voice is softer now but is still underlined with an unreleased fury.

Licking my cracked lips, I wince as the cut opens again, the wet taste of copper coating my tongue.

"I just need somewhere to stay for a couple of days." My voice is hoarse. I try to swallow to clear my throat, but it feels so raw.

Noah pats Caleb on the shoulder. "I'll go grab a bottle of water. Let us give her a minute," he says, and I close my eye, working on my breathing. Every single breath is becoming more of an effort now.

Caleb rubs his thumb in small circles over the back of my hand. I have no idea whether he's doing it subconsciously or intentionally, but I do know that slight touch is comforting.

I jerk awake, or back to reality, when Noah asks me if I'm thirsty.

I nod slightly, and Caleb reaches over and helps me sit up. I bite the inside of my cheek against the sharp pain. Noah holds the bottle to my mouth, and I manage a few small sips, the cool water like heaven. But I'm too afraid to drink anymore because it might make a re-appearance.

"T-thank you," I say, my teeth chattering, and I shiver. So bloody cold.

Noah glances at Caleb and then back to me.

"We need to get you out of those wet clothes."

I know he's right, so I give myself a moment and then try to push myself up and groan at the pain shooting up my wrist and arm. It's as though my senses are coming back to me. Everything is hypersensitive, and now I'm feeling everywhere he hurt me, everywhere his anger touched me and caused me pain.

"Here, let's just get the hoodie off you for now," Caleb says, and between him and Noah, they ever so carefully extract it from my body. They decide to leave my t-shirt and help me into an oversized sweater. It feels so soft, like cashmere, and smells expensive. I should feel bad for soiling their clothes and bed, but I'm too damn grateful to be out from the cold and wearing something dry.

I'm lulled into darkness again, drifting, being dragged under, when I hear voices, more than two, and the sound of footfalls pulls me back, there's a stranger staring down at me. I attempt to scoot back, but Noah stops me, his hand on my shoulder, gaining my attention.

"Don't panic, sweet girl. He's a friend and a doctor."

I stare from him to the stranger and then at Caleb, who gives me a curt, reassuring nod.

"Jessica, I'm just here to check you over and see your injuries. Is that okay?"

The thought of him seeing me in all my tragic glory makes me humiliated to my core, but at this point, my pride is the least of my worries.

Chapter Two

Jessica

I'm wary, of course. This man is a stranger. A doctor, yes, but even though I now know him to be Mitchell, it still does nothing to ease my nerves. I couldn't even trust the man who claimed to love me. And yet Mitchell is here for me, doing Caleb and Noah a favour, of that I am sure.

He studies my face and then lowers himself into the chair beside the bed—a tactical move, I think—his attempt to ease my anxiousness.

"Jessica, if it would make you feel more comfortable, Caleb or Noah can stay in the room while I examine you."

My heart beats faster, drumming in my ears. I have no idea to the full extent of what he might find. I just know that the pain is becoming even more unbearable with every passing moment. I'd rather it was just me and the doctor. Even though the thought of having him touch me is the last thing I want, even in a professional capacity, but what choice do I have? Going to a hospital is out of the question—I can't risk it.

Resolute, I exhale sharply and reply, "No, it's okay." But to my dismay, my voice wobbles.

Still on the opposite side of the bed, Noah takes my hand

gently in his. "You'll be fine. We'll be just outside in the hallway. If you want us to come back in at any time, Mitchell will call for me or Caleb."

I swallow, my throat protesting, and give a slight nod. I'm afraid it will all become too much if I speak, and I won't get through this next part.

"You're safe here, sweet girl. I swear it. And we trust this man with our lives, otherwise, he wouldn't be here. You're in safe hands."

I glance over and see Caleb standing ramrod straight, his hands tightly clenched into fists, his entire body practically vibrating with tension. His face softens when his eyes shift to mine, and he gives one curt nod before stepping out into the hallway.

Noah bends down and kisses the back of my hand before letting go, and I watch him follow Caleb, the sound of the door clicking closed behind them.

Mitchell leans down, opens a bag I didn't notice, and pulls out a blood pressure cuff.

"I will start with your blood pressure and ask you some questions. Is that okay?" he asks, wrapping the strap around my upper arm and closing it tightly, causing me to flinch.

"Sorry, let me loosen that a fraction." He loosens it on my arm and then presses something. The cuff begins to puff up with air as he squeezes a small pouch in his palm. "Is there any particular place you're experiencing more pain? And don't worry, I can give you some pain medication to help with that as we ascertain the extent of your injuries."

My hand automatically moves to my throat, and I touch the tender skin. "My ribs, it hurts to breathe."

He pushes his glasses up the bridge of his nose, and I notice a scar underneath his left cheekbone as he begins sanitising his hands, rubbing them together.

"I'm going to examine you now. Are you okay if I touch you?"

This is his profession, yet he still asks me for consent. The act alone causes my throat to thicken with building emotion, making it impossible to speak, so I nod my head once instead.

Starting with my head and face, he gently presses along my throat before asking me to open my mouth so he can look down my throat.

"The hoarseness you're experiencing in your larynx is likely due to the trauma you experienced. Rest your voice as much as possible and drink plenty of fluids to prevent dehydration."

He continues to let me know before he touches me as his examination moves to my torso where he raises the sweatshirt, exposing my midriff, and begins pressing lightly, prodding over the area. As he moves closer to where the pain is worst, I let out a hiss between my teeth.

And then his eyes lower to my shorts and the marks visible on the inside of thighs.

He pauses to look at me. "May I ask, is there any chance you could be pregnant?"

I shake my head. "No, I have a contraceptive implant."

Nodding, he glances to my thighs and then back to my face before clearing his throat. "I can see you have some abrasions. There's no easy way to ask you this, Jessica, but were you sexually assaulted?" The question causes bile to rise, and I don't know how to respond, even if I could find the words.

"It's okay. Just take a moment."

He reaches for the bottle of water and hands it to me, helping me sit forward to take a few sips before speaking.

"Honestly, I'm not sure, but I think so." My cheeks heat—not from embarrassment, but shame.

"All right, in that case, would you like me to take some swabs? We can rule out any potential STDs, and also, if you do decide to press charges, it could later be used as evidence."

Of course, he's right. I have no idea who Curtis might have been with besides me. He constantly harped on about how I was likely cheating on him, but it would no longer surprise me if he was just projecting his indiscretions onto me. Why can I see so much more with a renewed sense of clarity?

Probably because he beat me unconscious, and it took waking up the way I did to act—even if running is the coward's way out.

It's not like I've been anywhere in the last few months. I lost my place at culinary school—I couldn't turn up covered in bruises. I'm so fucking ashamed of myself, and I fight hard to keep my sob at bay, but it's no use.

Mitchell touches my shoulder to comfort me as I cry, and then he passes me some tissues. I wipe at my cheeks and under my nose, angry with myself and Curtis.

Eventually, I manage to speak around a hiccup, "I think it's better to be safe than sorry." The words taste bitter. If I'd had the guts to leave him sooner, I wouldn't be in this sorry state. I only have myself to blame.

He studies me. "Hey, you've done nothing wrong. You know this isn't your fault, right?"

I scoff at that. Easy for him to say; he wasn't the one who allowed this to happen. No, that's all on me.

"Do you want me to give you a few minutes?"

His bedside manner constricts my chest even more, his kindness almost too much.

"No," I reply in a rush. "Thank you, let's just get it over with."

Unable to look at him any longer, I roll my head back onto the pillow and stare at the ceiling. I listen to him as he gathers whatever he needs, and then I start counting in my head. I don't even stop when he asks me to spread my legs. I'm on autopilot now as I attempt to hide inside my mind, which would work better if I couldn't feel him taking swabs.

I close my eye and breathe, the pain from my ribs overpowering the stinging from between my legs.

Why did I wait so long before finally leaving the bastard? Oh, that's right, because for some reason, I believe in second and third and fourth chances, it would seem.

I hate to admit the fact this could have been prevented after the first time. I should have walked away. Instead, I allowed him to gaslight me as though it were my doing, that he wasn't in control of his fist. His anger had always been verbal until the first time he hit me. I think I was in shock.

Before that, it was always with his words, psychological and emotional.

He grovelled after and brought me a bunch of my favourite flowers, ruining those for me too. Then he actually got on his knees and begged me to forgive him. I did. Now that I think about it, I don't recall him saying sorry.

Not my greatest moment, but we live and learn until we don't. You hear about women dying at the hands of their abuser. Still, until you're one of those statistics, someone on the receiving end, you don't realise the severity until you pass out and wake up throbbing in pain in a ball on the bathroom floor, bleeding, battered and bruised. It's only then you see you were, ironically, the fucking lucky one because you woke up.

Tonight, when I finally managed to gather myself enough to pry my body up off the floor, I gingerly made my way back into the bedroom, my heart like thunder the entire time. I could hear the TV downstairs, the volume always so obnoxiously loud, blasting from the monstrosity the length of the living room wall that he insisted we get.

He always made the decisions; even when he asked for my input, it was a moot point.

I snuck down the stairs as quiet as I could be. I don't think I ever took that much care making sure to avoid every step that creaked. Even though my entire body felt broken, I was jacked up on shock and adrenaline. He was snoring heavily, passed out in the armchair, an almost finished bottle of Jack sitting on the floor, and at that moment, I knew it was now or never. I had to leave.

But even after all of this—the revelations, the hindsight—I still feel responsible.

The doctor interrupts my thoughts and brings me back to the present.

"I'll get these rushed through to the lab and let you know the results as soon as they come in."

I try to nod, only my neck hurts too much. "Thank you."

"Of course. In the meantime, I want you to rest. Your body has been through a traumatic experience. You have a sprained wrist, bruising to your larynx, and a laceration to your right temple. Hopefully, the butterfly stitches will suffice. Just be careful when washing your hair and face."

He pulls out some pain medication, the pills rattling around in the white plastic bottle, and leaves them on the bedside table.

"These should help somewhat with the pain, but they're strong, so don't take them on an empty stomach. You've broken a couple of ribs, and they'll take about six weeks to heal. So, I mean it, *rest*."

I silently watch Mitchell as he finishes tidying up and closes his bag. He reaches down and places his hand on my forearm. "And deep breathing exercises for your ribs. If anything changes or you start to feel worse, have one of the guys call me or get yourself to the hospital."

I try to force a smile, but all it does is aggravate my lip. "Thank you, you've been very kind." At no point did he judge me, and for that, I'm grateful. Goodness knows I'm doing enough of that myself.

I wait until the door closes and I'm alone. I carefully swing my legs over the edge of the bed and stare at the floor. The urge to cry is there, but I don't know if I can. Breaking down in front of Mitchell was terrible enough, but if I really let go, if I let it all out, I don't know if I'll be able to stop.

Mason will be so disappointed in me when he sees what I allowed to happen. I'm stronger than this, yet my broken body contradicts that. All I want to do right now is get clean, if that's even possible.

I can't stop thinking about all the things Curtis has said, all the things he's done to me. It's like a veil was hiding what was right before me. I wouldn't be in this position if I'd left him sooner. I know I only have myself to blame for being so weak.

And now I've dragged Caleb and Noah into this. The sooner I get myself together and find somewhere to stay, the better this will be for everyone.

Chapter Three

Caleb

I pace up and down the hall, only coming to a stop when Noah reaches for my arm. I end the call again as it rings out and goes straight to voicemail.

"Fuck."

Noah takes my phone from my hand, knowing I am on the verge of throwing it against the wall. It wouldn't be the first time.

"I'll get one of my guys on it. We'll track him down."

Noah is a fucking genius hacker, and he has a lot of people who owe him favours. Ironically, it's how we met Jessica's brother, Mason.

"How long do you think that's been happening?" I wave my hand in the direction of the guest bedroom. Mitchell has been in there for over twenty minutes, which only adds to my frustration. I have to keep telling myself it's because he's being thorough and doing his job.

Noah shakes his head, eyes trained on the closed door as if he can see through the wood.

"Fuck knows." He rubs his palm over his face and lets out a heavy sigh.

"I'm going to kill the fucker." If I get my hands on him, he'll wish he were dead. I clench my fists, and Noah grabs my wrist, tugging me towards him.

"I'm sure there'll be a queue, but we need to ensure she's all right first. She's the priority." Of course, he's right. He is always the voice of reason. Where I can be hot-headed and quick to act, he's the strategist.

"There's no way in hell her brother would have allowed her to be with him if he knew," Noah says, as he brings my clenched fist to his mouth and kisses my knuckles, grounding me in a way only he knows how. Sometimes it still blows my mind that this man is mine.

I don't deserve him, not even a little bit, but I'm a selfish bastard. He got under my skin and weaved into my inner reaches, connecting with my heart and soul on a level I never thought possible.

Before him, I would have continued to fuck my way through random men, but he changed me. Some might say you can't change people, but I'd have to disagree. Until Noah, I was never my true self. He changed me for the better.

Gripping the back of his neck, I squeeze. His eyes are stormy, his nostrils flaring.

I know long-hidden demons of his own are trying to surface, so I offer him the only thing I can now—me.

Covering his mouth with mine, I don't hold back as I force my tongue past his lips, demanding entry.

It's so easy to get lost in his touch, his tastes, his warmth. Where I'm a cold son of a bitch, he's warm and affectionate. Sure, I am those things, but only for him. What others see isn't what he sees, because this man will always get all of me, no holds barred.

Until him, I never believed in showing public displays of affection; to a point, I am still quite private. But Noah needs reassurance more often than not; his love language involves touch, so if he needs me to kiss him in a room full of people, then so be it.

Of course, there are more particular things I like to partake in, but that will be in the safety of a club we frequent or at home, just the two of us in our bed.

The handle of the door jiggles, and I pull out of the kiss. Noah's hand is still wrapped around my wrist when Mitchell steps out into the hallway and closes the door behind him with a soft click.

"Is she okay?"

"How bad is it?"

Noah and I speak at the same time, and Mitchell holds up his palm towards us, signalling for us to give him a chance to speak, as he walks further away from the door.

"She has a couple of broken ribs, bruising, swelling, a bump and laceration to her scalp, and a sprained wrist. That girl needs to rest. I've left some pain meds for her, but should anything change, you call me or get her to accident and emergency."

I clench my jaw as I tally all the ways I want to hurt the prick who did this to her.

"I'll rush the results from her internal examination. Shall I call her here with the results?"

Internal exam?

Noah nods. "Yeah, please, as soon as you have them. I don't want her worrying about that on top of this." He waves towards the door.

Mitchell edges towards the staircase and angles his head until we move away from the door.

"Listen, that poor girl has been through quite the trauma. She should have been seen at a hospital, but she's terrified. Just be there for her as best you can. She's going to need time to heal, not just physically but emotionally, too."

We hardly know her, and yet I have this overwhelming urge

to protect her from any more harm. And from the look on Noah's face, he feels the same.

Noah clears his throat, and his eyes roam to me and then back to Mitchell. "Hold on, when you said internal exam, are you saying she was sexually assaulted?"

"Yes, it would appear so. She has a little bleeding and bruising on her inner thighs."

I have to inhale a deep breath. The man was dead before, but now I want to skin the fucker alive.

Noah visibly swallows and gives a curt nod. "I'll show you out. Thanks again for coming, man." He reaches into his jean pocket to pull out his wallet, but Mitchell shakes his head.

"Hell no, I don't want your money. No way am I going to profit from her trauma."

I shake his hand and leave Noah to see him out as I return to the guestroom door. All I want to do is find the cunt who did this to her and smash his face into a brick wall repeatedly.

After I rein myself in and take a few deep breaths, I rap my knuckles on the door and wait for a beat before pushing it open and pausing. "Can I come in?" I wouldn't usually ask, but under the circumstances, it's imperative she feels safe.

"Yeah," she says, her chin dipped towards her chest as she sits on the edge of the bed.

"You okay?"

I instantly want to slap myself. Of course, she's fucking not.

"I'd be better if I could shower."

We managed to get her into a clean sweater, but apart from that, she's still in the rest of what she arrived here in. Our main concern was getting her checked out.

"Yeah, of course, no problem."

She pushes to her feet, trying to hide her hiss of pain. Her movements are sluggish, and before I can think better of it, I reach out and cup her elbow. "Let me help you."

I can imagine the last thing she wants is someone she doesn't know touching her, but I can't bear to see her struggle, not like this. She looks so frail.

She gives a soft nod, and then I wrap my arm gently around her waist and cup her under her knees, lifting her as carefully as I can into my arms.

"I can walk," she protests, but from how she says it, I'm not sure she's even convinced herself. Without entertaining her with an answer, I walk us into the en-suite.

I feel Noah's presence before he speaks.

"Let me get that." He opens the shower door partition and turns the knobs to get the jets working in the overhead shower.

Jessica takes a deep breath and watches his movements with one good eye.

I sit her on the bathroom countertop, removing my hands from her but not stepping back in case she needs me again.

"Okay, do you need a hand getting undressed?" Noah asks.

Her hands tremble as she reaches for the sweater's hem and begins to shuffle uncomfortably, her face contorting with the effort.

I cup her face between my hands and get her to focus on me. "Let us help you. You can trust us, Jessica."

She studies my face, searching for a lie with her good eye. Her other one is so swollen I don't think she'll be able to open it for days. Fortunately, Mitchell says there doesn't appear to be any severe damage, but once the swelling goes down, we're to get it checked out if she has any issues. And yet her injuries look fucking horrendous, her face hardly recognisable.

It's obvious she can't lift her arms higher than her waist, and I'm not surprised with her broken ribs and sprained wrist.

"Lean forward." I manage to get the sweater off her, and it's only now that her bruising is accentuated in the light of the bathroom.

"What the fuck?" Noah's voice radiates with anger, causing

Jessica to flinch. My eyes go wide as I stare at him in the mirror with what I hope conveys a *calm the fuck down* expression. That is usually his job, but this is a trigger for him.

He swallows hard, shaking his head once. "I'm sorry, I need a minute."

Chapter Four

Jessica

I try to breathe through my inner turmoil. This is so bloody humiliating I can't even bring myself to watch as Noah exits the bathroom, the door clicking closed behind him.

"That bad, huh?" I ask, my voice shaky. I avoid eye contact with Caleb, who is lifting me gently off the counter and back on my feet.

"Has this happened before, Jessica?"

I wrap my arms over my chest and hold on to my elbows like an anchor, my nails digging into my skin.

"Yes," I reply, but it's barely above a whisper. "But not like this, I thought…" I trail off, not finishing that thought out loud. I thought he was going to kill me.

His hands move to my shorts.

"May I?"

Under any other circumstance, I'd be nervous, but all I feel is utter desolation and shame.

Shame for what happened.

What I allowed to happen.

I grit my teeth and nod my head slowly.

He lowers my shorts, and I stare straight ahead, focusing on the beautiful ice-white tiles opposite me.

Whatever he just said, I didn't hear. I must have tuned out because suddenly, we're both standing in the walk-in shower. A moment of panic swells in my chest at the realisation he's in the shower with me. I lower my gaze and let out a breath when I see he's still fully clothed except for his feet.

I study his bare feet as he guides me underneath the spray and directs me to sit on a built-in wooden seat. It's a weird sensation, being here yet not feeling present. Almost like I'm detached from myself.

Everything's distorted, almost like none of this is real, only in my case, it is real, *very real*.

He begins pulling some bottles down from a nearby shelf, and when I don't move, he crouches down so his face is level with mine.

"Do you want some help?"

Clearing my throat, I try to answer, but the words are frozen on my lips.

I want to wash every single part of me, scrub myself clean, rid myself of everywhere that bastard ever touched. But truth be told, I don't know if I'll ever feel truly clean again.

His hands reach under my armpits, gently guiding me back to my feet. Once he's satisfied I won't fall over, he begins to wash my body, meticulously working over my exposed flesh using a soft satin loofah. He's gentle and attentive but avoids my breasts and between the apex of my thighs. There's no way he can't see the bruises.

He adds more shower gel to the loofah and passes it to me before turning his back, giving me some sort of privacy. Now that his back is to me, I find myself admitting it out loud.

"He raped me," I say, my voice cracking. Caleb's shoulders tense, but he remains facing the tiles. "I was passed out, unconscious when he did it."

The thought alone makes me want to vomit. It must have happened after he shoved me and I hit my head on the cabinet. I blacked out after that, and in a way, I'm grateful because violating me like that on top of everything else is too much.

"I woke up with my shorts around my ankles." I don't know why I'm telling him this, but I can't stop the words spilling from my lips. "He used to be so attentive, but that didn't last long before I met the monster."

I scrub the loofah between my legs and drag it over my chest, but it's not enough. There's no way I'll ever be clean again.

Angry with myself, I scrub even harder, another gut-wrenching sob catching in my throat, but a strangled cry escapes me. I'm unable to catch my breath now; the pain in my ribs slices through me, making it even harder for me to breathe.

"Hey, look at me, Jessica."

My face is between Caleb's calloused palms, and his touch is firm yet gentle, grounding me.

"Breathe for me. I need you to take a slow, deep breath."

He holds my stare, his eyes an intense blue with flecks of yellow and green around his pupils. I've never seen blue eyes this colour before, and for a tiny moment, I'm captivated long enough to inhale a staggered breath.

"That's it, little one, slow and deep. Breathe and release," he says with one of his palms pressed softly against my ribcage as he continues to breathe in and out with me.

I rest my forehead against his chest, tears streaming down my face. His hand cups the back of my neck as my body sags against his. If it weren't for his other arm around my lower back, I'd be a crumpled mess on the shower floor by now.

My tears eventually subside, and he pulls back, cupping my face softly, his thumbs wiping away my tears.

"Do you want me to try and wash your hair?"

I clear my throat, but my voice comes out hoarse. "Yes, please."

He says nothing in response as he ushers me to sit back down and carefully lathers my hair with shampoo. I close my eye as he works his fingers deftly and carefully over my scalp, doing his best to avoid the laceration on my head.

I don't recall him turning off the water or wrapping me in a towel, but we're no longer in the shower, and he's guiding me out of a steamed-up bathroom and back into the bedroom. He walks me over to a gorgeous white wooden dressing table and lowers me onto the small stool.

"I'll be right back," he says, glancing at Noah, who comes into view before he leaves the room.

Noah walks towards me with a small towel, kneels beside me and starts to dry off the excess water from the ends of my hair. Then he reaches for a small brush and combs through the ends, detangling the knots. He rustles through a drawer, retrieving a hairdryer and plugs it in, switching it on before waving it over my hair for a few minutes. It won't be enough to dry it thoroughly. My hair is too thick for that, but I'll take damp hair over soaking wet any day.

When he switches it off, I miss the warm heat and let out a shiver, my teeth beginning to chatter.

"Here, let's get you out of that wet towel and into some dry clothes."

He helps me put a t-shirt on, slipping it over my head as I push one arm through and then the other, keeping the towel in place. It helps that the shirt drowns me. He hands me a pair of boxers and then turns around. It gives me a moment to dry my body, a small hiss escaping as I pat gently between my legs. I slip the boxers on, having to roll them at the waist since they fit me more like a pair of shorts. Even though these clothes are too big for me, I'm thankful for them, for the way they hide the markings of my mistakes.

"Thank you," I whisper, my voice weak as I hand him the towel.

He turns and heads to the bathroom and I find myself inhaling deeply for the first time. The soft cotton of his shirt smells like him and it's strangely comforting.

"Have you managed to get hold of Mason yet?" I ask.

I know the kind of work my brother does involves him going off the grid. He's in the MI5, but that's all I know. He's always been very cloak and dagger. I've questioned him multiple times, but I am still none the wiser. He's always trying to protect his naive little sister, and yet here I am.

"No, not yet, sweet girl, but we're on it."

"It's my fault," I say and move to stand up. "I should have left after he hit me the first time."

Noah's expression turns hard, cold even, and I go to step away, but the back of my calf connects with the stool I was sitting on, and my arms flay.

Noah reaches for me before I fall onto my arse and pulls me into his chest. "Sorry, I didn't mean to startle you, fuck."

He brings a hand to the back of my head and holds me there. "I never want to hear you say it was your fault. You got that?"

I can hear the back-seated anger in his voice, but I realise it's not directed at me, and I relax a fraction.

"The only one to blame is him. I can guarantee you he will not be getting away with what he's done."

My body tenses. "You don't understand. I can't go to the police."

Panic grips me again, fear holding me prisoner.

"Shhh, I've got you. You're safe here."

I inhale a slow, deep breath. Fucking hell, it hurts. I try to concentrate on anything else. Like how Noah smells like floral leather, both sophisticated and elegant. Intense, robust, and powerful.

Noah walks me over to the bed and urges me to sit, fluffing the pillow against the headboard.

Caleb clears his throat as he enters the room. He's wearing a plain black T-shirt and a pair of grey jogging bottoms. Ones that I would probably pay more attention to in any other state, but all I want to do is curl up in a ball and sleep for a month, pretending like today didn't happen.

He places my bag at the end of the bed.

And I know I need to plan what my next steps are.

Chapter Five

Noah

The room is thick with tension with the shock of Jessica turning up on our doorstep, but at the same time, I'm glad she did. The thought of her out there alone, running scared, has my entire being alight with anger.

"I'm sorry to put you both out like this," Jessica says, her head dipped low. "I'll be out of here tomorrow."

I glance at Caleb, who raises a brow, and I speak up before he does.

"Yeah, no, you won't. You'll stay here until you're well enough to make your next move. And just so you know, you're not putting us out."

She visibly swallows, raising her head, and I notice, not for the first time, the bruising on her throat. I clench my fists. I'm usually the voice of reason, but I'm struggling to keep a harness on my own emotions. I've seen first-hand what can come from domestic abuse. The controlling incidents, coercive, threatening, and violent behaviour, the list goes on and on and on. I should know, I had front-row seats for years growing up.

Talk about a mind fuck.

Caleb walks over, his presence intimidating if you don't know him. Hell, even if you do know him. It's different for me; I know him intimately, and he still has the power to take my breath away.

We'd only met Jessica once when we had a get-together here for Mason. But she left a lasting impression in her wake.

"Why didn't you come to us sooner?" Caleb questions. I see the tensing of his jaw, the clenching of his fists, and the pulsing of his heartbeat in his throat.

I widen my eyes at him when he shifts his focus entirely on Jessica, his nostrils flaring.

"Because I hardly know you," she admits, her voice low and as defeated as her posture.

Caleb shakes his head and grips the bridge of his nose. I stand in front of him and cup his shoulder, his gaze moving to my face once again.

I nod in the direction of the door before moving past him. He sighs, his heavy footsteps following close behind me.

When we're in the hallway, I pull him out of earshot.

"You need to calm down and stop giving the poor girl the fifth degree."

His eyes turn to slits, and it's taking everything in him to rein in his anger, not with Jessica, but with the situation. I can understand why his instinct is to protect, and I know he feels helpless. His go-to is to react, but since the target of that anger isn't present, he's transferring.

"I barely recognised her when I answered the door," he says, his eyes dark with repressed rage.

Yeah, it took me a minute for my eyes to catch up with my brain when he yelled for me. Seeing her in that state was beyond a shock to the system.

The last and first time we met her in person, she was laughing and smiling. But she's a shell of the person we met.

I should know; it's not like she never crossed my mind since then. Hell, Caleb and I had talked about her for hours after the party ended, when she left with Mason.

I shake away the thoughts.

"Listen, just let her settle and get her bearings. We need to make sure she knows she's safe. She'll open up, I'm sure of it."

He visibly swallows, his eyes dark and stormy, his body so fucking tense.

"That's just it. She did when I was helping her in the shower, and she said how he... raped her while she was unconscious."

Caleb is pacing back and forth. I can feel his rage like a live wire ready to spark into a flame at any given moment.

"She couldn't even defend herself."

I have no words, it's not like we haven't crossed paths with sick individuals in our line of work, but still, this is too close to home.

Mason is a good friend. We promised should anything ever happen to him, we would make sure Jessica was all right. Even though this isn't our fault anymore than it is Jessica's, I already know without Caleb voicing it that he feels somewhat responsible. How could he not? It's ingrained in his being to look after others. His cold exterior is just that; he cares more than most people I know.

I take hold of his hand. "We'll take care of her together, okay?"

He clenches his jaw again. "Yeah, and then we'll take care of that mother fucker too."

Caleb would go to war for her, as would I.

I grab his face and pull him in for a hard kiss. My back hits the wall with force, a grunt leaving my lips as the air is knocked from my lungs, teeth knocking as he dominates my mouth. When he draws back, he rests his forehead against mine, inhaling deep, sharp breaths.

"Let me speak to her while you sort us both out a drink. I think we both could use one."

He nods, squeezing the back of my neck, and stalks off down the hallway.

Turning back to the room, I take a deep breath and tap my knuckles against the door before poking my head inside.

"Can I come back in?"

"Of course." Jessica tries to scoot back into a sitting position with a wince. I reach her in less than three strides and cup her shoulders, gently easing her so she's half lying back down, propped up by the pillows.

"Rest."

She scrunches the duvet between her fingers in a tight grip, her knuckles losing all colour.

"Is he really mad?"

Her one good eye peers over my shoulder before blinking and making eye contact with me again.

"Yes, but not with you, sweet girl."

He's angry on her behalf, and mine, probably. After everything that happened to my own mum, seeing Jessica like this was the last thing either of us envisioned.

"Don't worry about anything, okay? You're safe here."

She licks her lips, and I watch the roll of her throat as she swallows, her bruises prominent.

I reach out slowly, giving her time to tell me to stop before I trace the marks along her throat and down to her collarbone.

"How long has this been going on, Jessica? Does your brother know?" I mean, it's a daft fucking question; if Mason did, the son of a bitch would already be dead.

She trembles as I slide my hand along her jaw and cup her cheek.

"No, I haven't been able to get a hold of him, and honestly, unless he was in front of me, I'm not sure I would have the courage to tell him. He's not been answering his phone or returning my calls. It's why I came here, not only because I had nowhere else to go, but because I'm worried about him," she admits.

I'll have to speak to Caleb to see what he can find out and ask some of our contacts if they can track his last known whereabouts. He's gone off the grid before, so maybe it's nothing to worry about, but better to be safe than sorry.

"I'll be out of your hair just as soon as I plan my next move. I just need a few days."

Frowning, I take in her forlorn expression. "Hey, I don't want you worrying about that now."

She goes to reply, but whatever retort I know was on the tip of her tongue turns into a low hiss.

"Let's get those painkillers. When was the last time you ate?"

Her skin takes on an even paler complexion. "Hmm, yesterday maybe, I think, but I'm not hungry."

I reach for the pill bottle and scan the label.

"I know, sweet girl, but these need to be taken with food."

It's hard not to miss the roll of her throat as she swallows. It wouldn't surprise me if she felt nauseous.

"Just enough to take these. Do you think you can maybe try some soup?"

Nodding softly, she says, "Yeah, I'll try."

Caleb returns and walks in, holding a tray in his hands. "Did someone say soup?" And that right there is why I love this man. "Chicken noodle okay? I figured it's not too heavy, just enough to line your stomach."

I smile and give Jessica a wink.

"Perfect timing, let's get you sitting up."

Jessica shuffles upwards, and I position pillows against the headboard until she's semi-comfortable. Caleb places the tray over her lap with a small bowl of chicken noodle soup, some bread, and a bottle of water.

"Do you need any help?" I ask.

"No, it's fine, thank you."

Her nose twitches, and she sniffs back tears.

"It's just soup from a can, don't go getting your hopes up," Caleb says.

She picks up the spoon, her hand shaking as she brings it to her mouth. It spills before making it past her lips.

"Shit, I'm so sorry." She starts fussing about with the napkin as she tries to soak up the spill from the tray.

Caleb covers her hand, stopping her movements. "It's fine, Jessica." He picks up the spoon and scoops some soup before holding it to her mouth. Her lips part, and he takes his time feeding her until he's satisfied she's eaten her fill, and then she washes down the pain meds with some water before resting against the headboard.

"We'll let you rest. We're just down the end of the hall if you need anything," I say and reach for the tray.

She licks her lips, and I wonder if she wants some lip balm—they're dry and cracked, and her upper lip is split.

"Thank you."

We head for the door, and Caleb reaches for the main light.

"Please, can you leave the light on?"

He looks over his shoulder and nods towards the bedside table. "Will the lamp be enough?" Flicking one switch off and another on, the lamp comes on as the main light goes off.

"Yes, thank you."

Caleb says nothing else as we leave the room, and he closes her door softly behind us. Pausing in the hallway, he clenches his fists.

"We need to find out everything we can about this arsehole and then decide how to handle the cunt."

The floorboard creaks behind us, and then we hear the click of the lock on the guest room door. Honestly, I can't say I blame her after what she's been through. With a heavy sigh, Caleb follows me back downstairs.

That arsehole is going to get the retribution he deserves and more.

Chapter Six

Caleb

Noah spent the rest of the evening between his two laptops, trying in vain to track down Jessica's brother, Mason. I had no luck with any of my contacts, which doesn't surprise me. If anyone can find him though, it's Noah.

"I can't get a trace on him at all," Noah says.

I sigh and crack my neck. I already know what's coming next if he's having trouble finding him.

"I'm going to reach out to Elliot, if anyone can help me track him down, it's him." Of course, he'd fucking think that. "Caleb?"

Ignoring him, I move to my feet and go over to the bar, pouring two fingers of whiskey then downing it. And then I pour another, swirling the amber liquid in the crystal tumbler.

Noah sits back and spins in his chair, crossing his arms over his chest. "You can't be serious?"

I sit and stretch my arm over the back of the sofa. "What? I didn't say anything."

He pushes to his feet and walks over to me, taking the glass from my hand and taking a sip. "You didn't have to."

I snag the glass back from him and down the rest, savouring the bitter-sweet cinnamon with the lingering taste of vanilla.

"He's just a friend," he says, with an exasperated sigh as he rubs his temples.

I shoot him a narrowed look. "A friend who is an ex."

Noah laughs. "Yes, and an ex for a reason, something you know all too well." He moves to his knees, hands on my thighs. "I love it when you get jealous."

My dick twitches. "Yeah, I love it when you have my cock buried down the back of your throat." It's a crass response, but it's also the truth. I think he knows I need an outlet with everything that's happened in the last couple of hours. This situation with Jessica, even though she's here now and safe, is still partly out of my control, and I fucking hate that.

He licks his lips and dips his fingers into the waistband of my jogging bottoms, arching a brow, but the moment is interrupted by a high-pitched, frightening scream. Without a word, we're both on our feet and rushing up the stairs towards the wailing noise coming from the guest room.

I push on the door, but it's locked. Without thinking, I shove my shoulder into it hard—once, twice—before there's a pop and a crack of wood as it slams open, hitting the wall with a loud thud.

Noah switches on the main light, and we both look around, expecting an intruder, worried the fucker found her here.

Jessica thrashes around, her body trembling, her cries and wails filling the room.

Noah rushes over to her, but I quickly search the room and the en-suite to ensure it's just the three of us.

He tries in vain to get her to calm down, but she's inconsolable, sweating profusely, her breathing heavy.

"Jessica, sweet girl, you're dreaming. Calm down. You're safe."

Still nothing.

I sit on the other side of the bed and pull her into my body, worried the thrashing around will cause more injuries than she already has.

Her good eye flutters open, but it's vacant, her pupil dilated as she stares at me. The other is still swollen shut, and I clench my jaw. Noah rubs up and down her arm as I rock her gently back and forth.

Her face is flushed, sweat coating her skin.

Noah goes to the bathroom, returning with a damp flannel, and presses it to her forehead.

A small whimper escapes her, and if she weren't in my arms, I would be punching a wall right about now.

"Jessica, can you hear me?" Noah asks as he gently brushes the damp hair away from her cheek before he cups it in his palm. "Jessica?"

She doesn't say a word.

"Should we call Mitchell?" I glide my fingers up and down her arm, hoping it will coax her awake.

Noah shakes his head. "She's been through a traumatic experience. Let's get through tonight and see how she is in the morning."

Her eye drifts closed, but her breathing is still heavy, and I worry about leaving her alone.

"Do you think one of us should stay with her in case she wakes up again?" I ask Noah. I move out from under her as gently as possible and lay her back on the bed. She tries to curl into a ball but lets out a hiss of pain, her pupil moving behind her closed eyelid.

"Yeah, I can stay with her," he replies. I'm torn between offering as well, but I've always been more intimidating than Noah, so he's probably the best choice.

"You sure?"

He reaches for my hand and squeezes it. "Yeah, you know I'll only check on her every ten minutes, even if you're with her."

I nod in response, knowing he's right, but I doubt very much that I'll be sleeping tonight. I want to send a few emails to reach out and see what I can find out about this arsehole boyfriend. There is no way in hell he's getting away with this.

"Okay, I will reach out to some of my contacts. And you're right; if anyone can help us track down her brother, it's Elliot."

He musters a smile and leans in for a quick kiss, but I don't let him pull back. I grab the back of his neck, taking control. He moans, and I swear if we weren't currently leaning over Jessica, I would have him bent over this bed, fucking him into oblivion.

I try not to let my mind wander about how I wouldn't be against the idea of Jessica watching. I groan and nip his lip hard, but not enough to break the skin before drawing back.

"Hold that thought," he says, his pupils blown wide, his nostrils flaring slightly.

Glancing down, I see his erection is prominent in his joggers. He shifts himself and the head peeks out of his waistband. He doesn't wear underwear when we're in the house, and I love having easy access.

I force my eyes closed, willing back the urge to take him in my mouth and rectify that before leaving him for the night.

"Do you want me to take care of you before I leave?" I ask, unable to stop myself, but as soon as the words pass my lips, I feel guilty for voicing it out loud.

He raises an eyebrow, and I hold up my palm. "Yeah, I already know, it was an arsehole thing to say."

Jessica stirs and lets out another whimper.

"Problem solved," he says, his eyes glancing down to his now flaccid dick. "But for the record, you're my arsehole, and I love you for it."

Even now, he's trying to make me feel better.

"Yeah, but still, it wasn't my proudest moment. And so you know, I love you, too."

And I do. He's the only person I have ever said it to outside my family and chosen family. For a long time, I thought I was incapable of love—honest, all-consuming love—but I was wrong, so fucking wrong.

Of course, when we met, I was the biggest prick to him. My way of protecting myself, I guess. Everything about him drew me in; insta-lust quickly turned to love. And to say I wasn't fucking ready was an understatement.

But I knew after we slept together the first time there was no way I would be able to fuck him out of my heart or soul.

We've had our fair share of hook-ups with women and men, but always together, never apart.

It would be like caging a beast if we didn't, but he's the only man I make love to. We've never had anyone else back in our home. We have a suite at a hotel, or there's the club we would frequent.

"I know you do."

I move to my feet and look down at Jessica; she looks so fragile and broken, and I have to swallow down my anger again.

"She'll be okay. She's got us to take care of her now."

Yeah, she does, but for how long? The thought of letting her go doesn't sit well with me. It's a feeling I can't even articulate.

"But for how long?"

He tilts his head as he studies my face. "I don't know, Caleb," he says softly. Emotion flickers in his eyes as his gaze roams back towards Jessica. "We need to help fix her first."

And there we have it—his need to fix, my need to protect.

Chapter Seven

Jessica

I try to kick off my covers. It's hot—too hot. Groaning, I try to roll over onto my side, but I'm pinned. *What the fuck.*

Panic infuses me, my heart beating rapidly in my chest. It's like someone is playing a drum in my head.

"Shhh, you're okay. It's me, Noah."

Noah?

"Come on, sweet girl. I've got you."

This is some seriously fucked up dream if ever there was one.

But something is pulling at my subconscious. Everything starts to come back to me like a tidal wave, and I struggle to catch my breath. I blink, but I can barely see out my right eye, the other swollen shut, as I try to gather my senses.

Curtis beat me.

I ran, but I was unable to find Mason.

I came here.

"Jessica." Noah's voice, though firm, is distant as the wave of dizziness assails me.

His touch moves to me, his fingers lightly squeezing my shoulder.

"You had some sort of night terror," he says, his thumb moving over my shoulder in a small circular motion. I concentrate on his touch as I will myself to calm down. "Do you not remember?"

I remember nothing past locking the door and crawling back into bed.

"No," I reply, swallowing, my throat dry.

He shifts, causing the bed to dip, and I realise he's in bed with me. No, I'm in bed, he's on top of the covers. My chest squeezes tight as it wells with emotion.

"We didn't want to risk leaving you alone if it happened again. You had a traumatic experience, so I'm not surprised." He twists the lid off a bottle of water and cups the back of my neck for me to take a few sips; the water is cool and refreshing. I want to guzzle it down, but I'm afraid it would make me sick.

I sit up, and everything hurts: my head and ribs, everywhere. I untangle my legs and plant my feet on the floor.

"Fuck, I feel like shit," I mumble more to myself than Noah as I push myself up. He is beside me in an instant, gripping my elbow. "I'm good. I just need to use the toilet."

He says nothing, but gently guides me into the bathroom. I've never been a particularly good patient, and it would appear even now, there's no exception.

"I've got it from here," I say, feeling self-conscious. "Thank you," I add, feeling like an ungrateful brat.

When he's sure I have my footing and won't stumble, he releases his hold and walks back to the doorway, stopping to look over his shoulder. "I'll be just out here. Call me if you need me." And then he closes the door behind him with a soft click.

Lowering myself to the toilet, I let out a slight hiss, sore as I relieve myself, remembering how I woke up in a haze with my shorts around my ankles.

Shivering, I check the tissue as I wipe myself, expecting to see blood, but it comes away clean, which surprises me considering the bruising on my inner thighs and how sensitive I am between my legs.

I try to sniff back my tears, but it's futile. The only time I've ever been this emotional was after my mum died. I move to flush the toilet. Blinking through the tears from my one good eye, I take stock of the room's opulence, feeling as though I'm tarnishing it with my mere presence. If this is the guest bathroom, I wonder what the main bathroom looks like. I didn't appreciate its grandeur when I arrived here yesterday.

But standing here, looking at my horrid reflection, I realise what a fucking mess I am. My jaw and throat are bruised, and my eye is swollen shut. I squint, trying to open it, but give up with a soft hiss as I wash and dry my hands on the fluffiest hand towel I've ever used.

Or maybe my sense of touch is just heightened. Who the fuck knows? I feel like this is all some weird dream.

I lift my shirt next, look down at my stomach, and then back to my reflection to see the bruising across my ribs.

As worried as I am about my brother, now seeing myself in the light of day, I'd hate to think what he would have done if he was actually at home when I arrived on his doorstep, all fucked up.

My cheeks heat when I recollect Caleb helping me clean up in the shower, even when I blurted out about what Curtis did to me. Shivering, I try to ignore the feelings it evokes and remember how he and Noah cared for me—practically a stranger.

I comb my fingers through my hair as best I can. Surprisingly, it's not as bad as it could be. Looking down, I notice a new toothbrush and a tube of toothpaste.

"Thank god," I mumble to myself. It's bad enough being here like this, but my dignity is already rock bottom. At least I can keep up with my hygiene despite still feeling dirty and tainted. In my haste to grab some essentials when I left, I didn't bother grabbing mine from the toothbrush holder.

Once I've cleaned my teeth and rinsed my mouth, I stare at my reflection again, unable to recognise the woman staring back at me.

But that's a moot point. I need to think of what to do next, and fast.

Fuck, what if he finds me?

He'll try and get me to come back. My mind fills with scenarios of what he'll do when I refuse, which makes me physically shake. Because if he was capable of all of that before, now that he's found me gone, he will be pissed. I know if there's ever a next time, it will be the last.

A soft knock at the door disrupts me from my thoughts, and I let out a startled breath.

"Hey, Jessica. You doing okay in there?"

I clear my throat, straighten my shoulders, and open the door.

My breath catches in my throat. It's easy to forget how handsome Noah is up this close, and it's not like I had time to appreciate him yesterday. When they threw the party for my brother, I spent a few hours talking to him and Caleb. Noah was the more chatty of the two. But still, they never once made me feel uncomfortable.

"I grabbed you a pair of my joggers." He holds them out towards me. "They're clean, I promise," he says with a smile.

My face heats with embarrassment because I realise I am openly staring. I take them from him and quickly close the door again without saying a word. I think I hear him laugh, but I can't be sure.

Slipping into the softest joggers I have ever worn, I roll the waist so they fit a little better. What washing powder do these guys use, seriously?

"Just come down when you're ready. Caleb made breakfast," Noah calls out.

I nod and then shake my head at myself because he can't see me, which makes my head pound even more. I softly rub my temples.

Waiting a minute or two, I try to collect myself as best I can, and then quietly, I make my way downstairs and towards the kitchen. I'm in as much awe now as I was when I came here the first time; their home is gorgeous.

When Caleb sees me, he moves to the counter and flicks on the kettle.

"Morning, do you want tea or coffee?" he asks. His hair is damp and slicked back like he's fresh out of the shower.

I clear my throat. "Tea, please."

"Sugar?"

"One, please."

This is so surreal, them offering me tea, like I didn't just turn their lives upside down less than twelve hours ago, showing up in the state I did.

Noah stands and pulls out a chair beside him for me to sit. My cheeks heat from the small act of kindness, and I mumble a thank you as I sit. I place my hands in my lap, gripping them tightly as Noah retakes his seat. He opens his mouth to say something when there is a sudden loud metal thwack sound, and I jump out of my seat, the chair falling backwards and onto the floor behind me.

My good eye darts around the open kitchen, hating how my vision is impaired; I feel as though I am at a complete disadvantage.

A hand lands on my shoulder, and I startle.

"It's just the toaster. You're safe," Noah says, his gaze roaming over my face.

I nod, my heart racing. Fuck, my nerves are shot to pieces.

"Come sit," Caleb says, righting my chair as Noah guides me into my seat.

Glancing down, I grip my hands together to try to still the shaking, my heart hammering heavily in my chest, but it's no use. I can't seem to stop my entire body from trembling.

"I'm so sorry," I say, unable to meet their eyes, but I can feel them watching me, and I bite the inside of my cheek to keep from openly breaking down.

Caleb crouches beside me, one arm on the back of my chair, as he tilts my chin with his thumb and forefinger until I have no choice but to make eye contact.

"Jessica," he says in a deep, calm voice. "You have nothing to apologise for. If you weren't skittish after everything you'd endured, then quite frankly, we'd be even more concerned."

I don't know how to respond, so I nod slightly, his fingers still holding my chin. He's close. I can smell his aftershave—fresh, earthy, but also masculine and powerful. It matches him perfectly, both rich and alluring. But the truth is I hate how weak I've become. I freaked out over the sound of the damn toaster for crying out loud.

Chapter Eight

Caleb

Jessica is petrified, her body trembling, and I hate that she even feels like that here, but as I said, it's perfectly understandable.

I watch Noah talking to her quietly as I make up the poached egg and avocado on toast. It's one of Noah's favourites. I didn't even think to ask her if that was okay.

Carrying the plates over, I balance two in my hand and the third in the other. It would seem that working as a waiter while in college still pays off.

"I hope this is all right?" I ask and place a plate in front of her and Noah. "If not, I can make you something else, or I think we have some cereal." Not that I eat it, can't stand the whole milk, cereal concoction, makes me gag, but that doesn't mean Noah can't have it, and he is a secret sucker for Cocoa Pops, so who am I to deny him?

I sit and reach for the pepper, sprinkling a little over my eggs.

"No, this is lovely, thank you." Jessica waits for me to pick up my knife and fork before following suit and quietly cuts into her food. I notice her slight wince, and then I recall her wrist.

"Let me." I reach for her plate and quickly cut it up so it's easier for her to eat.

I glance at Noah, who winks, and a small smile graces his lips before cutting into his own. Yeah, yeah, I know. He's one of the few people who ever sees this side of me.

"Thank you."

We eat in what appears to be a more comfortable quiet, the only sound is from the stereo quietly playing in the background.

"Those are your painkillers," I say, sliding the small dish beside her orange juice. "For once you've eaten."

Once everyone has finished, I push my plate away, pick up my fresh orange, and finish it off before laying my palms flat on the table and focusing my attention back on Jessica.

"We haven't been able to track down your brother, but Noah has a friend working on it."

He raises his eyebrows, and I want to flip him off but decide against it under the current circumstances.

"You know people who can do that?" she asks, her voice small.

I nod. "We do. How much do you know about what your brother does for a living?"

She gives a slight shrug. "Not much, to be honest, I know who he works for, but he told me it was sensitive information, and for safety reasons, the less I knew, the better."

That makes sense, as it's just the two of them, and he's an undercover operative for the MI5.

It's how we all met. "Well, as you probably gathered, it's how we met."

"Do you think he's all right?" I hear the concern in her voice, and the last thing I want to do is worry her, but I'd be lying if I said I wasn't worried, too. The last thing we need is her fretting over that with everything else.

"I do. He's likely deep under surveillance."

Noah taps the table, and Jessica turns her attention back to him, moving her head, no doubt so she can see him.

"We need to discuss you not wanting us to contact the police or taking you to a hospital last night."

Her body tenses, and she sits up straighter as if ready to flee.

"Can I ask why?" he asks.

She clears her throat and takes a deep breath, tucking her lips between her teeth before letting out a soft puff of air.

"Because he is the police," she replies quietly.

I already found that out last night. While Noah was watching over Jessica, I was on my laptop until the early hours, getting as much information on him as possible.

If Mason had this information on the prick, he would've gotten her far away from him double quick.

He has a history of poor conduct and reports of both assault and sexual assault, but for some reason, it never progressed.

Noah, of course, isn't surprised. I summarised everything I learned with him this morning before Jessica came down for breakfast.

"We know, and we've found out. He doesn't have the best track record."

She scoffs out a humourless laugh. "Yeah, don't I know it."

Noah squeezes her hand with his, saying, "Hey, come on, stop that already. He's the problem, not you."

And if I have my way, I will happily take him out of the equation—permanently.

"You're worried they won't believe you over him. That the authorities won't take you seriously?" I say.

Her good eye moves back to me. "Something like that. He told me before that they wouldn't believe me if I ever considered reporting him. He said he knows many people, and I'd live to regret it."

She lets out a visible shiver, and her skin drains of colour.

"Yeah, well, it's not about quantity," Noah says. "And just so you know, he will not get away with this."

"He has some kind of little dick affliction," I say out loud, causing Noah to let out a quick chortled laugh, but he cuts himself off quickly when Jessica's jaw drops open, and then she laughs too.

It's the most beautiful sound I think I have ever heard, and for a fleeting moment, I am mesmerised.

As though it registers, she quickly covers her mouth with her hand.

But somehow, my off-handed comment seems to have broken some of her tension.

I gently pull her wrist until she drops her hand from her face.

"I'll take that as a compliment, seeing as I'm not usually known for my humour."

She worries her lip, but at least the colour in her cheeks has returned.

"You know we will make sure you're safe. Whatever you decide, we'll support you," Noah says.

Yeah, we will, and then I'll rip the bastard a new one because there is no way he'll be walking away from this intact, that's for sure.

"But what if he comes after me? I don't want to drag you guys into it. You hardly know me. I already feel bad enough turning up the way I did, but I didn't know what else to do."

She's already questioning herself, and I hate that. She's not the same carefree young woman she was when we met her.

"I honestly believed him when he said he'd change. Maybe that makes me a fool, but relationships aren't just about the good, are they?" she asks, looking for validation.

"No, they take work, compromise and communication. But abusive behaviour, verbal or physical, is not what relationships are built on."

Well, unless there's pleasure where there's pain and consent.

But what he did was none of those things.

"Social pressure exists to be in a 'perfect relationship'." Noah uses his forefingers and middle fingers to emphasise.

"That's bullshit. I bet to anyone on the outside looking in they think he's this great guy, right?"

She swallows, and my eyes roam over her visible bruises.

"Listen, I know you're questioning yourself...*don't*. None of this is because of what you did or did not do. It's all on him."

Jessica doesn't agree nor disagree, but give me time, and I'll help her find that confident young woman who left us with a lasting impression.

Chapter Nine

Noah

Jessica seems as though she might be ready to bolt at any moment, and I can't say I blame her. Caleb is managing to harness his usual brass self, and honestly, I couldn't love this man more if I tried.

"Yeah, but—" I cut her off before she can continue.

"Sweet girl, where will you go?"

She shakes her head. "I don't know. I have a little saved. I could use it for a hotel or bed-and-breakfast."

"And why would you do that when we have a perfectly good room here, where you'll be safe and looked after at least until we track your brother down?"

I just can't bear the thought of her being out there alone, especially not in her state.

Her shoulders slump, her chin lowering as she contemplates my words. I hate that I'm causing her to withdraw. Making her feel weak and vulnerable is not my intention, but letting her leave is not an option.

Caleb kneels beside her, his finger raising her chin until her eyes meet his. "Your brother would never forgive us if we let you go, and neither would we," he says. "Just stay long enough to heal, and then we'll discuss your options. How does that sound?"

She glances at me and then back to him, giving a soft nod of her head in agreement.

I almost scoff at that. Discuss my arse. He's backed her into a corner, playing her brother's card, crafty fucker. Like he will let her go and fend for herself, not bloody likely. One of the many reasons I love him.

"Come on. Those painkillers are strong. You should go lay down and rest, so your body can start to heal."

He stands to his full height, holding out his hand for Jessica. As always, he exudes power. She takes it and slowly rises to her feet, and I notice how small her hand is compared to his. Everything about her is so delicate and fragile even while standing there beaten and bruised. She's one of the strongest women I've ever met because she's a fighter, a survivor. I know how hard it was for her to run, especially in her physical state, but she found the strength. She's a fucking warrior.

She glances at me and smiles timidly as I stack the plates, her open eye darting to the table.

"Let me do that," she says, trying to pull her hand free from Caleb's hold.

"Jessica, go rest."

I can see her wanting to argue, but she's no good to anyone in her current state, and what kind of people would we be if we allowed her to do that? She's our guest and under our protection.

Caleb leads her away and back upstairs as I quickly load the dishwasher and wipe down the table and countertops.

My phone vibrates, gaining my attention. Unfortunately, it's just an automated message from the phone company, not her brother, as I had hoped.

"Anything?" Caleb asks, coming up behind me, resting his chin on my shoulder as he wraps his arms around my waist, pulling me against his chest.

"No, and if I'm being honest, it's a bit disconcerting. But I don't want Jessica to worry."

Caleb sighs into my ear. "Yeah, she needs to focus on healing and feeling safe."

I turn in his arms. "Did she say anything to you?"

He shakes his head. "Nope, just kept apologising. I want to skin the mother fucker alive."

Clenching my jaw, I take a deep breath. When we saw the bruising covering her torso, it was too much. One minute we were waiting for our takeaway; the next thing, we had Jessica lying beaten and bloody in our guest room.

"Same, and she has nothing to apologise for, but it's not hard to notice apologising is a trauma response. I don't even want to think about what she's been enduring at the hands of that arsehole."

If I think about it too much, it takes me to a dark place. Somewhere I don't want to be, because if I lose my shit, I'll want to hunt the cunt down. There's a deep thrum, just under the surface, begging to come out to play, but I'll taper it down and concentrate on Jessica.

Because if I need to worry about anyone being volatile right now, it's Caleb.

"What's your schedule like for today?" he asks, his hand moving to palm the back of my neck. "I have a meeting, but if I need to get Matt on it or postpone, I can. After what we just witnessed, I think at least one of us should stay home with her for now."

He's the CEO of Knight Risk Management Solutions and is sought out by some of the largest corporate companies in the world. The fact that he's considering delegating or postponing says a lot about his concern for Jessica, and this man doesn't like to reschedule or relinquish control. Even with his trusted employees, he wants to be the centre of all major risk management, and to him, every meeting is important regardless of the scale or size of the client's business.

"No, I know how much you hate setbacks. I'm good to work from home. There's nothing I can't do from here for the next few days." I'm the co-founder of a software development company and have a fantastic team of developers who work for me. I can always set up Zoom meetings.

"Okay, but only if you're sure?"

I nod. "I'm sure."

I thread my fingers through his hair, pulling his head closer to mine as I close the gap. I tease his lips, and he opens for me, taking control of the kiss. A guttural moan escapes me. This man never ceases to evoke a physical reaction from me in the best possible way, but it can wait, and I know how much he enjoys delayed gratification. I rub up against him, his arousal evident.

He slows down the kiss, pulling a breath away as he speaks against my lips, his voice deep, dark and delicious. "You're insatiable," he says, nipping at my chin, his grip on the back of my neck tightening just a fraction.

"As are you," I reply.

He thrusts into me once and then gives me a chaste kiss before dropping his hand and stepping away with a smirk. But it's not hard to sense the tension. It's so taut.

"I'm going to reach out to Elliot," I say. The last thing I want to do is piss him off, but I've exhausted all other options. So, the sooner Elliot is on the case, the better, and we can hopefully get a trace on Mason.

He gives a curt nod in acknowledgement, his jaw tensing.

Elliot has always been a sore subject between us, even though he has nothing to worry about. I mean, I get it to an extent. When I met Caleb, my relationship with Elliot was complicated. Hell, we weren't even together. So, I guess you could say I was on the rebound, but everything worked out the way it should. And even though Caleb acts like a hard bastard, he has insecurities. Up until me, he'd never been in a relationship. But he tolerates Elliot for me as best he knows how, anyway. Don't get me wrong, it does flatter my ego that he gets possessive over me, jealous even, but he has no reason to worry.

He's the one I love.

"Okay, keep me posted." He glances at his watch, his eyebrows drawn in before he looks back at me. "I need to get my arse into gear and get dressed if I'm going to make it in time."

I have no doubt he will. After all, he's never been one for tardiness.

He turns away, but I call after him, "Caleb?"

Peering over his shoulder, he cocks a brow.

"No detours afterwards, okay? We'll decide what to do about her ex once we have everything else figured out with Jessica."

I wouldn't put it past him to pay that fucker a visit once his meeting is dealt with. I watch as he clenches and unclenches his fists.

He doesn't reply, and honestly, I can't say I blame him, but I'm hoping he'll weigh the pros and cons while he's on his way to work and think better of going in hot-headed.

One way or another, Curtis will get his dues. It just depends on when and how.

I decide to grab a bottle of water for Jessica, an excuse to check on her, but before I do, I grab my phone and pull up Elliot's number. He answers on the second ring. Because the fact I'm even calling him means it's important.

Chapter Ten

Jessica

I don't know how or when this became my life, seeking refuge with two men I barely know while hiding out from someone who claimed to love me. How could I have been so damn naive? I always was a fairy tale kind of girl. I even grew up believing in happily ever afters, which is pretty pathetic now that I think about it. I walk into the en-suite and stare at my reflection.

I hardly even recognise myself, and I'm not talking about the bruises or the split lip staring back at me. But the weak version of myself I have become.

I pull up my top and stare at the marks marring my skin and take a deep breath. It's a weird contrast because the pain reminds me I'm alive, yet I've never felt so strangely detached or numb.

My lips pull into a straight line. "I hate you," I whisper.

"I hate you. I hate you. I hate you…" A sob catches in my throat because it's true, I have never hated myself more than I do now.

My vision blurs, and I'm unable to keep the tears at bay as I slide down the wall and wrap my arms around my knees, pulling them into my chest. I'm bombarded with vivid memories. I just want to disappear. The self-loathing is so overwhelming, breathing becomes even more of a struggle. It's suffocating.

I cover my ears, trying to drown out the voices in my head as I rock back and forth. My head is pounding, my body aching, and my heart feels as though it's fractured beyond repair. I wish I had the strength to pull myself together, but I don't.

How could I when this is all my fault?

I let this happen and became a victim.

I should have stood up for myself.

Left him sooner.

I only have myself to blame. This is on me.

Repeating the same things to myself, over and over again, is exhausting, and I find myself lying down, the tiled floor cool against my skin. I'm hot, and yet I can't seem to stop shivering.

What is wrong with me?

My stomach churns, the urge to vomit and purge everything terrible about me pulling at my insides, but I don't have the energy.

A hand on my shoulder startles me, my heart racing in my chest as I blink up to find the concerned face of Noah.

"Jessica, what are you doing on the floor?"

Before I can even conjure an answer, he swoops me into his arms.

"Fuck, sweet girl, you're freezing."

I swallow, trying to find my voice, but my throat is raw from all the crying. I feel exhausted on so many levels.

There's a sound of heavy footsteps nearby.

"Noah, I'm heading out…"

Deep low rumbles of voices echo around me, but I can't make heads or tails of what they're saying. All I know is I want to sleep with no dreams, just darkness, a void where I am nothing and no one.

Sitting bolt upright, I clutch the soft linen within my fist as I attempt to gather my whereabouts. My heart is beating angrily in my chest and my temples. My breathing is heavy and erratic, but not from the kind caused by physical exertion; my laboured breathing is thick with fear. There's a small lamp beside the bed, the light dim but enough to make out the room. I glance to my right and choke on a staggered breath. Noah is seated in a chair beside the bed.

He holds up his palm, as one would with a wild or scared animal, and although I may not know him or Caleb as well as my brother, in a stranger whereabouts kind of way, I have this feeling deep down that I'm safe with them.

I wipe the sweat from my brow and tuck my tangled hair behind my ears, my fingers going to my wrist, seeking a hair band. And then I remember how *he* used to say it was tacky, so I stopped doing it for the sake of arguments.

"Are you okay, sweet girl?"

Noah leans forward, his gaze probing as he takes in my appearance. I find myself nodding, even though I don't think I'll ever be all right again, not truly anyway.

I never realised just how unhinged someone could be until *him*.

"You don't have to pretend, not with me or Caleb."

His palm cups my shoulder softly.

"I don't know who I am anymore…" I admit.

Caleb enters with a phone to his ear, his shoulders tight under his suit jacket; his joggers and casual t-shirt are long gone. Not a wrinkle in sight. He looks down right powerful and ready for business. His posture relaxes a fraction when he notices me sitting upright.

"No, yeah, she's awake, okay, will do. Thanks, man." He pulls the phone away and ends the call.

My chest constricts for an entirely different reason. "Was that Mason?" I ask in a rush, my voice hopeful.

He shakes his head. "No, it was Mitchell."

My hope dissolves, my heart still racing as I sink back into the mattress. "Oh." It's hard to hide the disappointment in my voice.

Noah reaches over for my hand, giving it a soft squeeze. "You had us scared there for a minute, and it was either call Mitchell or get you to the hospital."

I'm about to protest, but he holds up his other hand. "Which we knew you didn't want, hence Caleb's call to Mitchell," he says, gaze flicking in Caleb's direction.

"No, of course, I hmmm… I don't know what happened." I pick at my thumbnail, the skin raw.

Caleb moves across the room and comes to stand beside Noah's chair.

"Mitchell says it was likely a panic attack."

Is that what that was?

The humiliation just keeps coming.

"I am so sorry. I know neither of you asked for any of this."

A deep noise emanates from Caleb's chest, almost like a growl. "You don't need to apologise."

"Sorry…" I cover my mouth with my hand because apologising has become second nature.

"Shhh, it's okay. And don't worry about Mason. We're working on it," Noah says, glancing at Caleb, where they have a silent exchange.

I clear my throat, my voice thick when I reply. "Thank you. But I don't want to be even more of an imposition than I already am."

"Sweet girl, you're not, I promise." Noah's words are full of sincerity. It's impossible to doubt him, but it doesn't stop the swell of guilt that swarms me.

"Listen, you rest, make yourself at home, help yourself to anything. And if you need anything, Noah is working remotely, so just ask, okay?"

There it is again, that sinking feeling.

Is he working from home because of me? I hate to be a burden.

Caleb's thumb hooks under my chin, tilting my face a fraction until I'm staring up at him.

"We know this is hard for you, being in a strange place. I can only imagine how vulnerable you must feel, but you can trust that we'll do whatever we can to put you at ease going forward."

And that's just it, they already have. Mason would have never said he trusted them otherwise. My conflicted feelings have everything to do with me and nothing to do with them.

"Try and sleep. Noah will make sure you're taken care of." Caleb kisses the top of my head before dropping his hand and righting himself. "I'll see you both later."

He squeezes Noah's shoulder, and I can't help but melt at how they catch each other's gaze. It might only be for a couple of seconds, but it's intense and filled with so much love I have to look away, feeling like I'm intruding on a very intimate moment.

One thing I know for sure is Curtis never looked at me that way. In company, of course, he was the perfect boyfriend. The rest of the time, his expression was filled with contempt. It didn't matter what I did or didn't do; I was never enough.

Chapter Eleven

Caleb

I want to track that motherfucker down and beat him until he's a bag of bones.

Leaving was nearly impossible, but I don't think I'd be good around Jessica in this state. I meant what I said. She needs to rest and take time to heal. Noah is better than I am at containing his anger over the situation. Me, not so much. It's taking everything in me not to make a detour and drive straight to his house. It's not like I don't have the address. I did a lot of digging last night while Noah watched over her.

I'm surprised Mason didn't come across it because he would have vetted the bastard. It would have been a straight red flag if he had delved deeper. As much as I hate getting Elliot involved, it's for the best. I need to put my petty jealousy to bed.

Pulling to a stop at a red light, I snatch up my phone from the centre console and shoot a quick text.

> Me: Everything okay?

I see the bubbles appear and tap my steering wheel with my other hand as I await his reply.

> Noah: Yes. Nothing has occurred in the past ten minutes since you left.
>
> Noah: And don't text and drive!

> Me: I'm at a red light, smart arse.

> Noah: You love my arse.

I can't help but smile, but he's also right.

> Me: True

I drop my phone back in the centre console.

Getting through this meeting will be excruciating, but at least I'll have something else to focus on, if only long enough for my anger to abate to a simmer rather than a full-on boil. I could use a good workout session, but that will have to wait until I'm home. I enter the underground car park near Tower Bridge, where my main offices are. Scanning my pass, I await as the barrier rises and make my way to my reserved space.

"Mr. Knight."

I look up as Benji stands there with a shammy leather in his hand.

"Benji, you look like you've grown a foot since I last saw you." I ruffle his hair, and he smiles wide, his braces sparkling under the fluorescent lights.

His dad, Carter, steps out from inside the valet bay. "Tell me about it. He needs to slow down. The kid has his SATS when he returns to school after half term."

Holding out my hand, I shake Carter's hand. "So, you're putting him to work in the meantime?"

Carter throws his head back and laughs. "Nah, believe it or not, he likes spending time with his old man, and you know he's a motorhead."

I glance up and see him peering through the driver's side window of my BMW 8 Series Coupé.

"Hey, Benji, you fancy giving my car an inside and out?" I ask, looking at Carter, who smiles with a nod.

He spins on his heels to face me. "What, really?"

"Absolutely. I'll be a couple of hours."

I hand my key fob to Carter and pat his back, listening to Benji's excited chatter as he tells his dad the specifications of my car, from the size of the trims to the colour, just from sight alone.

Heading into my building, I say hi to Tim, the security guard, and Felix, my reception manager.

"Morning, Mr. Knight."

"You dye your hair again?" I ask. Last week it was violet, this week it's teal.

Running his fingers through the short strands, he smiles. "Yeah, my girlfriend is working on her ombre."

"Well, tell her I said she did a good job." Not that I know anything about hair.

When I reach my floor, I smile at Wendy in greeting, her headset plastered to her ear, talking as she types a mile a minute on her keyboard.

Entering my office, I undo my suit jacket and sit, starting up my PC. Minutes later, Wendy walks in with a cup in each hand and her iPad under her arm.

"Morning, Caleb," she says, handing me my drink.

"Morning, Wendy-Bird."

Rolling her eyes, she sits opposite, placing her iPad on the desk.

"Come on," I say, sipping my coffee. "I'd be a lost boy without you."

She laughs. "That you would." She rubs over her stomach, and I swear she popped overnight—went home on Friday, and came in on Monday with a full baby bump. "You still haven't entered the baby pool," she says.

I bring my finger up to my lip. "That's because I'm still deliberating." What can I say? I'm competitive.

"Hmm, well, don't take too long. My maternity leave will be here before you know it."

Wendy has worked with me for ten years; honestly, she's not only an employee but a friend. She was there for me when I struggled with my feelings for Noah.

"Don't remind me. We still have interviews lined up for maternity cover next week?"

She nods, sipping her herbal tea and pulling a face. "I miss freaking coffee."

I shrug and then take a huge gulp of mine.

"Anyway." She reaches for her iPad and flips the cover, swiping the screen. "Your meeting is on schedule for Ten AM. I've already set up the conference room, and the slides are ready."

"See, lost without you."

She glances down. "Yeah, you can prove how much when you and Noah come to my baby shower." She slides an envelope towards me.

Snatching it up, I work my finger under the seal and read over the date. "We'll be there," I say, but I worry about Jessica in the back of my mind. If she's still with us, there is no way I'm leaving her alone.

"I might need to add a third person if that's okay?"

Glancing up, she eyes me. "Of course. Anyone I know?"

I shake my head. "No, a friend's sister will be staying with us."

"Which friend? I know all your friends."

There's no point in hiding it from her.

"Mason's sister, Jessica."

Her eyebrows pull up. "Oh, I didn't know you were close."

Fuck it. I get up and close my office door before returning to my desk.

"We're not, just between us. She turned up on our doorstep pretty banged up." And that's putting it lightly.

Wendy straightens in her seat. "Shit, what? Was she in some kind of an accident?"

I shake my head. "Boyfriend—ex-boyfriend." Soon to be hung, drawn, and quartered.

"What the fuck?" She covers her mouth with her hand. "Is she okay?"

Her bloody and bruised image comes back in vivid detail, and I have to force down my anger.

"No, not really."

"Fuck, what did the police say?"

I shake my head, scrubbing my palm over my jaw. "She didn't want them involved. She's terrified. It doesn't help that Mason is unobtainable, either; it's why she came to us. She had nowhere else to go."

Wendy's eyes go wide. "Shit, do you think it's a coincidence?" Any other time I'd laugh; Wendy loves a conspiracy theory.

I glance out the window overlooking The River Thames—not a cloud in sight, the weather so calm and still. It's a complete contradiction to the storm brewing inside me, waiting to erupt.

"No, but Noah is on the case."

She cocks her head to the side. "Well, if you need anything, you know where I am."

As much as I appreciate her offer, I don't want her involved in any way, shape, or form. It's clear this prick Curtis is unhinged, and if he's capable of hurting someone as amazing as Jessica, who knows what else he is capable of?

Chapter Twelve

Noah

I left Jessica to rest whilst I checked my emails and touched base with my team, though the urge to keep checking on her was driving me hard. But the last thing I want to be is overbearing. I don't want to suffocate her. She's already been through enough.

The sound of the front door has me out of my seat in a flash, and it's only when I make it to the hallway, I see Maggie hanging up her coat on the rack.

She turns, not seeing me standing there, and I startle her. She stifles her scream, covering her mouth with her hand, dropping the carrier bag, the sound of glass breaking, echoing.

"Shit, sorry, Maggie." I rush forward. "I didn't mean to frighten you."

Bending down, I grab the carrier bag off the floor, touching her forearm. "Are you okay?"

"Better than those pickles from the sound of it."

I cringe. "Sorry." She waves me off, taking the bag from me and rushing toward the kitchen, but comes to a halt as I almost walk straight into her.

"What on Earth?"

I see Jessica standing there, her face ashen, her arms wrapped around her waist, and her body visibly trembling.

She opens her mouth to speak, but only a strangled sound escapes her. I move around Maggie and hold up my palms facing Jessica as I approach, blocking her view from Maggie.

"Jessica?"

Her bottom lip wobbles, silent tears falling from her one good eye and before I can think better of it, I gently pull her into my chest, her body stiff, shaking beneath me.

"I heard a scream. I thought…" she stammers.

I cradle the back of her head against my chest. "Shhh, I'm sorry, totally my fault. I startled Maggie. She's our housekeeper and family friend," I say softly, stroking my other hand up and down her back, hoping to soothe her. "You're safe."

Maggie reappears behind Jessica with a tray in her hands. "How about some tea and biscuits?"

Pulling back, I look down at Jessica. "Sound good?"

She worries her lip, eyes assessing me, and I give her an encouraging nod.

"Yeah, okay."

I drop my hand to her lower back and lead her towards the living room. Maggie is leaning over the small table, already unloading the tray's contents.

"Maggie, this is Jessica, Mason's sister," I say in the way of introduction. "She'll be staying with us for a while."

Smiling, Maggie stands to her full height, barely five foot two, and holds her hand out to Jessica.

"Yes, I believe I met you briefly at the party."

Jessica shakes her hand. "Yes, you made the cake. It was delicious."

Maggie waves off the praise and then takes a seat. "Oh, shoot, I forgot the sugar," she says, her eyes flicking to mine.

"I'll get it."

I glance at Jessica and give her what I hope is a reassuring smile before I fetch the sugar. My phone vibrates in my back pocket, and I pull it out to see a text notification.

> Caleb: Is she okay?

> Me: Yeah, apart from me forgetting Maggie was here this morning. I scared the shit out of her when she came through the front door. Jessica panicked.

> Caleb: Fuck.

> Me: Yeah, Maggie made tea. I've been sent to get the 'sugar', code for I need to check on her woman to woman.

I grab the small bowl of sugar cubes and stuff my phone back into my pocket. When I return, Maggie is sitting next to Jessica, who wipes a stray tear, but as I approach, Maggie moves back to her seat.

My phone buzzes again, and I pull it free before sitting beside Jessica.

> Caleb: Maybe it will put her a little more at ease being around Maggie.

> Me: One can only hope.

Swiping out of my messages, I place my phone on the coffee table and, using the sugar tongs, I grab one and drop it into a mug, stirring it before passing it to Jessica.

Her cheeks flush, and it's the first bit of colour to grace her skin…other than the bruising.

"Thank you," she says quietly, blowing on the contents before taking a timid sip.

I catch Maggie staring, and she quickly makes herself busy

with her tea, but I know she has questions. Thankfully, I know she'll refrain from airing them in Jessica's presence.

Maggie fills the silence with easy conversation until we've all finished our tea and then excuses herself to take care of the housework.

Jessica sinks further into the sofa cushions with a vacant look. I wish I could tell her we had some news on Mason, but I can't.

"Hey, you doing okay?"

She doesn't acknowledge my question, and I wonder if she can hear me.

I kneel in front of her and hook my finger under her chin. She blinks as I come into focus.

"You okay?" I ask again.

Swallowing, she nods her head. "Yeah, sorry."

Dropping my finger from her face, I reach for her hand, giving it a gentle squeeze. "I'm the one who should apologise for managing to scare both you and Maggie simultaneously."

Instead of replying, she glances towards our hands, and I'm about to let go when she squeezes a little tighter.

"Is there anyone else you want to call? Let them know where you are. That you're all right." Which is bullocks, she's anything but all right.

She shakes her head. "Honestly, there's no one else. Not anyone I still talk to or who would notice me gone. And if they did, it's likely they're Curtis's friends, not mine."

I can't imagine how isolated she's been over the last few months—not having anyone to turn to until she was desperate.

"Well, you're safe now, and that's all that matters." I don't know how many times I've told her that since she turned up, and yet I keep reiterating it, if anything, to prove to myself that she is indeed here and safe.

"Thank you. Both you and Caleb have been extremely hospitable under the circumstances."

I notice she tries to stifle a yawn, so letting go of her hand, I push to my feet.

"Come on, you. You need to go get some more rest."

Gingerly, she shuffles forward and stands up; a soft groan falls from her lips followed by a sharp hiss through her teeth as she stands.

"How about a nap, and then when you wake up, I'll make us both some lunch."

She licks her lips. I noticed she didn't touch the biscuits.

"Yeah, okay."

When we return to the guest room and step inside, I take in the fresh linen on the bed, extra pillows, a fluffy faux fur throw, and a small vase of flowers on the dresser.

Maggie is an absolute gem of a woman. It gives the room a more comfortable feel, less generic guest room. Jessica runs the tips of her fingers over the throw before gently lowering herself to the bed.

"If you want to watch TV," I say, reaching for the remote. "Just press the power button. It's built-in with the bed frame," I say, pressing the button and watching the TV rise from the foot of the bed before handing her the remote. "You can watch any channel. There's also a selection of music and radio stations in case you just want background noise."

She's still watching the TV rise, not that I can blame her. It's a fair old size.

"Thank you, I might watch it for a while."

Of course, if I had my way, I'd just sit in here with her, but the last thing I want to do is seem as though I'm hovering.

I nod, lean down, and kiss the crown of her head.

"Do you want the door open or closed?"

Her eyes scan the door and then the room quickly. "Closed, please. But only if that's all right with you?"

I have to grind my jaw to keep my anger at bay, not with her but with the question.

What the actual fuck?

From now until further notice, it's my goal to ensure she's the one who is indeed comfortable.

Chapter Thirteen

Jessica

I was mortified at my reaction when I heard that startled scream. I wasn't sure what to think, and before I could even stop myself, my feet were moving until I found myself in the hallway, staring at a vaguely familiar face.

As soon as Noah left to get the sugar, Maggie came and sat beside me and told me if I needed anything at all to let her know. She didn't ask me what had happened, but something tells me it was pretty apparent from the way she not so subtly took stock of my appearance.

I glance around the room, and my chest tightens at the added personal touches. Even though I don't plan on staying here for long, I appreciate the gesture.

Noah gave me a look I couldn't quite decipher before he left me alone. I worry I'll say or do the wrong thing, and I already feel like so much of an imposition. I'm a mess. It doesn't help that the one person I want to see is unobtainable. At this point, I just want to know he's okay.

My bag is still at the foot of the bed, so as carefully as possible, I suck in a deep breath and lift it onto the mattress. I grabbed my favourite framed photo of Mason and me.

Brushing my thumb over the glass, I trace our smiling faces. He's always had a way of making everything better, even while growing up. I'm sure the last thing he wanted was to have to raise me practically, but he did and never once complained about it.

It was easier once I left school, and even more so when I turned eighteen. My mum wasn't interested when she could no longer get money for me—sad, but it's the truth.

She already had a widow's pension from our dad. He died of cancer when I was eleven. I vaguely remember things being good before then, but my memories now are overshadowed mainly by what came after. I don't know what would have become of me without Mason, yet here I am, seeking refuge in his friend's home.

Is he okay? Where is he? Will he be disappointed in me?

All these questions play on a loop as I pull out my most prized possessions and lay them on the bed.

There are three more photographs. One is of me with my mum, dad, and Mason in Blackpool. That was our last family holiday before Dad got sick. The other was one of me bungee jumping in Ibiza when I went on a girl's holiday before I met Curtis, and the last one is me with my group of friends from culinary school, even though we've lost touch.

My passport, birth certificate and purse are all here. I flip through to see how much cash I have on me: two twenty pound notes and a couple of quid in loose change. I have all my bank cards and driving licence, even though I don't have a car. Thankfully, apart from a joint account with Curtis for bills, the rest of my money is my own. I have a couple grand in a savings account and a few hundred in my current account.

I stare at my iPhone and pick it up, turning it over in my hands, tempted to turn it on, but I'm not ready to face whatever messages might await me from Curtis, and the last voicemail I left for Mason said I was coming here. And there's my laptop which has seen better days; I'm surprised it still works after one of Curtis's blowouts.

Going back in the bag, I feel around, and my heart begins to race; in my haste, I didn't grab any charging cables. I only grabbed a bra, a couple of pairs of underwear, some T-shirts and leggings, and an oversized cardigan. Also my Guns n Roses t-shirt that has seen better days and a beautiful scarf with foil embossed black roses that my mum got me one year for Christmas. She usually gave me cash and then asked me to borrow it back. I never did get it back.

My white Steiff Teddy bear, Lotte, was a gift for my eighteenth birthday. A small jewellery box inside holds my Rolex, a twenty-first birthday gift from Mason, and a couple of other items of jewellery, a charm bracelet, a rose pendant necklace and some earrings, the running theme, all of these were gifts from Mason. Anything from Curtis I left behind. He didn't like me wearing anything that wasn't from him, so it wasn't difficult to grab my box and leave the rest behind.

This is my life. My worldly possessions might seem pathetic to anyone else, but they're everything to me. I'll need to get some trainers. I wasn't thinking of practicality when I grabbed my clothing. I think that was evident from how I arrived here.

Putting the contents carefully back into my bag, I place it at the foot of the bed. Picking up the framed photo of Mason and me, I stand it on the bedside table and bring Lotte to my chest, cuddling the soft, familiar teddy.

There's a soft knock on the door, and I startle awake, my heart racing, ribs aching. I glance at the TV, the credits rolling. I couldn't have been asleep too long. I was close to the end of the film.

"Can I come in?" Noah's voice calls through the closed door.

I move to sit up, clearing my throat. "Yes."

The door opens, and his head appears first before he enters, balancing a tray in his hand.

"I hope you don't mind. I took the liberty of making lunch."

"Thank you."

He places the tray on the foot of the bed and hands me a plate with a sandwich.

"Cheese salad. Hope that's okay?"

I nod. "Yes, thanks."

He places a glass on the coaster beside me and eyes the photo before reaching for the other plate and pulling the chair closer to the bed where he sits. "Thought I'd join you. Caleb is always telling me off for eating lunch while I work."

I pick up the sandwich and wait for him to bite into his before I bring mine to my mouth and take a tentative bite.

"If you want me to make you something else, I can."

Shaking my head, I cover my mouth with the back of my hand before speaking. "No, it's nice, thank you." Even if I was telling the truth, I just don't have much of an appetite.

His eyes glance at the TV.

"Marvel fan?" he asks before taking another bite of his sandwich.

"Yeah, but Curtis was a DC fan."

I quickly take another small bite of my food. I have no idea why I even told him that.

"Nah, Marvel for the win," he says good-naturedly, and I notice he's already eaten half his sandwich, and I've barely taken two bites of mine.

He grabs a packet of crisps off the tray and rips open the packet, adds some to his plate, and holds up the bag towards me.

I shake my head. "I'm okay with just this, thank you," I say with the sandwich clutched between my fingers.

He falls silent for a beat as we both eat; the only sounds are of his crisps crunching or me chewing. It probably feels like it sounds louder than what it is.

He's finished quickly, and I can barely manage to finish half of mine.

"If you've had enough, you can leave that, don't worry. It won't go to waste. If you're worried about that, I'll eat it."

"Thank you," I say, passing him the plate as he hands me the glass of juice from the bedside table.

"Nice photo."

I can't stop the small smile that curves my lips. "It was a good day," I reply, reaching out for Lotte and placing it beside my pillow, but not before he sees it. He says nothing as he picks up the rest of my sandwich and finishes it in less than three bites.

"Hollow legs," he says with a shrug. Where Caleb is filled out, with broad shoulders and thick thighs, Noah is the leaner of the two.

When I realise I've been staring, I glance back at the TV.

"Want to press play on Captain Marvel? I'll watch it with you for a bit before I go back to work."

Without answering, I grab the remote and select the film. When it begins to play, the subtitles pop up and he says nothing, but I do turn the volume up a couple of notches.

An unusual sense of calm washes over me, his quiet presence a welcome support.

Chapter Fourteen

Caleb

I arrived home later than I would have liked under the circumstances. I know Jessica is fine with Noah, but still, I didn't like leaving her. So much has happened in the last twenty-four hours.

Just as I undo my tie and the top button of my shirt, Noah emerges from Jessica's room, quietly closing the door behind him. He sees me and smiles, holding his finger to his lips before he leans in to give me a chaste kiss. Then he angles his head towards the hall, and I follow him to our room.

"How is she?" I ask, pulling off my tie and wrapping it around my knuckles before leaving it on the dresser.

"She's sleeping. I made her lunch, she didn't eat much, but it was better than nothing. I sat with her and watched some Marvel before giving her more painkillers, knocking her for six." His fingers find the buttons of my shirt as he begins to undo them.

I cover his hands with mine. "Any news from Elliot?"

Noah looks at my bare chest through the gap in my shirt. "No, but he's on it, and he said he'd let us know as soon as he finds out anything, no matter how small."

I start walking him back towards the bed, and as the back of his thighs touch the frame, he sits down, moving his hands to the waist of my trousers, where he begins to unbuckle my belt.

Placing my hands on his shoulders, I push him back until he's lying down and then bring a knee up as I bracket my hands on either side of his head, rubbing my nose against his.

"And what else did he say?" I can't help asking. I'm strung so damn tight right now.

His jaw tenses. Noah is patient with me for the most part, but he's also still only human. He arches a brow. "Really, Caleb?"

Yeah, I'm being super obtuse, that much is evident.

"Humour me," I say with a deep growl as I move my mouth to his ear, where I flick out my tongue before tugging on his earlobe and biting down gently, thrusting my groin against his.

"It was pretty much what I said. I asked him to help us locate Mason, and he said he'd be in touch, and I replied with a thank you. It was polite communication."

I lick the side of his throat, and he shivers. It's impossible not to love everything about this man, the way he tastes, how he smells—how he feels when he's wrapped around my hard cock.

The urge to take him is like a predatory need to show him who he belongs to, but I'm aware we also have Jessica in our guest room at the other end of the hallway. I'm not against having sex while visitors stay over, but the circumstances are different in this case.

"Want to go down to the gym for a quick sparring session while Jessica is asleep?"

Having the gym in the basement is definitely one of our better ideas. I push myself up and finish stripping out of my suit. Noah sits up, resting on his elbows, watching me as I grab a pair of workout shorts and pull them on, my erection evident in my boxers.

Then, without a word, I turn and make my way downstairs to the basement. Some of the good things about it is its fully air-conditioned, divided into sections for training and has a steam room and hot tub. But the best part is its soundproof.

I grab the remote and turn on the sound system, but lower the volume as Noah appears in his workout shorts.

"Want to spar?" he asks.

Walking backwards, I move to the small ring in the corner and pull off my socks before slipping under the rope. My eyes are fixated on Noah as he follows suit and joins me.

There'll be no sparring; neither of us is wearing gloves or mouth guards, for that matter.

I circle Noah, and he watches, his gaze intense, his pupils blown wide. I move towards him until his back hits the rope.

My hand slips under his shorts. "Hmmm, someone forgot their boxers," I say, bringing the pad of my thumb to the head of his cock, rubbing it over his pre-cum before raising it to my mouth and sucking.

"I'd say sorry, but I know what you need, and they would have just slowed us down." His fingers find the waistband of my shorts and boxers, and he shoves them down my legs, dropping to his knees right in front of my erect cock.

And then, without any fanfare or warning, he grips my arse cheeks and takes me into his mouth, straight to the back of his throat. I let out a deep groan and throw my head back.

"Fuck." I grab the crown of his head, running my fingers through his hair before gripping it and tugging him even closer as he slides a hand to my balls. When I look down, he's already looking up at me expectantly. He knows what I need without me even needing to ask.

"You ready for me to fuck your face?" It's a rhetorical question, but still, he hums his consent, the vibration heavenly against my already throbbing dick.

This man knows how to draw pleasure from me, allowing me to be who I need to be in the moment, and let go of my inhibitions. The way he knows me like no other, and yet he loves me regardless, says so much about him as a person. But the way he trusts me...something about that makes me feel both powerful and cherished.

I slow my thrusts as tears spring to his eyes. Reaching down with the pad of my thumb, I wipe one away and bring it to my mouth, licking off his sweet and salty essence.

His fingers continue to play with my balls, his need to give the release I so desperately crave his intent. I stare down as he pulls himself free with his other hand and begins to stroke up and down his length, matching my punishing thrusts. But I no longer want to come down his throat. Clenching my jaw, I pull out of his mouth and grip myself hard at the base of my dick. I tug on his hair, my fingers still buried in his scalp.

"I want to come together," I say, my voice deep.

He smiles before licking his lips. I love how swollen they look as he moves to his feet, his fist still wrapped around his dick, his head leaking pre-cum. He's just as wild for me as I am for him.

Reaching for his hip, I tug him forward, adoring the hitch of his breath as I do, and then I knock his hand away, so we're flesh on flesh, and he bucks against me.

I'm already wet, having been inside Noah's mouth, so I spit into my palm before pulling back and taking his cock in my hand, lubing him up before wrapping my hand around both our cocks, and then I grind into him. He thrusts back, meeting my every move. Our foreheads touch as we both stare down. Our gyrations become even more erratic, frantic even.

"Don't you fucking dare come," I say through clenched teeth. "Not until I say."

I continue working the both of us, the pressure almost painful as his arousal glistens. He's so ready to combust at any moment, the way his dick throbs and continues to harden. His nails dig into my arse cheek as he thrusts his hips against mine with wild abandon.

We're grunting now with every single thrust.

"Who do you belong to?" I growl out, my pleasure and need for release mounting.

He's about to lose it. I can tell by the way he hardens. "You, always you, Caleb."

"Then prove it and come for me. Right. Fucking. Now."

With a roar, he throws his head back as he erupts between us, his cum coating us both. And then I finally give in, chasing my release, my cock thickening as I continue to thrust, not relinquishing my hold on Noah as I drag every last drop from him. Fountains of my cum join his as I move even faster, panting and hissing through the powerful release. He twitches in my grip as I spasm the last of my semen, covering my stomach and hand, mixing with his arousal.

"Fuck, I love you," he gasps out, catching his breath.

"Fuck, I love you," I say, my breathing ragged as he looks up at me through heavy lashes.

"Not as much as I love you," he replies.

His entire face is relaxed and sated as he gives me one of his killer smiles, both his dimples prominent, his eyes piercing as he stares back at me. The look alone is one filled with adoration and love.

I brush my lips against his, the kiss gentle and tender, contradicting the savage need that consumed us only moments before.

We need to clean up, but for now, I'm content in this embrace, savouring that he is *indeed* mine.

Chapter Fifteen

Noah

It's been almost a week since Jessica's life turned upside down. Apart from her first night here when she woke screaming and had a panic attack, she's been quiet. Honestly, too quiet.

She naps throughout the day, which Mitchell said is perfectly understandable under the circumstances, but still, the silence bothers me the most.

Some days she'll come out of her room for lunch, but for the most part, she stays in her room. The only meal we manage to get her to join us for every day is dinner. Maggie has been by three times this week, clearly concerned for Jessica's well-being. We're doing our best to be here for her, but Caleb is just as worried about her silence as I am. She says her pleases and thank yous and replies to conversations at the correct intervals, but she's so removed from herself that it's making our concern for her heighten.

After the first two days, her bruises transformed into blue, purple, and purplish-black—so angry in colour that they were even more alarming than how they appeared upon her arrival. Caleb gave her some arnica salve to help, and I think it did. They're much less prominent than a few days ago, now turning yellow and green. Her wrist seems a lot better. She's not favouring the other hand as much, but it's clear her ribs still cause pain and discomfort.

I find myself watching her. She still avoids making eye contact for too long and tries to shrink herself down in size, her shoulders hunched. The more we see a shell of the young woman we first met, the angrier we're both becoming. We try our best to keep this away from her, but I'm sure she must pick up on the growing tension. Caleb prides himself on communication in all aspects of his life, so I know this is a lot harder for him, but we're also trying to be as respectful to her needs and healing as possible. I just worry that, mentally and emotionally, she's not healing at all.

"Hey, sweet girl, how are you feeling?" I ask when she emerges from her room wearing one of my shirts. It wasn't long before we realised her essentials consisted of the bare minimum. It is not lost on me how, apart from the framed photo she now has on her bedside table, she still keeps her bag at the foot of her bed like she's ready to flee at any moment.

"Yeah, I'm okay, thank you." It's a monotone response, one lacking emotion, but sadly one we're becoming accustomed to, but still, it's better than complete silence.

"It's a nice day. Did you want to eat outside?"

Her body stiffens at my suggestion.

I reach out and pause, waiting for her reaction, and then I softly touch her shoulder. "Just on the roof garden terrace," I add for clarity.

I realise in the week she has been here, she's only been in her room, the kitchen, or the living room. At least the skylights from the kitchen give some natural light with it being on the lower floor, and she's at least not completely closed off to daylight even while she's closed off to the outside world.

It's why we're so desperate to find out why we've been unable to track down Mason. Whatever he's doing must be a top-level secret. But hearing from him, knowing he's okay, will give her the boost she needs.

She twists her hands in front of her and looks away. "Yeah, if that's what you want to do," she replies.

I almost let out a sigh. "Only if you'd like to, no pressure. I just thought you might have a touch of cabin fever, and the fresh air would do you good."

Her gaze lifts to mine for a moment, and I notice the moment her posture relaxes.

"Yeah, that sounds nice."

I smile as I turn towards the kitchen, the sound of her feet padding softly behind me. I noticed how the first few days, she almost always walked on tiptoes, literally. But she's been doing that a little less; maybe it's from always walking around on literal eggshells around her pathetic excuse of an ex. At this point, any progress is better than no progress.

"I hope you like macaroni and cheese. Maggie brought her homemade one, and it's delicious."

Using the oven gloves, I remove the casserole dish from the oven and place it on the counter. Peering over my shoulder, I notice a small smile grace her lips. "I do. Two of my favourite food groups. Cheese and pasta." As soon as the words leave her lips, her mouth turns into a straight line, like she can't believe she said that out of the blue.

I turn to face her, slipping off the gloves. "That's good to know. I can't wait for you to try this," I say, pulling out two dishes and spooning out two generous servings.

She quietly moves beside me and pulls cutlery from the drawer before grabbing some serviettes as I load the dishes onto the tray.

"What would you like to drink?" I ask, moving to the fridge and opening the door. Maggie always brings some groceries with her even though it's unnecessary. "We have orange juice, apple juice or some sparkling Elderflower." When I poke my head back out of the fridge door, I notice her eyes light up.

"Elderflower?"

"Yes, please," she says, reaching into the cabinet for glasses, but before I can tell her I'll do it, she lets out a hiss of pain.

The fridge forgotten, I rush to her side and reach over her head for the glasses that are just out of her reach and lower them to the counter.

"I keep forgetting myself," she admits, her cheeks tinged with a flush.

I wrap my arm around her shoulders and kiss her temple without thinking before stepping away and grabbing the bottle of Elderflower.

"How about you pour, and I'll get the ice?"

She smiles gratefully and does that before I load up the tray, and she follows me up the stairs and out onto the decent-sized terraced roof garden.

I move to the oval cast aluminium table and unload the tray.

"Take a seat," I say, tilting my head to the chairs, all with curve back cushions.

Her eyes scan the area. "Wow, it's lovely up here," she says as I sit opposite.

Smiling, I grab my fork. "Thank you. Caleb got the hot tub. I got the roof garden."

Picking up her fork, she looks past me and then to her left and right.

"The hot tub is in the basement, where we also have a gym and a steam room."

Her mouth gapes open. I nod to her food and load up a forkful of mine. "I'll show you once we've eaten, give you a proper tour."

I pause with my fork to my mouth, waiting to see her reaction to this gooey goodness, and it doesn't disappoint when she closes her eyes and lets out a small moan as she chews, her eyes springing open.

"Oh my god, it's so good," she says, swallowing and digging back in for more.

"Told you," I say before diving into mine. It's good to see her other eye open. Although it's bruised and the white of her eye is bloodshot, her eyesight seems to be all right for the most part. Mitchel told us to have her gently ice it a couple of times a day. Two days later, we had him come back to check it out. He said her sight appears fine, but if she gets any issues seeing spots or her vision seems impaired at all, she needs to see a specialist.

In a couple of weeks, her bruises will fade, but it's the emotional damage I'm more concerned about, but right now, it's a conversation for another day, one I'm hoping she'll be the one to broach. I want her to know she can trust me and Caleb. I don't ever want her to feel coerced or cornered.

All I know is in the space of a week, my protectiveness towards her is only increasing. I always knew she was special, but it's something more than that, maybe something I'm not willing to even admit to myself or Caleb, maybe not ever.

Chapter Sixteen

Jessica

Noah wasn't kidding when he said that Maggie's mac and cheese was delicious. I devoured it all, and even though my stomach aches, it was worth it. Something about eating food that I love has me feeling nostalgic.

Noah quickly clears the plates and loads the dishwasher before taking me on a tour of the rest of the house, which seems almost daft. I've been here a week and visited for Mason's party, but it seems there's more to see.

That terraced roof garden is so beautiful, and the aluminium slate dining table and chairs set it off perfectly. One thing I can't deny is these men have style in abundance.

"Okay, you ready to come see Caleb's pride and joy?" he asks, his voice holding so much warmth, my chest aches. I love the obvious way they're so in love with one another.

I don't know what I expected when he brought me here, but it wasn't this. Being in a basement, I would have thought it would be dark, but there are spotlights in the ceiling and lights lining the outskirts of the long room.

"Weights, rowing machine, running machine, cross trainer," he says as we begin to walk the length of the room, coming to a stop. "Here is the small boxing ring," he says, grabbing the rope, a smile curving his lips, one I'm not privy to but has my mind wandering to places I have no business being. I let out a shiver. My nipples harden under the thin material of my t-shirt.

He grabs a remote from the wall. "Let me turn the air con down. Sorry, it can get really hot down here."

"It's fine," I say, my voice catching for some reason unbeknownst to me. There are two rooms on either side. One has a round tub, which is clearly the hot tub, and the other has benches which must be the steam room, with clear glass and mirrors. There are a lot of mirrors.

"Yeah, Caleb has a thing for the mirrors," Noah says close to my ear, causing me to turn too fast, but he steadies his hands on my shoulders before he gives me a playful wink and drops his hands.

It's only then I realise my comment about the mirrors wasn't just in my head—mortified.

"Do you use it a lot?" I ask, trying to sound casual but failing miserably.

He nods and leads me to the room with the hot tub, opening the door for me to follow. There's a partition behind that I didn't see from outside.

"Yeah, pretty much daily. It's a good stress reliever. There's a wet room in here, as well as in the steam room, too."

I let out a low whistle. "Wow, that must have cost a bomb," I say, immediately wanting to duck and run. "Shit, I'm sorry. I have no idea where my manners have gone."

Noah laughs, the most beautiful sound I have ever heard. How can a man laugh and look like that? Not all men were created equal, and this man right here proves it.

"Don't be, it was a lot of money, but it made sense. It was a good investment in the long run. And helps with a good work-life balance. Otherwise, we'd be taking more time away from each other to go to the gym, and between us, the gym helps with our mental health." He moves towards the hot tub and presses a button. It lights up and starts bubbling up. "We get to work out and see each other, so it's a win, plus it has its perks for a little rest and relaxation, too."

I reach down and put my fingers in the water; it's already warming up, and the bubbles tickle my skin.

"You're welcome down here to use the hot tub any time you want and, of course, any of the equipment when you're given the all-clear."

He makes it sound as though I'll still be here. The truth is, I need to start thinking ahead and make some decisions about what comes next. Pulling my hand out, I accept the small hand towel he passes my way.

"Thank you."

I dry my hands and look around, wondering where to put it. He shows me a laundry basket built into the counter, hooks, and the soft-close cupboards that hold towels and toiletries for use in the wet room.

He lets out a soft chuckle. "It's okay. I get it. This is all a bit overwhelming. Caleb nor I grew up with a lot of money, so believe me when I say it might look a little extreme, but we don't take it for granted."

I quickly turn to face him. "I wasn't... I didn't... I didn't mean to offend you." I avert my eyes, worried my reaction was unintentionally offensive. And after all they've done for me.

"Hey, Jessica, look at me." His finger tilts my chin up until I'm staring back at him. "You didn't offend me. Why would you think that?"

I try to form an answer, but I can barely catch my breath.

"Jessica, breathe with me, okay? In through your nose." He inhales. "And out through your mouth." He exhales. Everything is muffled, his voice, my surroundings. Everything feels disjointed, uneven, and out of place. But in the recesses of my mind, I can hear him as he continues to coax me through it, bringing me back to the present until I feel like I can finally breathe again and then I realise I'm sitting in his lap on the floor.

"Sweet girl, you back with me?"

I bring my trembling fingers to my face, and when I pull them back, I realise I've been crying.

"I don't know what happened. I'm sorry."

Noah is gentle as he holds me in his arms, cradled in his lap, but it's not lost on me how he's being gentle not to hurt me.

"You had another panic attack. Was it something I did, something I said?" The worry in his voice is almost devastating.

"No, not at all. I don't even know what happened," I admit. Because it's the truth, one moment we're talking, and the next we're on the floor.

"Come on, let's get you back upstairs," he says. I go to move, but before I do, he's already somehow standing with me still in his arms, and now my heart is racing for another unknown reason.

"I can walk, but thank you."

He studies my face for a beat before nodding and carefully setting me back on my feet. He waits to make certain I won't fall. Then, with a palm resting on my lower back, he gently grips my elbow as we go back upstairs.

"Here, let me get you some water. Do you want any painkillers?" he asks as he grabs two bottles of water from the fridge.

"Yes, please."

He passes me them both, and I shake out two tablets from the bottle and unscrew the water lid before swallowing them. There's a bitter aftertaste that causes me to scrunch up my face.

Silently he sips his water, leaning against the counter, as I shift from one foot to another.

"I might go and have a nap if that's okay?"

He pushes off the counter and steps towards me, nodding. "Of course. You sure you're all right after what just happened?"

Saved by Two

"Yeah, I'm fine," I say, giving what I hope is a believable smile, and then I turn and make my way back to the guest room.

I've been finding that napping in small intervals throughout the day helps, seeing as I've been unable to sleep at night. I don't know if it's from the fear of having nightmares or because I feel safer sleeping in the day. Instead, I find myself quietly prowling between the living room, kitchen, and the guest room at night. Sometimes I sit in the small window seat and try to read one of the many books Caleb and Noah have. They have bookcases full of so many different books. Or I watch Marvel, my comfort films, or anything to try and keep my mind busy. But the truth is nothing keeps my attention for long before my mind drifts to places I'd much rather it didn't. If Caleb and Noah have noticed, they haven't mentioned it, so hopefully, my restlessness isn't disturbing them.

Biting my nails has become a new pastime of mine, too. Keeps my hands busy. Usually cooking and baking would have been my go-to, but I'm already intruding on their hospitality enough as it is, and I don't want to start taking over their kitchen as well as their guest room.

I climb into the bed and tug the duvet up to my neck, a big yawn escaping me as I press play on the TV. Between lunch and the panic attack, I'm exhausted and can barely keep my eyes open.

Chapter Seventeen

Caleb

Noah and I agreed to rotate our work schedules so one of us would always be at home with Jessica. We don't want it to seem like we're crowding her or for her to feel suffocated. I know I can be a force to be reckoned with at the best of times, so hovering over Jessica while she begins to heal is something I don't want to do, even if it does go against my nature.

When I arrive home, Noah is already in the kitchen in front of the range cooker.

"Something smells good," I say, approaching him from behind and wrapping my arms around him before leaning over his shoulder to see what he's making.

"Yeah, thought I'd get a start on dinner."

I kiss his temple before stepping back and undoing my tie.

"Thanks, it's been a long day, and local traffic was murder."

Shrugging out of my suit jacket, I look around to see any sign of Jessica.

"How was she this afternoon after what happened in the gym?"

He turns the heat down on the pan and reaches for his glass

of wine. "Quiet. She's not come out since she went to take a nap."

I look in the fridge, grab a bottle of beer, and twist off the cap, taking a huge gulp.

"I'll check in on her before I go change."

Grabbing my jacket, I head through the hallway and stop at her door where I listen for a sound. There's the TV's low hum, so I gently tap my knuckle on the door and wait before pushing it open.

A few pillows prop up Jessica, but she seems to be able to lie down more than when she first arrived, having to sleep sitting up. A bear is cradled under her arm, her hair fanning the pillow. But even from here, I can see the dark circles under her eyes, so quietly I step back, not wanting to disturb her.

Once I've showered, I return to the kitchen just as Noah starts setting the table for three.

"Dinner's almost ready," he says, glancing up.

"Don't suppose we know any more about Mason?" I ask.

Noah grabs the cutlery and lays it out beside the placemats.

"Elliot seems to think he's on an undercover case, but from what he's uncovered, he might be on security for a high-profile client, so he's going by an alias."

I grab the open bottle of wine from the fridge and top off Noah's glass before pouring myself one, and I leave it on the table for when Jessica comes for dinner.

"That would make sense why he's been unreachable, but it still doesn't help when I know how much Jessica, at the very least, could do with hearing his voice."

Noah grabs my hand and squeezes. "Yeah, I agree, but honestly, because she was with Curtis, he probably thinks she's okay, if that makes sense."

I lean in and give him a chaste kiss. "Yeah, yeah, I know, and you're always the voice of reason."

It's like an itch I can't scratch—wanting to go and pay this guy a visit, but I made a promise to Noah. It doesn't mean he'll be getting away with it scot-free. And Noah knows this too; we're biding our time now.

"Can you let Jessica know dinner is ready?"

The image of how tired she looked, even asleep, makes me pause. "Maybe we should let her sleep. We can cover her dinner and heat it when she wakes up."

He nods. "You've noticed how exhausted she is, too?"

"Yeah, and I've heard her moving around in the middle of the night. You know what a light sleeper I am, but I figured it's how she copes."

I watch as he dishes up three plates, covering hers with tin foil.

"Do you think we should say something?" he asks, walking over with our plates of creamy chicken carbonara.

Pulling out Noah's chair first, I take both plates from him so he can sit, placing them on the placemats before I join him.

"No, let's wait it out a little longer. I might be a little more worried if she wasn't sleeping during the day."

Picking up his glass, he holds it up, and I grab mine. We chink them together as we both say cheers and take a sip.

"Do you think she's afraid she'll have nightmares like she did on the first night?"

I swirl some of the pasta around my fork. "Maybe, I just want her to feel like she has a semblance of control. Though I'm sure under the circumstance she feels differently—her entire life has been turned upside down."

Light footfall catches my attention, and sure enough, Jessica pads into the room, her hair in a messy bun on the top of her head. She's wearing a pair of leggings and one of Noah's t-shirts.

"Hey, sweet girl. We didn't want to wake you. Are you hungry?" he asks.

"Yeah, I can get it," she says, her eyes darting towards the kitchen counter.

Noah goes to push his chair back, but I put my hand on his shoulder.

"No, you eat," I say, moving to my feet. "You sit, Jessica. I'll get it."

She moves around the table and takes the seat opposite me and closest to Noah.

I uncover the plate and, satisfied it's still warm enough, bring it to the table and place it in front of her. "What did you want to drink?" I ask and notice her eyes dart to the bottle of wine and then to her plate.

"You can have a small glass if you want to, Jessica. You're an adult."

Any injury to her vocal cords seems to be okay.

"Yes, I'll have some wine then, please," she says, her voice small.

Noah doesn't hesitate as he pours her a glass and then fills a small tumbler with some water for her.

"Thank you." She smiles genuinely, not forced like the others I've seen her use. "Another one of my favourites," she says, eyeing the pasta.

"Probably not as good as Maggie's macaroni and cheese," Noah says more for my benefit than hers, I'm sure.

"Please say you saved me some?" I ask.

Noah laughs. "Of course."

"Thank you. And just for the record, your carbonara is just as good as Maggie's."

His cheeks flush from the compliment, and I squeeze his thigh under the table.

"Hmmm, this is good," Jessica says around a forkful.

"Now you're both just stroking my ego," Noah replies, sipping his wine, looking heavenward with an overdramatic eye roll.

I raise my eyebrows as I move my hand higher on his thigh, and he coughs around his wine.

But the sound of Jessica laughing now has our full attention.

"No, I tried a lot of food in culinary school, and I wouldn't lie. This is really good."

Neither of us reply, caught in the sweet afterglow of hearing her at ease for the first time in a week.

She tilts her head slightly when she glances up and notices us both looking at her. "What?" She runs her tongue over her top teeth. "Do I have something in my teeth?"

Noah is the first to break out of whatever spell she has us under.

"No, sweet girl, it was just good to hear you laugh," he admits.

Her cheeks flush; even with the bruising, the glow beneath her skin still shines.

"Oh." She tucks a loose strand of hair behind her ear, and for the first time in what seems like forever, we fall into a semi-comfortable silence.

Chapter Eighteen

Noah

"Thank you, that was delicious," Jessica says, resting back in her chair, her shoulders relaxed as she covers her stomach with her hand.

"You're welcome."

Caleb starts stacking all the plates, and before Jessica can even think to help, he tells her he's got this, giving her a wink.

"You'll have to let me cook for you both as a thank you for having me."

I reach over and touch her arm. "You don't have to do anything to thank us. But I'd love to try anything you'd be willing to cook for us. It's not every day we have a chef at our disposal."

Her look is wistful. "Not quite. I missed out on my diploma. But I'd love to cook for you both regardless."

"You can always go back though, right, finish and get your qualification?" Caleb asks as he tops up all our wine with the tipple left in the bottle.

"Yeah, maybe," she says, picking up her glass and swirling the rose-coloured liquid like it holds all the answers.

"You can do anything you put your mind to. I have no doubt."

My eyes follow Caleb as he returns to the kitchen, and I mouth, "I love you."

He returns with dessert. "Tiramisu," he says.

"Okay, now you're really pulling out the big guns. At this rate, I'll never leave."

It's such a contrast to see her coming out of her shell again and being relaxed; honestly, she can stay as long as she needs to. I don't think either of us is in a hurry for her to leave any time soon, and from Caleb's glance, it's clear he feels the same way.

"Well, full transparency, this is shop bought. Neither of us can bake, so you need to submit any complaints directly with Marks and Spencers."

She laughs again, the sound so carefree. It reminds me she's only twenty-two. Eight years younger than myself and twelve years younger than Caleb.

"And for the record, you can stay for as long as you need, just so we're clear," Caleb says, glancing at me and then back to Jessica. This is why I love this man. I know he thinks he's hard to love—but he's not—loving him is easy. Relationships are hard, there's a lot of give and take, but at the end of the day, being with him is worth it.

This time when our plates are empty, Jessica insists on clearing the table. I give Caleb a look that says, let her do it.

"So Jessica, where are you on your Marvel-thon?" I ask.

I watch as she loads the dishwasher, making sure she's careful. Hell, it hurt her to reach for a glass earlier. It's why I moved them all to the lower shelf and rearranged everything so it's easier for her to reach. I'm sure Caleb will say something once he notices because he doesn't particularly like change. Everything has its place. I'll happily toss my dirty clothes into the laundry bin, yet he'll fold his.

"I was getting ready to watch Thor."

"Fancy some company?" he asks, his eyes roaming to mine. I raise my eyebrows, and he shrugs.

Joining Jessica in the kitchen, I dig around the cupboard and pull out a box. "We even have popcorn."

She glances between us both. "You don't have to watch it with me," she says as I unwrap the packet and place it in the microwave.

"We want to," I assure her. Well, probably more me than Caleb. He's usually the more restless of us, but if he knows how much I love something, he'll make it work. And I know he wants Jessica to spend more time out of her room with us. Because it's clear something seems to have shifted, not by much, but enough to ease some of the heavy tension of the past week.

"Yeah, okay."

Caleb claps his hands together. "I'll go get the TV ready while you're waiting for the popcorn," he says.

"Shall I get us some drinks?" Jessica asks.

"Yes, please. Caleb and I'll have a coke."

When we make our way into the living room, Caleb has the film ready to go and the ambient lighting for our viewing pleasure.

He pats the spot next to him for me and points to the other side for Jessica, so I'm in the middle.

"I thought you might like the pouffe footstool, and there's a blanket in case you get cold."

She smiles and sits as I help adjust some of the cushions behind her back until I'm sure she's comfortable.

I pass out the bowls of popcorn, and then Caleb hits play.

Twenty minutes into the film, he's already asked me about fifteen questions. It's a love-hate trait and probably why we never go to the cinema. But he's making an effort for Jessica.

I love that she's patient and answers some of his questions, how comfortable she is with us.

I realise she's asleep only when I feel her head on my

shoulder. I go to move, but Caleb squeezes my knee. I glance at him, and he shakes his head.

He holds his finger to his mouth before whispering in my ear, "Let her rest while we watch the rest of this." He kisses my temple, his attention moving back to the screen.

A heavy weight across my lap pulls me from sleep, and I blink away the fogginess as I peer down to see Jessica's head resting on the cushion in my lap.

A hand squeezes my shoulder, and I turn my head to face Caleb.

"Shit, what time is it?" I ask, stretching my neck.

He glances at his wrist. "Just after six."

I look down at the sofa and notice her legs are up, and she has another throw over her.

"I covered her when I got up to use the toilet, and when I returned, you were out, too."

And that's when I notice a throw covering my legs. "Did you sleep?" I ask.

He shrugs. "A bit."

I reach down and stroke the hair away from Jessica's face. "Did she stir at all?"

"No, she whimpered a little, but once I moved her head onto your lap, she settled."

Jessica takes that moment to blink awake, looking up at me from my lap. A smile breaks out on her face, and I half expect her to panic, but instead, she surprises me when she says, "Sorry, did I crash out on you guys?"

"It's okay, little one, you don't snore that much," I say, flicking the tip of her nose.

She laughs and lifts her chin to see Caleb from where she is and blushes before she moves into a sitting position, holding her ribs as she does.

"Considering I took over the sofa, I have to say I slept really well," she admits sheepishly.

Saved by Two

Somehow, that knowledge makes me breathe a little easier.

Chapter Nineteen

Jessica

It's strange how time can move so differently, from one week to the next. The first week I was here, it was as though time had stood still and now not so much. It's been three weeks, and I feel like I can breathe somewhat easier, even though my ribs still cause discomfort. My bruises are now a dull yellow as I begin to heal from the wounds inflicted by my abusive ex. And little by little, their presence has started to chip away at the walls I built, allowing rays of light to filter into the darkest corners of my broken heart as I struggle to come out of my shell and rebuild my shattered self-esteem.

The gentle hum of the city outside provides a comforting backdrop to my thoughts as I sit on the plush carpet of the living room floor, surrounded by the warmth of Caleb and Noah as they sit on the sofa. Both have become such unwavering support, allowing me sanctuary from the storm that engulfed my life, offering me safety. Their home has become my haven and not just because of its luxurious walls but because of the two extraordinary men who reside within them. They're salvation I never knew I needed.

With his protective nature and uncanny ability to make me

feel safe, Caleb has been coaxing out my inner fears and insecurities lately. If I startle at a sudden noise or flinch at an unexpected touch, he whispers soothing words to chase away the lingering fear.

Noah is the epitome of patience. He possesses a calm demeanour that always puts me at ease. The silence is no longer as loud—before it was excruciating—but now there's solace in the quiet, an unspoken understanding between us acting as a salve to my wounded spirit. Noah's smile is infectious. He always has a way of making me forget my pain, if only for a moment.

Together, Caleb and Noah are a force to be reckoned with, balancing each other out in their own unique ways, making my road to recovery a little less lonely.

They encourage me to be me again, to find peace with who I am and not what I was forced to believe I was, which was pretty much worthless, according to Curtis. They are a source of both strength and comfort. They've shown me what it means to be treated with kindness and respect, something I almost forgot existed—having lived with Curtis for nine months—as I open up to them little by little.

Being in such close proximity to Caleb and Noah, our lives have become intricately woven, even in such a short space of time.

The sun begins to set, casting an amber glow across the living room. With my back against the sofa, I glance back to Caleb and Noah on either side of me on the sofa, both engrossed in the film; it's become a nightly routine. My heart swells with gratitude for these two men who have seen me at my weakest and are helping me to find my inner strength.

The more the days pass, the more I know I'll need to venture out into the real world at some point. It's one thing living in the safety net they've created, but it's another facing those fears outside the confines of these walls.

"What has you thinking so hard, sweet girl?"

My cheeks heat from his term of endearment. Lately, that's all I do around these two men, but if they notice, they never comment.

"I've decided I want to start taking back my life. I want to look into maybe getting counselling." I've been toying with it back and forth the last couple of days, now it's something I finally dare to voice out loud.

Noah nods his agreement, and his eyes fill with a tenderness that touches my soul. "I think that's a courageous step."

"You do?"

Caleb sits forward and touches my shoulder. "Yes, we both do. You have a resilience that is rare, Jessica. You're one of the strongest people we've ever met."

Tears well up in my eyes, and for the first time in what feels like a long time, they aren't tears of pain or despair but gratitude and hope, a testament to how much these men have helped me.

"Get up here," Noah says.

He lifts his arm as I settle between them. Then he tugs me close to his side before kissing the crown of my head. Caleb takes my hand, entwining my fingers with his. It seems strangely intimate and yet not strange at all.

I wipe under my nose and fight back the tears.

"I can help you with that," Caleb offers. "I can get it all arranged for you and have something set up."

Shifting so I can see his face, I shake my head. "You don't have to do that," I say, my voice steady despite the rapid beating of my heart.

He holds my chin gently between his thumb and forefinger with his free hand. "No, but I want to. I can help you find a therapist who specialises in trauma and abuse. You don't have to go through this alone."

My eyes meet his. "Thank you, Caleb," I whisper, my voice

filled with gratitude. "I honestly don't know what I'd have done without you and Noah both."

Noah squeezes my shoulder. "We're in this together."

He leans over, snatches up his laptop from the coffee table, and sits it on my lap.

"In that case, I think it's time we sorted you out with a few extra items for your wardrobe, don't you?"

I nod because I don't think the slippers I arrived in constitute outdoor footwear. "Yeah, you're right."

"Password is Formidable."

I stare at him in disbelief. "Why would you share your password with me, and why Formidable?"

He smiles, showing off those dimples I've come to love. I quickly swallow down the thought. I'm allowed to appreciate his dimples. That's all. There's nothing untoward or creepy about it.

"Because I trust you, and as for the name, it's the club where Caleb and I met."

I lick my lips. "Thank you. Formidable, I've never heard of it," I say, typing in the password and pulling up a Google search engine.

Caleb lets out a small chuckle, and I quickly turn to look at him. He laughs even less than I do, so I'm intrigued by his response.

"It's a very exclusive club, let's just say…for members with very particular tastes."

His pupils dilate as he stares at me with that penetrating gaze of his, which, if I were standing, would have my knees buckling beneath me.

"It's a sex club," Noah whispers into my ear, causing goosebumps all over my skin.

"Oh," is the only articulate response I can muster.

"Anyway, we've digressed. Let's get you online and get yourself some new outfits."

Caleb moves to his feet. "And while you're at it, find something dressy. I think it's time we took you out."

The thought of getting dressed up and going out brings on my anxiety, and the laptop almost slips off my lap, but Noah catches it.

"Hey, one step at a time, outfits first, and we'll discuss outings later," Noah says, giving Caleb a narrowed look.

"I don't want you overthinking this, sweet girl."

I let out a deep breath. "It's okay. I know I can't stay hidden in here forever, just sometimes the thought of stepping back into the outside world fills me with fear."

Caleb crouches in front of me, peering over the top of the laptop. "You're strong, Jessica; this is all part of you reclaiming your life. But believe me when I say you have nothing to worry about. We'll be with you every step of the way. You're not alone."

"We've got you," Noah says.

And just like that, without even trying, they've given me something back that I haven't felt in a long time—hope.

Chapter Twenty

Caleb

After reaching out to someone I know, I've set up some counselling sessions for Jessica; even with me calling in a favour, the first one is still two weeks away, so I'm incredibly grateful I got her an appointment. The sooner she starts, the better. When she spoke up and told us that she was thinking of doing it, her voice was tinged with a mixture of vulnerability and determination, which both touched and emboldened me. I couldn't have been more proud of her in that moment.

I see a flicker of that indomitable spirit she had when we first met, and even with the pain that still radiates from her, it's there, ready to resurface.

My reaction to support her every step of the way is instinctive, born out of a deepening connection over the last few weeks, but I feel that pull, one that is more than friendship.

I've found myself drawn to her in ways I'm still struggling to comprehend fully, and I'll need to address it with Noah soon because I'm sure I'm not alone in this—he has my heart, and I will always be honest. But I see it in him, too, how he's so attentive to her. His silent reassurance is a testament to his growing feelings towards her.

Sometimes bonds form that are out of your control.

> Me: I need to talk in private when I get home.

> Noah: Gym?

I smile, as much as I'd love another one of those 'talks', that will have to wait.

> Me: Yeah, see you soon x

> Noah: xx

As soon as I enter the house, I'm greeted by the smell of steak. I find Noah in front of the stove, his back to Jessica, sitting at the counter, laughing at something he just said to her over his shoulder.

I take a moment to appreciate just watching the two of them. They're yet to notice I'm here, and something about how much more relaxed Jessica seems to be in our home brings me joy. I only ever thought I'd care about the happiness and well-being of Noah, but somehow that shifted, and now that very much includes the happiness of Jessica.

I still get this deep-rooted need to go after her ex, but Noah anchors me. He's right. I know he is. We need to bide our time.

But still…

After steak and chips, we all settled in the living room and watched a cooking show with Jessica before she excused herself to go to her room. I haven't heard her as much during the night, so I think she's finally getting the rest she needs—those dark circles under her eyes have almost faded, and I'd like to think Noah and I are the reason behind it.

"Did you want to talk downstairs, or is here okay?" Noah asks once we're alone.

"Here is fine," I reply as he pours two fingers of whiskey each, passing me a glass before sitting in the armchair opposite.

Taking a sip, I sit forward. "It's about Jessica," I say, waiting for a reaction. He tilts his head, cocking an eyebrow as he peers over the rim of his glass, waiting for me to continue.

"First, I want to preface this by saying I love you more than anything. So regardless of what I say next, if it's a hard limit for you, I'll understand, and we'll work through this as a couple together like we do everything else."

He smiles. "Duly noted."

My pulse begins to race, somehow discussing this with him out in the open will make this all very real. "I think it's obvious we both like Jessica, but I will admit the lines are blurring for me, and my feelings are no longer platonic. So, what I want to know is, how do you feel about her?"

He swallows his whiskey before swiping his tongue over his lips, licking a stray drop before answering.

"I think you already know, but I realise full transparency is necessary, so yes, I'll admit my feelings towards her are developing beyond friendship."

For some reason, hearing him say that out loud eases the tension in my gut and helps me breathe a little easier.

"But the question is, what do we do about it?"

I swirl the whiskey in my glass. "Honestly, I don't think it's something we can pretend isn't happening or ignore how she's making us feel. But I also don't think she's ready for one of us, let alone both."

He nods his agreement. "It would be a lot to navigate for all of us, and that's only if it's reciprocated."

I can't help but smile.

"What?" he asks, raising his eyebrows.

"The attraction is there, I have no doubt, but we need to tread carefully," I reply. "I'd never want to ruin the trust and friendship we've built with her. My concern for her well-being will always outweigh my selfish wants and desires."

"As will mine," he agrees.

We're already secure in our relationship. We like to play and have needs that we fulfil, but none of them have the emotional variety, they're sexual, and we both know one another's limits.

"So, I guess we need to talk to her," he replies as he rests his leg on his thigh, swirling the amber liquid in his crystal tumbler, staring at the swirls of golden hues.

"I know that's the next step, but I'm still not sure she's ready, and I don't want to scare her off. She has a safe haven here, and I'd be lying if I didn't say a small part of me is worried she'll bolt."

He lets out a soft laugh. "I don't think she will, but communication is important. What do her body cues tell you?"

"That she's attracted to us, but this will be a huge step emotionally and mentally."

Noah nods. "I think that's a given."

"And yet we can't keep ignoring it."

"So, we'll talk to her together and hope for the best."

A glint touches his eyes when he stares back at me. "When do you want to talk to her?" he asks.

I lift my shoulders. "As soon as the moment seems right."

Which I hope is sooner rather than later. I want all our cards on the table and pray that she doesn't retreat into herself when we do.

Chapter Twenty-One

Noah

I saw the signs that Caleb liked Jessica. He has these tells usually only reserved for me, so I figured it would be a matter of time before he broached the subject. I'm glad it's more than just physical, though, because whatever this is, I know for a fact I couldn't—wouldn't—start anything with Jessica without my feelings being involved.

We also need to, at some point, discuss what that would mean for us and her brother, Mason, but that's something for another day. It's a moot point until we've tracked him down anyway.

These growing feelings for Jessica in no way take away from my love for Caleb, but something about her fits so effortlessly with us in our home. Yes, the circumstances that brought her here are not ones I would ever wish upon her or anyone else, but maybe it's happenstance. If Mason had been home, she never would have come here. As cliche as it sounds, things happen the way they do for a reason.

I know Jessica has said something about wanting to take a bath. Otherwise, I'd be knocking on her door right now, asking her to talk to us, but the fact she's now comfortable enough to take a bath and relax fills me with pride.

Taking a sip of his whiskey, Caleb looks over the rim of the glass, his lips so full and inviting, as he stares at me with abandon, the tension building into something else entirely—damn this man and the effect he has on my libido.

I shift in my seat.

"You keep looking at me like that, and you know what will happen." His voice is deep and smoky.

I smirk. "That is exactly what I was hoping for."

A deep moan vibrates through his chest, his eyes deep pools of darkness as his nostrils flare.

My verbal response gave me the reaction I was hoping for.

He spreads his thighs, the bulge between his legs impossible to ignore. With his elbow resting on the arm of the sofa, he holds the glass in his palm in such a relaxed pose, but with so much power.

"How about you put that smart mouth of yours to work."

Finishing my drink, I place my glass on the table before pushing up from the armchair. I make my way over, his gaze fixated on me. It's predatory, and yet he hasn't even moved. I lower myself to my knees, run my hands over his thick thighs, and then reach between his legs, cupping his hard erection through the material of his joggers and massage him gently.

"Hmmm, someone is ready for me," I say, tugging at the waistband slowly, releasing his hard length from his joggers. I love that he's commando, too. He shifts, raising his arse, allowing me to tug them over his thighs and legs. I want to feel his flesh underneath my palms.

Taking the glass from him, I take a sip of the amber liquid before placing it on the coffee table and then reach under his t-shirt, pushing it up his torso. His abs tense as my fingertips graze over his hot-as-sin skin.

I pull it over his head until he's naked before me, sitting there in all his masculine glory. I'm aware that Jessica could walk in at any moment, and so is he, but something about that is thrilling and only turns me on even more.

"You're so fucking perfect."

I stroke his thighs, watching his dick jump from the contact—the wet tip engorged, enticing and inviting—studying his length before I dive in. My dick hardens at the thought; giving this man head always turns me the fuck on. I wrap my fist around his generous girth, loving how hot he feels beneath my palm.

"I could spend hours stroking you, licking you, teasing you," I say, keeping my eyes on him as I speak.

"Noah, enough talking already. You know what to do."

Indeed, I do.

And I want it.

To give this man an earth-shattering blow job while I'm still fully clothed and he's naked and at my mercy has my dick pulsing in my trousers, begging to be set free.

Slowly I lean forward, his breathing the perfect acoustic to my descent as I softly kiss the tip, a slow lick as I circle his head, lapping up his pre-cum.

I take my time, the tip of my tongue sliding down the underside of his cock, his breathing heavier as I move on to pepper light and gentle kisses up and down his length. I feel the tensing of his thigh muscles, and his erection grows even harder. And then I start licking, his taste so fucking tantalising I can never get enough.

I can feel him throbbing with anticipation, but he's resolute in his self-control. How he refrains from grabbing my scalp and fucking my throat raw, I have no idea, but it's all part of the foreplay and one of the many things I love about him.

His dick jumps, leaking even more pre-cum, and I know he's more than ready as I take him into my mouth. He lets out a deep moan as I slowly work him, taking him to the back of my throat and relaxing just as he likes it.

The sound of his breathing grows heavier as I work him over. Looking up through my lashes, I love how he watches me with his heated gaze.

He arches his bottom up as I cup his balls and slide a finger to his perineum.

Caleb is hung, but I still suck in air, pulling my cheeks against my teeth, creating more of a vacuum suction. His fingers delve into my scalp, gripping my hair, the sting welcome.

This is where I feel him become more unhinged, deep-throating me as he slides his dick past my larynx into my throat.

My eyes begin to water. His finger reaches out and catches a tear with his thumb, and he brings it to his lips, sucking on the pad.

He eases back as I play with his balls, lightly flicking them with my finger. He grunts, and I groan, both emitting sounds of pleasure.

And here it comes, the moment he's about to let go and fuck my face. I love the power exchange, and he loves this position of power.

Using my mouth for all it's worth, he gives over to his desires. It's objectifying, intense—degrading even—and sexy as hell. It's the thing about being a switch I love the most.

Caleb is hard-wired to be dominating; he rarely relents, and when he does, I know it's only because he's allowing it, but even then, he still tops from the bottom. Knowing our preferences and talking about them early on helped build the foundations of our sexual relationship.

Caleb comes with a deep groan, emptying himself down my throat as I swallow every drop.

Nothing turns me on more than giving myself over to him, and this man brings my body to life like no other.

It's as though now that he's admitted his growing feelings for

Jessica, he's opened Pandora's box and is ready to come out and play.

I love Caleb, adore him, and worship everything about him, even when he's an insufferable arsehole. He's moody and possessive, but I love him all the same.

He never shies away from what he wants—or needs. And he always gets it eventually. It's how he got me.

But there's something uniquely alluring about Jessica, and now it's obvious we both feel it—this possessive need to protect her, adore and worship her.

It's deeper than sexual gratification.

Her bruises have practically faded, and her ribs are still healing, but the scars we can't see—the ones that affect your mental health—are the hardest to mend.

And although Caleb might not believe you can truly fix people, he does believe with time, we grow around our trauma. I think the internal scars Jessica carries will only make her stronger, and like a phoenix, she'll rise from the ashes and be reborn.

Trauma changes us, sometimes irrevocably. It can harden us to the world around us, make us cynical, and sometimes we withdraw from the world, become shadows of our former selves.

I had unresolved issues from my childhood, things I've only ever told my therapist and Caleb. He helped me more than he knows, and together I believe we can do that for Jessica.

When we lose that innocence, the vulnerable part of us—the inner child, inevitably destroyed, it changes how we see the world. Because healing isn't linear, it's complex and multi-dimensional; it's a work in progress.

Chapter Twenty-Two

Jessica

The house is quiet when I come downstairs, which is a first. Since I've been here, either Caleb or Noah have always been home with me.

Home. I don't know when I began calling it home, but I remind myself it's *their* home, not mine.

I make my way over to the kettle and flick the switch, the neon light coming to life. My heart swells when I notice my favourite mug sitting on the counter, a tea bag and sugar already inside and a spoon sticking out. I get a pang in my chest and a flutter in my lower stomach—something I have no right to feel around either of these men. They're together; I would never want to come between them. But the thought of being between them now has my entire body heating. I've seen them in scarcely any clothes. I'd be lying if I said I hadn't secretly admired them both, and like the steam flowing through the nozzle of the spout, I'm hot just thinking about them.

I go to the fridge, retrieve the milk, and notice a sticky note with my name on the side of a Tupperware container. I lift the lid, smiling when I see freshly sliced fruit.

Because Noah knows I like it on my porridge.

A girl could seriously get used to this.

But the thought scares me—this was only meant to be temporary. It was never going to be permanent.

And yet somehow, I've found myself swept up in how these two men each take care of me in their own unique ways.

Maybe I'm foolish, pretending it's more than what it is. After all, it's not like I could ever choose between them; they've already chosen one another.

I busy myself making my porridge and then sit at the breakfast bar when the doorbell rings, causing me to flinch and drop my spoon, splashing myself with porridge in the process, shit.

My heart races and my hands shake as I take my bowl back over to the sink and grab some kitchen roll to wipe my hand as I peer at the door-cam on the kitchen wall and let out a breath—it's Maggie.

I go to the front door and pull it ajar ever so slightly.

"I'm so sorry, dear. I forgot my keys. It's been one hell of a morning already," she says, squeezing through the gap and then closing the door behind her. She shrugs off her coat and hangs it on the hook before facing me.

"Everything okay?" she questions, her eyes dropping to my trembling hands, which I quickly hide behind my back.

"Yeah, of course, I'm fine."

I'm fine—the universal code for absolutely not okay.

She reaches out and rubs her hand up and down my arm gently. "Well, you can always talk to me, dear. Living with two men, I know you're a little outnumbered, and we women need to stick together."

I smile as she drops her hand. "Thank you, but Caleb and Noah have been great and very hospitable, allowing me to stay here while I get back on my feet. I hate to be a burden."

She arches one of her brows. "They're both very good men.

Even with Caleb's hard exterior, he's a pussy cat. Besides, you could never be a burden."

Maggie gestures toward the kitchen, and I follow the floral scent of her Chanel number 5. It was my nan's signature scent, and it fills me with nostalgia. I kept her half-empty bottle after she died and would spray a little on my favourite cushion just to keep her scent alive. The empty bottle is in a box with some family photo albums Mason kept.

I love how Maggie feels at home as she helps herself to tea before starting the housework.

"They only hired me as a favour to my late husband, and they pay me way more than the job I do, and yet Caleb is like the son I never had."

She picks up my porridge. "It's still warm. Did I interrupt your breakfast?"

"Yes, but it's no bother." I take the bowl from her and retake my seat.

"How about I join you with my cuppa and a custard cream before I start?" She's already reaching for the biscuit barrel and a plate.

I smile, grateful for the company.

"You know those men dote on you, don't you," she says, pouring water over her earl grey tea bag. "I'd say they're well and truly smitten, if you ask me."

My porridge goes down the wrong hole at her proclamation, and I cough and pat my chest as I try to catch my breath. She pats my back firmly a few more times; she might be getting on in years, but she has one hell of a palm.

"Let me get you some water."

After hacking up my airways and what feels like a lung, I can finally catch my breath enough to take a few sips of water, the cool liquid heaven on my raw throat.

"Maggie, they're just protective, and besides, they're together."

She raises an eyebrow and lets out a 'hmmm' sound as she stirs her tea and then joins me.

"Have you any plans over the Easter bank holiday weekend?" I ask in the hopes of steering this conversation elsewhere.

"I'm visiting with my sister in Wales. My youngest niece had a son; I've only met him on Zoom. I can't wait to give him a big snuggle from his Great Aunt Mag."

Her smile is contagious, and I can't help but to return it.

"Me and Jeff might not have been blessed with children, but we've been fortunate with our nieces and nephews."

The thought of her and her husband being unable to have children is heartbreaking.

I clear my throat. "Did you ever consider adopting or fostering?" As soon as the question leaves my lips, I instantly want to take it back. "Sorry, that was rude of me even to ask that."

She reaches for my hand and squeezes. "Oh, no love, not at all. On the contrary, it's interesting you should ask. We fostered. It's how we met Caleb."

I have no words.

"But no, we never adopted, not because we didn't want to but because we felt we could help more by fostering. We only stopped when Jeff got sick. But even to this day, I still keep in touch with every child who stepped over our threshold."

My eyes well with emotion, tears streaking down my cheeks before I can get a handle on them. I can only imagine the positive effect Maggie had on so many, the way she nurtures so naturally.

"I didn't know that about Caleb," I say, wiping my face. She passes me a tissue, and her eyes soften.

"No, not a lot of people do. He's built those walls high. But that's not my story to tell."

I nod in understanding; I wouldn't want someone else talking about my past, either.

"So dear, what do you have planned for today?"

Pulling the recipe book closer, I flip through and stop on the page, turning it towards her.

"Oh, that looks delicious, and what will you make for dessert?"

Biting my lip, I shake my head. "I have no idea, to be honest."

"Well, sticky toffee pudding is one of their favourites."

Now that I can do.

"Have a quick look in the fridge and pantry. If you're missing anything, we can pop the shop before I leave."

The hairs on the back of my neck stand on end. I haven't left the house since I've been here, and the thought sends my mind reeling with turmoil.

Chapter Twenty-Three

Caleb

My meetings ran later than I would have liked, and I know Noah's day was fully booked. The thought of Jessica home alone eats me up inside. The need to protect her runs riot as I sit in local traffic. Bloody typical. It wouldn't usually leave me feeling so disgruntled, but I haven't even managed a phone call to check in with her.

I know she's a grown woman, but after everything, it's impossible to ignore how much she affects me—affects us.

She might have arrived in her moment of need, and I wish it were under less dire circumstances, but the fact of the matter is, she belongs with us. We've been tiptoeing around our attraction for weeks while she's also been healing physically and mentally. How will she react? Is she ready to cross the line? Because there is no going back once we do.

Parking up, I grab my laptop and jog up the steps to the house. My car automatically locks behind me as I pull out my door key.

The first thing I notice when I step into the hallway is the smell of cooking, causing my mouth to water and my stomach to grumble.

I can hear the faint sound of music as I kick off my shoes and loosen my tie, popping the top button of my shirt as I make my way to the kitchen.

Jessica is slowly swaying her hips along to the beat of the music as she stands in front of the stove, stirring something in a saucepan.

I'm transfixed as I watch her entirely in her element, and my heart staggers an irregular beat in my chest.

She turns to grab something from the counter and must catch me in her peripheral vision; a shriek leaves her lips as her hand knocks over a glass of juice that shatters when it hits the floor.

Her hand shoots to her mouth as her eyes go wide, and I immediately rush forward, but my reaction only spooks her more, and her bare foot crunches on the broken glass.

A sharp hiss escapes her lips.

"Shit," I say and move around the shards, grabbing her gently by her hips and lifting her onto the counter.

"I'm so sorry," she says in a rush, tears springing to her eyes. "I'll clean that up and, of course, replace the glass." She tries to slide off the counter, but my hand holds her thigh, keeping her in place.

"No, you'll let me take care of your foot, Jessica. You're bleeding."

Drops of blood fall to the tiled flooring.

I lift the back of her calf and bring her foot up on the counter's edge.

"Don't move. I'm just going to grab the first aid kit."

I glance at her face, she's pale, tear-streaked, and I fucking hate it.

Cupping the back of her neck, I pull her towards me and whisper. "It's all right, little one." I brush my lips over hers in a brief kiss before pulling her into my chest. Her small fingers grip my shirt, a shiver rolling through her.

"I'm sorry I startled you."

A small sob escapes her; my fingers thread into her hair softly, and I tilt her head back so I can see her eyes.

"You never have to fear me. You know that, right?"

"I know. I'm sorry," she says with a slight hiccup.

I hate she's even still apologising to me. It's my fault, but seeing her reaction was a sucker punch to the gut.

My palm rubs up and down her back, before I pull away and move to the cupboard where we keep the first aid kit.

Grabbing one of the breakfast bar stools, I slide it closer to her and pull her foot into my lap.

"I hope you're not ticklish, little one. I don't fancy a kick to the gut."

Unzipping the kit, I locate the tweezers and, as carefully as possible, I remove the tiny shards of glass.

"It started over the most minute things," she says hoarsely. I peer up to look at her face, but she's staring at her foot, yet her focus is removed far from here. "Once, I buttered the bread of his sandwich, and he lost it and threw it against the wall. It was the first time he shouted at me." She huffs out a laugh but is anything from amused. "And yet I was the one who apologised and cleaned up the mess."

I squeeze her calf softly, wanting her to know I'm here and she's not alone.

"And then the little things became the big things. My makeup, the way I dressed. Or how I organised the cupboards. Nothing was ever good enough, yet I wanted to please him. Can you believe that?"

Pausing what I'm doing, I reach up and grab her hand.

"He's an abusive sociopath. This is all on him." And there will come a day when there is a reckoning, when he'll pay for what he's done.

She looks away, and I return to cleaning and dressing her foot. Luckily, it's superficial.

"I just don't know who I am anymore," she admits, looking so damn defeated.

Before I can stop myself, I pull her into my arms and across my lap. There's a slight hitch to her breathing when I do. That one small sound pumps pure adrenaline through my veins.

"You're still you,. You've lost yourself, and that's to be expected. But you're still in there. I see you."

Her palm presses to my chest, covering my heart, and I wonder if she can feel how it's an erratic staccato beat.

With a tilt of her lips, almost forming a smile, she asks, "What do you see?" Her eyes trail over my face in a soft caress against my senses.

Covering her hand with mine, I hold her gaze. "You are strong. Resilient and powerful in your own right. Because you're not a victim, Jessica, you're a fighter, a survivor. Your compassion still shines through. You've not lost your ability to still be kind."

Moving my hand from hers, I cup the back of her neck, my thumb stroking across her cheekbone. It's now free from bruising, but I'll never be able to forget how beat up she was, and I know that kind of hurt doesn't always heal as quickly on the inside. She's beautiful, but it's more than what's on the surface; there are so many layers to this woman, and I want to learn every one of them as I unwrap her like a special gift.

I move my thumb lower, tracing her soft, plump bottom lip. There's that smooth intake of breath, causing my dick to stir. It's impossible not to when she's perfectly cocooned in my lap.

Pulling her closer, my head moves of its own accord, my lips kissing the corner of her mouth and she turns her face just enough that if I move my lips just a fraction, they'll meet hers fully.

And then the buzzer on the oven goes off, causing her to startle, followed by a nervous laugh.

Moving to my feet, I sit her on the stool and turn off the

buzzer. "Do you want me to turn off the oven?" I ask, peering over my shoulder.

With a shake of her head, she says, "No, I need to put the garlic bread in." She's already sliding off the stool when I hold up my hand.

"Nope, hold tight, little one. Let me get this glass cleaned up first."

She glances at the shattered pieces, grimacing. "I can do that."

Moving back in front of her, I stand between her thighs, cupping the back of her neck.

"I was the one who startled you, so I'm going to clean it up." I leave no room for argument as I lean in and kiss her forehead before quickly cleaning up the mess.

The front door opening and closing lets me know Noah's home, followed by the echo of his footsteps.

"It smells delicious, by the way. What are you making?" I glance at the covered pan.

Moving beside me, her cheeks flush with a slight blush. "Chilli con carne and homemade garlic bread," she replies as she takes the baguette and slides it onto the tray in the oven. "And sticky toffee pudding for dessert."

"That's it. We're keeping you forever."

I adore how her skin flushes, and the thought of seeing her entire body blush like that makes me smile.

Noah walks over and smiles at me in greeting as Jessica glances over her shoulder.

Picking up on the tail end of the conversation, Noah says, "Damn straight we are." Placing his palm on her lower back as he kisses her temple.

Chapter Twenty-Four

Jessica

My insides melt at their words, my emotions so conflicted. The way they talk to me has my stomach doing summersaults. I'd love to stay safe in this sanctuary they've created. But there is only so much of their kind hospitality I can keep indulging in before it's time for me to get back on my feet.

Cooking today reminds me how much I love it; ultimately, my goal is to return to doing the things I love. Which means at some point, I need to start living again.

Noah lights some candles as Caleb sets the table. I watch how they move around one another so in tune. It's beautiful. I don't even think they know they do it—like magnets, there's an invisible pull, a once-in-a-lifetime special connection.

I turn back to plate up our dinner and try to ignore the deep-rooted longing, the pang in my chest, the wish to one day only have an ounce of the love they share. Being here, it's easy to pretend I am part of it, but then I'm consumed with guilt. They're a couple, yet I can't deny how drawn I am to them. They're both so different and yet complement one another. And not just on the surface, they are each handsome in their own right, but it's more than that.

The way Caleb told me what he sees when he looks at me triggered feelings I thought were dormant before those words. I felt a strange numbness, a disconnect, with that part of myself and yet slowly, these two amazing men have breathed life back into me.

"What has you concentrating so hard, sweet girl?" Noah asks as he picks up two plates off the counter and carries them to the table.

He nudges his head for me to sit, and Caleb tucks my chair in once my butt hits the soft padded seat.

I blush at the action, something about it so chivalrous.

"I was thinking about my next steps. Maggie mentioned going to the supermarket today, and I realised I've not left the house apart from the roof terrace. Maybe it's time I started getting my life back."

Noah nods at the same time that Caleb frowns as he pours us all a glass of wine.

"Maybe you should wait until we know your ex is no longer a threat." He glances towards Noah as he takes his seat.

"Or maybe we should support Jessica in whichever steps she feels she's ready to take," Noah says, reaching for his glass and holding it up. Caleb and I mirror him.

"To new beginnings." We all clink our glasses. It's delicious as always; Caleb has such a fantastic palate.

I pick up my fork and wait, my eyes flicking between Caleb and Noah as they take their first bite.

Noah closes his eyes in appreciation, and then a deep, satisfied hum rumbles up his throat. Caleb's eyes widen as he swallows.

"Fuck me, this is good," he says, taking another bite.

Pride swells deep inside the crevices of my chest cavity, and I smile around my forkful. I can't remember the last I felt proud of something I had done.

"I can see why you wanted to become a chef," Noah says, reaching for some garlic bread. "This is food heaven."

The compliment warms me unexpectedly because I know that every word these two men speak is the truth. It was clear early on that neither of them said things they didn't mean.

I love how the only sounds are hums of enjoyment and cutlery scraping against the plates as we eat. The guys both have seconds, and I half expect them to lick their plates clean.

"I hope you've saved some room for dessert." I stack the plates, but Noah ushers me away and takes them into the kitchen to start loading the dishwasher.

"Believe me. We always have room for dessert." The way Noah throws that comment over his shoulder, with a smirk on his handsome face and a wink, makes me wonder if that was some kind of innuendo.

I clear my throat and look away, but when I do, Caleb is staring at me, his gaze intense, turning me inside out.

"So, is that what you want to do, become a chef?" he asks, bringing the rim of the glass to his mouth.

The fullness of his bottom lip momentarily entrances me… and how his tongue sweeps over his top lip after he takes a sip. And how his adam's apple is so prominent as he swallows.

My lower stomach tightens with need.

"Yes, that's why I was in culinary school. I only had four months left until I would have received my diploma. It was a combined course with an internship."

I glance into my lap, squeezing my hands into fists, my pulse racing. Sadness and anger fight for my attention—my culinary dreams were something I ended up losing because of my arsehole ex.

"Hey." Caleb leans over, his forefinger hooking under my chin until I'm staring back at him.

"That can all be worked out if you still want to do it. We can help make it happen."

Noah comes over, his hand squeezing my shoulder. "I think you'd be robbing the world of your talent if you didn't."

My entire body heats from their lightest of touch and encouragement.

The oven buzzer goes off, and I'm grateful for the reprieve. Caleb drops his hand, and Noah releases my shoulder as I push to my feet.

"I'll dish up dessert," I say, unable to hide the catch in my throat.

With my back to them, I make my way into the kitchen, but with the open space, I feel their eyes on me, causing the hairs on the back of my neck to stand on end and my nipples to stiffen beneath the lace of my bra.

As I slip on the oven gloves and open the oven door, I'm hit with a wave of heat, adding to my already traitorous body as I slide out the baking tray.

Unable to stop myself, I glance over to see Caleb staring at Noah intently as he whispers something to him—words I'm unable to make out above the noise of the extractor fan and the sound of music playing from the radio.

The connection I have with these two men I've never had with one person, let alone two, and that might be the most terrifying revelation of all.

Chapter Twenty-Five

Noah

The connection we share with Jessica has deepened beyond friendship, and we find ourselves yearning for something more. Yes, her arrival in our home was unexpected. She needed a safe place to heal physically and emotionally, and we know the emotional part is ongoing. But little did we know that her presence would fill a void in our lives we didn't even know existed. It's a complex situation, but we're willing to navigate it together.

At first, it was about making her comfortable, seeing that she had everything she needed. Over time, she's opened up to us, conversations have deepened, and then something profound happened. She started to smile, her laughter filling the house, the trust she felt toward us developing before our eyes.

We know that exploring this newfound connection won't be without its challenges, but the rewards seem infinite. Caleb and I have discussed our desires and boundaries extensively, making sure we're on the same page. Open and honest communication has become our lifeline, and it's time to include Jessica.

"Are you ready for this, Caleb?" I whisper, reaching over and taking his hand in mine.

He nods. "Yes. We can't ignore this bond we both feel. She must feel it, too. And I want to explore what this could mean for all of us." His voice fills with deep tenderness. Caleb's grip on my hand tightens, and a smile tugs at the corners of his lips. "We know better than anyone that love is love, and whatever this is, it's time we embrace it fully, which means being honest with her."

I squeeze his hand back before letting go, a silent reassurance that we're in this together just as Jessica returns and places a bowl of sticky toffee pudding in front of Caleb and me before returning for her own.

We all eat and exchange small talk, but there's an undeniable tension in the air.

"Thank you, little one. I've eaten in Micheline star restaurants, and I have to say your cooking is up there with the best of them."

Her cheeks glow at Caleb's praise, and I can't help but agree with him. She really is gifted.

"I'm going to get this cleared up, and then Caleb and I would like to discuss something with you."

She nods, but it's impossible not to see the uncertainty in her eyes.

"It's nothing bad, sweet girl," I say, hoping to reassure her. "Caleb, why don't you pour us a drink, and I'll join you both in the living room once I've loaded the dishwasher." The truth is, I need a moment to collect myself. I'd be lying if I said I wasn't nervous. This could go one of two ways. I just hope she's on the same wavelength as Caleb and me.

Moments later, I walk into the living room, and Caleb is standing beside the fireplace, tumbler in hand. Jessica is in the armchair, flicking through the TV. A shy smile graces her lips when she notices me. She looks radiant, and my heart skips a beat at the sight of her.

Caleb walks over, handing me a glass of whiskey from the coffee table before leaning in, giving me a chaste kiss.

He gives me a nod, and we both move to the sofa.

"Jessica."

Here goes nothing.

She mutes the TV and turns to face us, giving us undivided attention.

I take a deep breath, my voice trembling slightly as I speak up. "Jessica, Caleb and I have been discussing something and wanted to share it with you."

She swallows, her eyes flitting between the two of us. "Okay." I can hear the wariness in her voice, and I hate that.

"Firstly, we know the reason you're here isn't necessarily one of your choosing. Let's say it was more happenstance," I say, glancing at Caleb, who squeezes my thigh, giving me the added support to keep talking, fully aware he can cut in at any time. "But that being said, we're glad you're here because we've developed feelings for you…if it isn't obvious."

Her lips pull into a genuine smile, which has my heart racing.

"I care about the both of you, too."

"We know, but what Noah is trying to say is our feelings," he says, waving his hand between us. "They go beyond friendship."

Jessica's eyes widen in surprise, a slight hitch in her breathing.

We wait maybe less than a minute for her to digest our admission, and it takes everything in me to stay seated, scared if I move, it will spook her.

I watch tears well up in her eyes, a shimmering mix of disbelief and hope. "You…you both feel that way?" she asks, her voice barely above a whisper.

I nod as hope fills my chest. "Yes, we do."

"So, what we want to know is if those feelings transcend to you too. Are we reading something into this that isn't there, or have you developed feelings for us as well?"

Bringing her thumb to her lips, she chews on the nail nervously.

"It's okay if you can't answer that or need time to digest what we've just told you."

She shakes her head, eyes glancing between the two of us. "I like you," she says, looking at Caleb and me. "Both of you, but I'm also a little confused."

"Is that because this doesn't conform to society's conventional standards?" Caleb asks, his voice calm, neutral even.

"I don't know, maybe. I've been conflicted, thinking it was all in my head."

"Not in your head," I say, hoping my words help ease any uncertainty she might be having. This is a lot to get her head around.

"We're not going to lie, little one. We know this is a lot. But we want to be honest with you. And if you're open to it, we'd like to explore the possibility of being with you."

Her eyes widen again, but now there's a small spark of intrigue and, dare I say excitement. We let the suggestion settle, giving her time to gather her thoughts.

"I've never had a connection like this with anyone, let alone two people."

Caleb moves to his feet and slowly walks to where Jessica is sitting before kneeling in front of her, his gaze unwavering. "And never have we. Yes, we've done things together as a couple that involve other parties, but feelings have never been involved before. This is new for us too, Jessica."

He slowly holds out his hand, and without hesitation, she takes it in hers, gripping his like a lifeline.

"The connection we all share is undeniable. And we'd like to see where this goes. Take some time to explore the possibilities. If that's something you'd be interested in doing?"

She nods slowly, and I already know he will need a verbal answer before Caleb speaks because communication is vital.

"Words, we need to hear the words, little one."

Clearing her throat, I see the moment her resolve kicks in—she pushes her shoulders back, that spark of determination front and centre.

"Yes, I'd like to explore this—with the two of you."

Relief floods through me, mingled with anticipation. We've taken the first step, but there's still a long road ahead; this is already a huge milestone: admitting our feelings.

Caleb rises to his feet and gently tugs on her hand until she joins him. He pulls her against him, holding her close.

"We'll take this slow. I can't promise it will be easy. But I know that you are more than worth the effort."

He kisses the crown of her head before stepping back, hands moving to her shoulders, and as she gazes up, her eyes are full of emotion.

The tension is still taut, but I think it's for entirely different reasons.

"How about we watch a film," I say, rising to my feet and taking her hand in mine before wrapping her in my arms, needing to close the distance. Holding her like this now seems so much more profound.

Caleb's nostrils flare as he watches, and the smile that breaks out on his face is enough to make me smile in return. Because I can see his relief, knowing she wants to explore this too. When I step back, lead her to the sofa, and lower myself, she follows suit and sits beside me. Caleb grabs the remote, taking up the seat on her other side.

I reach over and tilt her chin until she's looking at me. "You need to breathe, sweet girl. Nothing has changed, we're still us, we're not about to jump you. We want you to relax."

She licks her lips, and my dick stirs to life, but I ignore it. It's not the first time I've been aroused in her presence, but right now, this is more than sexual need or desire.

It takes a while for her to relax, and when she does, it's with her head on my shoulder, legs tucked up. Caleb's palm rests flat against her thigh, his thumb making small circular motions. I can't help but feel an overwhelming sense of gratitude. This is just the beginning, and yet it feels so right. And as we all sit cocooned on the sofa, I know deep in my heart that we've made the right choice.

The film ends all too soon, and Jessica lets out a yawn.

"Come on, sweet girl, let's get you to bed."

She stands, followed by Caleb and me, his palm going to the small of her back as we walk her towards her room. As much as I'd love to have her nestled between us tonight—just to hold her—we agreed to take this slow.

When we stop at her door, Caleb pushes it open.

Jessica's lips part, but no words follow. She tries again, but still nothing.

"What is it, little one?" Caleb asks in a low murmur, his thumb and forefinger softly gripping her chin.

Her cheeks heat, her eyes cast down, and for a moment, I think she's not going to answer, but then her eyes flutter to mine and then back to Caleb.

"I want to know if I can kiss you both?"

I swear my heart wants to break free of my ribs and rip out of my chest.

He smirks and nods his head for me to step forward. This is, after all, Caleb, and I know how much he loves delayed gratification.

"You never have to ask," he says, stroking his thumb over her jaw before dropping his hand. "Noah, do you want the honours?" It's a rhetorical question.

Without preamble, I move in front of her, Caleb close behind me as I palm her neck and guide her until her back is flush with the wall. Her small hands move to hold onto my hips.

I bring my other hand up to her face and stroke her cheek with my thumb, loving the blush of colour highlighting her cheekbones.

I wait until she's staring back at me.

"I'm going to kiss you now, sweet girl." And then, slowly, I inch forward as her tongue swipes over her lips in invitation before her eyelids flutter closed, and I lower my mouth to hers.

She parts her lips as our mouths connect, and I take that as an invitation, my tongue seeking entry, meeting the tip of hers with mine. My tongue moves against hers with slow and gentle strokes, the pressure light, but I feel it in every cell of my body.

I shift my focus to her lips, adding a little more pressure, and a deep moan escapes her, causing my dick to strain in my trousers.

Her hands slide between us, gripping my t-shirt and pulling me closer. And I groan as the kiss increases in intensity.

It takes everything in me to slow it down before gradually pulling away, her breathing heavy as her eyes flutter open, pupils blown wide.

The smile that fills her face has me desperate to dive back in and do it all over again, but I can feel Caleb's heat at my back, and I know as much as he prides himself on his self-control, he wants to kiss her just as much as I did.

Squeezing the back of Jessica's neck, I give her one more peck on the lips before stepping back and allowing Caleb to take my place.

He's a couple of inches taller than me, and Jessica has to tilt her head back to look up at him. He wraps his arm behind her back, tugging her into his body, causing a catch in her breath as he cups the back of her head, eliminating any unnecessary space between them.

And then his mouth is on hers. I love watching how

responsive she is to him and him to her. She moves her hands to his back as if he's still not close enough. And then he pulls back, eliciting a desperate moan from Jessica that doesn't last long because he plants a series of kisses along her jawline and collarbone.

I have to adjust myself. Watching the two of them, consumed in their kiss, slays me in the best possible way. Seeing how sensitive and responsive she is to his touch is the most beautiful thing to witness.

It takes longer than it should to finally part ways because we want nothing more than to be buried inside her, but we can wait because the reward will be worth it.

Chapter Twenty-Six

Jessica

It's been two weeks since Caleb and Noah told me their feelings went beyond friendship. They both walked me to my room, and I didn't know where I found the courage to ask if I could kiss them, but I did. Being so close to these two men after discovering I wasn't alone in my attraction towards them gave me the courage.

Each touch and glance holds a newfound significance, and it's electrifying. And yet it's only been light kisses since then—nothing like the first time. They've been patient with me, guiding me and supporting me when I had my first counselling session. Caleb insisted on taking me, escorting me into the building and was in the reception area when I came out, which I was grateful for. His presence alone was the anchor I needed. I was surprised at how much it took out of me physically and emotionally. When we returned home, I was exhausted. Caleb insisted I nap, and I slept until the following morning.

I'm finding myself going to bed hot and bothered by the time we part, wishing I wasn't going to bed alone and that they would join me.

Thirsty and having woken from a restless, fever-like dream, I slip out of my room and head downstairs. I pad towards the kitchen when a sound from the front room catches my attention.

I creep in the direction of the door ajar, light flickering from the lit fireplace, and at first, it takes a moment for my eyes to adjust and my brain to catch up to what I'm seeing.

Caleb and Noah are kissing, and both are completely naked. I gasp at the two gods in front of me. I should back away, get my water and return to my room, but I can't move.

Noah takes himself in his hand, and if my mouth weren't already dry like the Sahara Desert right now, I would be salivating.

The man is hung.

Caleb takes over, fisting both their erections together as he works them up and down, and the combined grunts and moans from them have me turning into a human jelly mould.

I squeeze my thighs together. I never thought I'd have voyeuristic tendencies until this very moment. But watching them as they engage in a sexual act has me transfixed.

Everything has my senses heightened. I almost feel dizzy. The heady mix of their aftershave and their arousal assails my senses. I can't remember the last time I felt sexually aroused like this, if ever.

The way they kiss one another with abandon has to be one of the most erotic things I have ever witnessed.

I can't move, and even if I could, would I want to?

Caleb's abs move as he works his fist over their erections in his large hands. I've never really appreciated the size of male hands until this moment.

Noah groans low and deep, sending a deep searing heat between my thighs.

Caleb pulls out of the kiss as though it pains him, tugging their erections hard before letting go.

"I want you on all fours, now."

I swear I forget how to breathe, how to swallow.

Noah shivers and then turns around, dropping to all fours in front of the open fireplace, giving me the perfect side profile, his skin glistening with perspiration. Caleb reaches for a small bottle on the mantle and kneels behind Noah, knocking his thighs further apart and cupping the globe of his perfectly toned arse as he drizzles some of the contents between his cheeks and then coats his erection. He gives it a few good strokes before he aligns himself at Noah's back entrance.

Fuck.

My breathing becomes heavier the longer I stand here watching. Wet heat pools between the apex of my thighs, and I have no choice but to clench them together, desperate for some kind of relief, to reach the ache, my breasts heavy. But I'm also very invested in watching as they both come undone.

Caleb trails a hand up and down Noah's spine, causing him to peer over his shoulder. "Are you going to fuck me or tease me to death?" Noah says, his voice breaking on the last word as Caleb edges closer, teasing his arsehole with the head of his engorged dick.

"Nope, I am going to fuck you," Caleb says, pushing in until he's buried to the hilt.

Noah lets out a deep moan, his head dipping forward. "Fuck," he curses.

"Yes indeed," Caleb replies.

Every sound in the room is amplified as he pumps into Noah, slick, hot, delicious.

My nipples pebble under my t-shirt, and my body breaks out in goosebumps.

Caleb keeps one hand firmly on Noah's hip, and reaching around with the other, he fists Noah's dick, pumping it up and down with vigour, all while still thrusting.

"Now tell me?" he hisses into Noah's ear. "Who do you wish was here right now, with their soft satin hand wrapped around your dick instead of mine as I fuck your arse?"

"You know who." He groans, pushing back against Caleb's weight behind him and then into his hand with a thrust.

"Yes, I do, but she doesn't, so say it," he says again, his movements harsher, deeper.

"Jessica, I wish it were Jessica."

Caleb's face turns towards me when he releases his dick and grips both hips. Until now, he was going easy on Noah. Now he's relentless as he pounds into him.

I can't look away, let alone move, as he keeps his eyes trained on me, his lips curving to a salacious grin, as his eyes roam over my body.

"Touch yourself," he commands.

I don't know if he's talking to Noah or me, but it's as though my hand has a mind of its own as I reach between my thighs, my naked core wet and wanting.

I glance between Noah and Caleb. Noah has his fist wrapped around his dick, straining with every stroke, and I slide a finger into my hot, waiting core, my lips parting on a low, deep moan.

"That's it, now fuck your hand."

Noah and I are Caleb's puppets, each adhering to his commands, and yet I shouldn't even be here. I intruded on their private moment.

"I won't ask again."

I am equally scared and turned on, not because I'm afraid he will hurt me, but because I'm nervous about letting go of my inhibitions. My body is coiled so tight. I know the moment I do as he says, my release won't be far behind.

And once I do this, there is no going back. It will make everything leading up to this very real.

I could force myself to walk away, return to my room, and act like I hadn't witnessed one of the hottest things in my life, but there would be no point. We've all been dancing around this for weeks, and I know that neither of these men will hurt me. My body is safe with them. My heart, on the other hand, that's a question for another day.

Biting on my bottom lip, I stop thinking and let myself feel, parting my legs when I add a second finger, hooking them inside as I begin to ride the palm of my hand, my clit a sensitive bundle of nerves.

My eyes drift closed, and two pairs of stormy eyes stare back when I open them.

Caleb is ruthlessly fucking Noah, his balls slapping against his arse as Noah fists his cock with abandon. I whimper. I'm so fucking wet, my insides a quivering mess in need of a release. It's right there on the edge, begging to be set free. My free hand reaches out for the doorframe, my legs almost buckling with the intensity of the moment.

"That's it, Jessica, fuck your hand as though you were fucking Noah's face while I fuck his arse." Caleb's voice is a deep tenor against my very core.

Because both of those things sound so forbidden, my ex never gave me oral, and he sure as hell never went near my arse, and yet he loved it when I gave him head.

"Whatever you're thinking, let it go. You're here, and it's just the three of us," Noah says, his voice strained. Even from here, I see the head of his engorged dick, hard and ready for release.

And he's right. They're proof that there is nothing wrong with both giving and receiving where pleasure is involved.

"Oh fuck," I hiss out as I start fucking my hand.

I hear one of them growl, but I can't be sure. This entire situation is so surreal that I can no longer think straight.

My orgasm is right there, on a precipice, ready to freefall.

"Come for me now, both of you," Caleb says, followed by a deep, loud groan.

Noah throws his head back, his dick swells right before he comes all over his hand. It keeps coming in short spurts, spilling onto the wooden floor. The sight has my breath stalling in my chest as I crest the orgasm ripping through me. My legs give out, and I fall to the floor, the soft rug a blessing beneath my knees as I convulse a wet hot release dripping all over my hand.

"Fuck," I say on a breathy exhale.

And then Caleb roars and I look up, my entire body shaking as he throws his head back and cums deep inside of Noah, who twitches from the force.

Chapter Twenty-Seven

Caleb

I don't think I have ever come so fucking hard before, my release relentless, my cum overflowing as I pull out of Noah. Leaning over, I kiss the nape of his neck and stroke the length of his spine, damp with sweat.

"Did I hurt you?" I ask.

I like to fuck hard, and it's so easy to get lost in him. It's why aftercare is so important to me.

"No, I loved it," he says. His body is still shuddering from the aftermath of my harsh fucking.

I glance over to Jessica. Her arms tremble as she pushes herself up and sits back on her heels, kneeling on the floor, her hands on her thighs, *shit*.

My dick twitches, still semi-hard, *what the fuck?*

At this rate, I'll be ready to go again within minutes.

I beckon her over with my finger and watch as she takes a deep breath, and I see a slight flinch. She's still not fully recovered from her broken ribs, but she's almost healed everywhere else—on the surface, anyway.

She moves to stand on her shaky legs and walks over to us slowly, her cheeks flushed, her expression nervous.

I stand to my full height as Noah uses a discarded top to clean himself up, even though I like the idea of my seed leaking out of him.

Jessica stops before me and tilts her head back until our eyes lock.

I grip her chin, wiping my thumb over her satin-soft lips.

"Did you enjoy watching me fuck Noah, little one?"

I love how her nostrils flare as she exhales, her pupils blown wide, both from her post-orgasmic bliss and my question.

She swallows, her voice raspy when she replies, "Yes."

Noah moves to stand beside me, his dick, like mine, is semi-hard. Reaching out, he takes hold of Jessica's hip, causing her to shiver.

"Are you cold, sweet girl?"

Her eyes dart between us as she pulls in a sharp breath. "No," she replies.

"Are we making you uncomfortable?" he asks, the concern evident in his voice.

She tries to shake her head, but I still have hold of her chin, causing her eyes to move back to mine.

"Of course not. I'm…umm, it's not that, it's… I'm—" she stutters over her reply, her cheeks glowing a beautiful crimson, her throat breaking out in a flush, and I wonder how far down that blush goes.

"She's aroused," I say, stepping back, still gripping her chin gently.

I make a slow appraisal, my eyes snaking down the length of her body, stopping at her bare thighs. "You look so hot in Noah's t-shirt."

My dick grows even harder, her scent captivating, evoking a sense of deep-rooted desire.

"I had to fuck his throat raw the first time he gave you one to wear. He knew what it would do to me, but he did it anyway. So, I had to punish him."

Her eyebrows jump up from my words, wrinkling her brow.

I swipe my thumb over her full bottom lip. "Oh, it's all right. I can assure you he enjoyed it."

Her nipples are hard against the soft cotton, and I bring my free hand up and play with one between my thumb and forefinger over the cotton. We've been going slow, trying not to rush her into anything she's not ready for, but when I felt her presence and saw her out of my peripheral in the doorway and then saw the desire reflected in her eyes, I wanted to test the waters. But her touching herself and us touching her are two very different things.

"If you want to stop at any time, all you have to do is say, stop, okay?"

She nods, but I let out a tsk sound, and Noah brushes his knuckle over her cheek.

"Words, sweet girl, we need you to use your words. What do you say if you want to stop?" he asks.

I pinch her nipple, and her lips part, her breathing heavier before I drop my hand back to my side, and her eyes dart between us.

She clears her throat and swallows before answering. "Stop, I say stop."

"Good girl."

Her tongue sweeps over her lips, touching my thumb in the process—the things I want to do with that mouth.

I glance at Noah and then back to Jessica.

"How about we ease you into this gently? You are, after all, still healing."

Noah takes her hand without missing a beat and gently leads her over to the sofa, easing her down.

Grabbing the bottle of water from the table, I twist off the lid, lean over Jessica, and tilt it towards her lips.

"Drink."

No hesitation, no question, so fucking obedient.

When she stops swallowing, I pass Noah the bottle and lower my mouth to hers, licking over the seam of her lips, seeking entry; she submits so beautifully.

I give her a small taste of what's to come, fucking her mouth with my tongue.

When I pull back, her eyes flutter open.

"Exquisite." I glance at Noah and smirk. "Care for a taste?"

I move back to sit beside her as Noah takes my place.

"Abso-fucking-lutely I do." He lowers his mouth over hers, giving me the perfect view before he claims her. He eases her back until she's lying down, and I watch as she opens up to him. Her tongue is duelling with his, and it's a sight to behold.

My fingers trail up the length of her thigh closest to me, slowly teasing over her decadent skin as she breaks out into the most delightful goosebumps.

A small moan works through her chest, her breasts and nipples pressing against the cotton t-shirt, but Noah's possessive mouth drowns out the sound.

I love seeing and hearing her reaction to our touch, our taste.

Her body is crying out for ours.

Noah's palm moves to her breast, causing her body to arch into his touch.

I move my hand underneath her t-shirt until I have her other breast in the palm of my hand, skin on skin.

"Jessica, have you ever had a breast orgasm?"

Noah pulls his mouth away from hers to allow her to answer.

Her eyelids open, focusing on him, and then she glances at me as we gently massage her breasts.

"Are you going to answer him, sweet girl? Caleb doesn't like to be kept waiting."

She jerks, and I can't hold back my smile as he pinches her nipple through the thin layer of cotton.

"Did you not hear his question?"

Her cheeks flush with another wave of heat.

"No, sorry," she says, her voice small.

Noah grips her chin, training her focus on him.

"Why are you apologising?"

It's a habit we've been slowly working on helping her to correct. When she first came here, she said it so much. All I wanted to do was skin her coward of an ex alive—I still do.

She licks her lips, her eyes looking between his, an unspoken understanding as she realises what he's asking.

"I was too caught up by the feel of your hands and lips," she admits, her gaze moving to me.

I smile. "We'll take that as a compliment. My question was, have you ever had a breast orgasm?"

Her eyebrows draw in and a low chuckle escapes me.

"Oh, believe me, little one, they're a thing, and seeing how beautifully you respond to our hands on your breasts, I am pretty sure we can help show you."

Noah's lips skim down her throat and to her chest, where he sucks her nipple through the soft fabric, and she pushes her head back into the sofa cushion.

"See, even with the material in the way, you still love his mouth on your nipple, yes?"

Her fingers dig into the cushion by her side. "Yes," she says on a low exhale as Noah continues to play and tease her stiff peaks.

Chapter Twenty-Eight

Jessica

I try not to squirm beneath their touch, but it's impossible. I'm hyperaware of their proximity, their intoxicating smell. Every touch is like a branding iron, heating my flesh in intense waves.

"Your breasts can swell up to twenty-five percent when aroused. Did you know that?"

It's hard to concentrate on forming an answer, but Caleb likes it when I use my words; even if it's not the most articulate answer, I know he'll appreciate it.

"No, I didn't," I admit. Though my breasts have always been sensitive to touch when I'm aroused, I never knew that was a thing.

"It makes your breasts super sensitive, creating a sexually induced hormonal surge."

Noah lets out a humming sound of agreement, the vibration making my lower stomach tighten with deep heat.

And then he leans back, and suddenly their touch is gone.

My eyes flash open. Caleb has his hand wrapped around the back of Noah's neck, his tongue fucking his mouth, and his other hand wrapped around his hard dick. Wet heat pools between my thighs, and I reach up to cup my breast.

Seeing them together drives me higher. I can't explain it—maybe because I'm attracted to them both, it spurs me on. I feel free to be myself at this moment without fearing judgement or guilt.

I love the way Caleb stares at Noah when they stop kissing. It's full of so many emotions: love, lust, and dominance.

And then they're both looking right at me with hunger in their eyes. They're the predators, and fuck me, I'm their prey.

I should be worried I won't survive the emotional fallout after this is over. I know I'll never be the same, and I don't want to be. They might destroy me, but not without healing me first.

"Take off your top, sweet girl," Noah says, his erection still being fucked slowly by Caleb's fist.

Sitting up, I pull the top off, the change in temperature causing my nipples to harden even more.

Noah reaches out and takes one of my nipples between his thumb and forefinger.

"Stunning," he says as he twists it just enough to get a reaction from me. "Nipple stimulation activates the same region of the brain you get from a clitoral, vaginal or cervical stimulation," Caleb explains as though he's my teacher and I'm his student. And as if to prove his point, he lets go of Noah's dick and reaches out to touch my other breast, using Noah's pre-cum as a lube while slowly circling my areola. "Shall we test the theory?" he asks, his dick thick and hard.

Eagerly, I nod and reply at the same time. "Yes." It's impossible not to hear the plea in my voice. Even though I just got off while watching them together, I need more.

"Noah, shall we?"

"Abso-fucking-lutely," he replies, tapping his chin in thought. "Hmm, how shall we do this?" he asks, eyes roaming over my naked form, leaving a blaze of heat in its wake.

I don't think he's asking me as much as Caleb, so I anxiously wait.

"Come sit in the middle," Caleb says, moving to allow me to swing my legs off the couch. Noah sits down beside me.

I'm bare between two equally aroused naked men who I haven't stopped thinking about the past few weeks. I tried to ignore my attraction. When they admitted they liked me, the flirting, the innuendoes, made me realise it wasn't one-sided.

I'm not given very long to ponder the thoughts further as both men lower their mouths to my breasts, and I almost shoot out of my seat.

"Shit."

My hands move to grip each of their thighs as they continue to play with my breasts like proficient musicians skilled in the art of sexual pleasure. So far, they've only kissed me and fondled my breasts, yet I've never felt more turned on in my life than in the last ten minutes.

I close my eyes, my head falling back against the soft padding. Falling prisoner to their attention, I'm surprised by how gentle and light their touch is as they alternate between circling my nipples and breasts—sensual and all-consuming.

"Fuck." My current vocabulary, it would seem, only consists of swear words.

Caleb licks my nipple with long strokes, and all my nerve endings are sent into a frenzy. Between the two of them, it's a symphony of pleasure, too much and yet not enough. And then I feel it shoot in my nipples and throughout my breasts, but it's most intense around my areola. I can't hold back as I cry out from the pleasure coursing through me.

"Oh my God," I say breathlessly, opening my eyes to find Caleb and Noah staring at me with fire in their eyes.

"Not quite, but close enough," Caleb says, his gaze unwavering.

"Well, sweet girl, I'd say it worked, wouldn't you?" Noah questions.

I nod, licking my lips, my entire body on fire.

"Yes, it was—intense."

Caleb drops to his knees. "Hmm, but something tells me you're not fully sated yet."

He opens my thighs, spreading me wide.

"Fuck, Noah, she's practically dripping."

I tense and try to close my legs. Having them see me on display like this…I'm worried I'll be a disappointment.

Caleb pins me with his penetrating stare. "Remember, all you have to do is say stop, and it all ends."

Shaking my head, I grab hold of his wrist just as he goes to pull away.

"No, I don't want to stop." And it's true. I need this as much as I need oxygen.

"Then open up, spread those glistening lips and let me and Noah see how wet your cunt is for the both of us."

I swear the way this man talks to me should alarm me, but if anything, it turns me on even more.

My entire body heats, and I know there is no way to hide my blush as they openly appraise me.

"Look at her clit all swollen for us," Noah says, tucking his bottom lip between his teeth.

"Do you want the honours of eating her pretty pussy first?" Caleb asks, his hand stroking Noah's spine.

My clit is practically throbbing now, and the urge to close my legs for an entirely different reason is mounting, desperate to bring myself some semblance of relief.

"Please," I whimper, squeezing my eyes closed. Unable to hold back any more, I slide my hand down my stomach and towards my clit.

A strong, calloused palm stops my descent, and I open my eyes to find Caleb shaking his head.

"As much as I'd enjoy seeing you fuck your fingers up this close and personal, it's not going to happen. We'll be the only ones bringing you pleasure."

A low moan works its way up my chest. "Then please, do it already. Please stop teasing me."

Noah throws his head back and laughs.

"Sweet girl, this isn't teasing. Caleb could edge you all night. Bring you right to the brink over and over again and still not let you come."

The thought makes me want to cry.

Noah lowers his head, kissing my thigh, sending tingles straight to my waiting core.

"Don't worry," Caleb says, his fingers caressing my throat. "I can guarantee you'll be coming tonight. There'll be no games, not tonight. Not until we know your hard limits."

I frown—what does he mean by *hard limits?*

But before I have time to ask him out loud, Noah's head is buried between my thighs, impaling me with his thick, hot tongue.

"Fuck, fuck, fuck," I chant as he spears it in and out, his thumb rubbing over my sensitive clit.

"Does she taste good?" Caleb asks. I glance up to see him kneel behind Noah, his nostrils flaring as he watches intently while his boyfriend continues to fuck my pussy with his tongue.

Chapter Twenty-Nine

Noah

Good would be an understatement, she tastes fucking delicious. I'm aware I never answered Caleb, but I'm too lost to her writhing against my face. The way her hot channel flutters around my tongue has my dick leaking pre-cum, and I think of how hot it would be to release my cum all over her swollen folds as she falls over the edge. The sound of a bottle cap popping open has me pulling my mouth away from her pretty little cunt and looking over my shoulder. Caleb is covering his dick in lube, and I already know what's about to happen. I am more than ready for it.

I glance over my shoulder as Caleb leans forward, catching my mouth with his as he spreads my arse cheeks and starts circling my arsehole.

I'm a little sore, but him fucking me while I lick and suck and devour Jessica's juicy, delectable pussy is more than worth it because the pleasure will outweigh the pain.

"Oh my god," Jessica says, her eyes blown wide with arousal as she realises what will happen.

"Does this turn you on?" I ask, hooking two fingers inside her, causing her to jerk in response.

A mewling of sound spills from her lips before she replies. "Yes, so much."

Caleb kisses my shoulder before signalling for Jessica to give him her mouth. She leans closer, my fingers stroking the spot deep inside.

"Fuck," she says right before Caleb captures her lips with his, my body wedged between them. I can feel his heart beating against my back. Her tight core continues to flutter and clench around my fingers. I take a nipple into my mouth, biting down gently. Her entire body arches into me, causing my dick to bob excitedly.

I reach my arm behind me, seeking out Caleb's stiff shaft and take him in my fist, working him in a few hard thrusts. He groans, ending the kiss with Jessica, leaving them both breathless.

"Are you ready?" I don't know if he's asking Jessica or me, but we nod as she leans back again, parting her thighs a little wider.

Caleb wraps his arm around my waist, tugging me backwards towards him. "Arse up," he grunts, circling my hole before pushing his thumb inside.

A deep moan escapes me. I will never tire of this man. Jessica's eyes gaze between the two of us with blazing intensity.

Jessica's body is sweaty. Her skin is flushed, and as desperate as I am to fuck her, I know there'll be time for that later.

Lowering my face back between the apex of her thighs, I inhale.

"Your smell is intoxicating." I pull my fingers free and stick them into my mouth, sucking before releasing them with a soft pop. "As is your taste." I push them back inside her with a deep thrusting motion and am rewarded with her wet heat.

"Have you ever tasted yourself?" I ask.

She shakes her head, biting her bottom lip.

"Here." Pulling my hand back, I hold out the two fingers. "Suck."

Jessica grabs my wrist and opens her mouth, hollowing her cheeks as she sucks on my fingers.

"You like?" I ask as she releases them.

Her nostrils flare as Caleb scissors my back passage. I moan, arching into him. His grip tightens against my hip.

"Stop trying to top from the bottom," he says, nipping my shoulder.

I circle my hips, groaning when I feel him touch my prostate, but just as quickly, he pulls his fingers free, replacing them with the head of his dick.

Lowering my face again, I lick up the length of Jessica's pussy before spreading her folds. As Caleb thrusts into me, I plunge my tongue into her hot waiting centre.

I reward Jessica with the same vigour with my tongue for every thrust of his hips. Her hands are in my hair, tugging, pushing, kneading.

Caleb is punishing me in the best possible way, and I know I need to take Jessica over the edge before I go. I replace my tongue with two fingers and then a third before my lips clamp over her swollen clit.

"Oh, Noah, please don't stop." Her voice is hoarse. "I'm so close."

Something about her saying my name is my undoing, and from how Caleb pounds into me, I'd say it was his, too.

"Come all over his face, Jessica. Show us your pleasure."

"Fuck, Caleb." Her entire body coils tight, her channel tightening around my fingers in a vice-like grip, and I reach down for my dick and squeeze hard, trying to hold off my orgasm as she comes all over my fingers, twitching and jerking from the explosion of pleasure.

Caleb continues to press against my prostate, and I can't hold back any longer. Pulling my face away from her swollen clit, I keep my fingers inside her as she continues to convulse. I work up and down my shaft, almost angry, as I push back against Caleb's deep thrusts.

"Do it," he says. "Come all over her cunt."

I pull my fingers free from her soaking wet heat and roar as my orgasm ricochets through me as I come in thick, hot spurts, my cum shooting all over her swollen pussy, coating her in my seed. It takes everything in me not to succumb and close my eyes, but I want to witness every reaction of the aftershocks from her orgasm. Caleb fucks me with abandon now, unable to hold back as he releases his inner beast.

I'm over-sensitive as he continues to pound into me, and the last of my orgasm leaves my spent body.

I sag and hiss as Caleb loosens his grip and slides free from my arse.

Gripping himself at the base of his dick, he moves beside me and pumps his shaft in hard, fast strokes. His balls draw up tight, the veins are prominent along his thick, velvety length as he tenses, and then he explodes. His cum squirts across Jessica's breasts, and then he angles his pulsing dick lower, his cum mixing with mine over her fleshy, swollen folds. Unable to help myself, I circle my fingers in our mixed pleasure as he continues to cum on her, and then I push my cum soaked fingers into her tight, hot channel.

Her back arches in the most erotic way as she cries out in pleasure. Caleb continues fucking his fist as the last of his orgasm leaves him, and then his thumb circles her clit.

Within seconds, she comes again, chanting our names between incoherent curses and soft sobs.

Caleb lowers his mouth to where my fingers are still pumping in and out of her. He licks a trail of our mixed juices, causing my dick to jerk in response, the action fucking filthy.

"Fuck," I curse out as he sits back, and I grab the back of his neck and pull him in for a soul-rendering kiss.

When we pull apart, we're both breathing harshly, and Jessica whimpers, her orgasm turning into tiny tremors of aftershocks. I remove my fingers, and she gasps for air.

Her eyes are hooded when they finally open, tracing over Caleb and me as if she can barely believe what happened. Her chest rises and falls rapidly from the exertion of chasing her pleasure, and she licks her lips, swallowing hard.

I reach behind me for the bottle of water and bring it to her mouth, urging her without words to drink, which she does eagerly, letting out a satisfied sigh once she's finished.

I sit back on my heels, Caleb's finger lazily stroking her thigh. Her eyes flutter closed, her head falling back against the sofa, the most magnificent smile gracing her lips.

Chapter Thirty

Jessica

I'm vaguely aware of deep hushed voices and the feel of a warm damp cloth between my thighs stroking gently over my sensitive flesh, causing me to shiver. I blink my eyes open, but they're heavy, my entire body sated.

"Shhh, sweet girl," Noah says and then I'm floating, no, I'm being carried. I feel safe. I rest my cheek against the firm, warm chest, releasing a contented sigh.

Suddenly, hands are wrapping around my throat, constricting my airways, making it impossible for me to draw a breath.

I thrash out my arms and legs, kicking with all my might, but they connect with nothing, an empty space.

I'm being suffocated. Is this how I die?

Suddenly the hands around my throat are gone, replaced with a heavy weight bearing down over my entire body, hands now pinning my shoulders.

I try to lash out again, but my hands are pinned above my head as I thrash back and forth.

"Jessica."

"Please don't do this?" I plead, but my voice is hoarse even to my ears.

"Jessica, it's me, Noah."

My body stills, *Noah*.

"That's it, sweet girl, wake up, come on, you're safe, I promise."

His words coax me back as I blink, his face coming into view, a frown marring his forehead, full of worry.

He lets out a heavy sigh.

"There you are," he says, releasing my hands and stroking my cheek.

He stares at me, his eyes filled with concern. My heart is racing, my breaths coming out laboured. I ground myself as I study his features—the flecks of green in his eyes, the way his nostrils flare ever so slightly, and the tiny scar above his right eyebrow.

His thumb wipes my cheek, and I realise they're wet with tears.

"Do you want to talk about it?"

My first instinct is to shut him down and evade the question, but a part of me knows that to truly heal, I need to stop hiding the darkest parts of myself. I look past him and realise I'm in their bedroom—the vague memory of being carried makes sense.

"He was strangling me," I say, my hand automatically moving to my throat as I shudder, the remnants of a cold, callous touch. "It felt so real."

The bed dips, and I turn my head as Caleb lays on his side, resting his head in his hand as he peers down, his fingers stroking up the length of my arm.

"But it wasn't. You're safe with us. This, this is real," he says.

I swallow as he trails his fingers up and down my arm. Noah continues to caress my cheek, spreading warmth throughout my body, chasing away the ice that had settled deep in my core.

"It's just you, me, and Noah, little one. You're safe with us. You can feel us, yes?"

Clearing my throat, I nod and allow these two men to ground me.

"It just felt so real. I couldn't breathe. I thought he found me," I admit. I'll never forget waking up my first night here with Noah spooning me, keeping me safe in his arms.

We've talked over the last few weeks, and I thought my nightmares were becoming less frequent because I haven't even been able to remember some of them.

"You're safe, little one. But if we're moving too fast and you need us to back off, we can do that. Your comfort is what's most important to us." Caleb leans over and kisses my forehead softly, the brush of his short beard against my skin.

As he draws back, I panic and reach for his wrist.

"Please don't ask me to leave." I've never felt as needy as I do at this moment. Maybe it's my connection to them both after such a short time. Who knows?

"We won't, but we can if you need space. You can stay in here, and we'll take your room." Noah glances at Caleb and then back to me.

Right now, the last thing I want is space, and maybe that's me being co-dependent. But after having their mouths on me, them touching me intimately, I want more to know I'm not this broken shell of a person, that my ex hasn't ruined me.

"Kiss me." My voice comes out strained, but I don't care. I need to feel them, know this is as real as Caleb assured me.

"My pleasure." Noah lowers his mouth to mine, sweeping his tongue over the seam of my lips before seeking access. I open up to him immediately, unable to suppress my groan as his tongue mingles with mine.

Fingertips dance over my collarbone in the most tantalising of touches, then work up and down my throat, causing me to break out in goosebumps. Then I feel lips tracing over my bare breast, and I arch my back, seeking more. I didn't know how much I enjoyed my nipples and breasts being lavished until now.

Noah pulls back. A complaint forms on my lips, but it's drowned out when Caleb's mouth meets mine.

And damn, can these men kiss. I have no doubt both men could bend me to their will. Caleb is hard and demanding. Noah is soft and slow. Together, the perfect combination.

A hand slips between the apex of my thighs, and even though I'm sensitive from earlier, I crave their touch, the need to be owned all over again. My legs part, and I hear a sound of approval as lips whisper over my lower abdomen.

"Would you like us to make you come, sweet girl, until you are so consumed with pleasure that you pass out?"

I doubt he needs my answer, but when Caleb pulls back, his mouth hovering over mine, I suck in a deep breath and find my voice. "Yes, please," I croak out. Caleb's eyes are dark as he studies me in a way I doubt anyone ever has, and at this moment, I don't know whether I want to laugh or cry.

"Such a good girl," he says, his voice full of reverence.

I shudder. *Oh my God!*

Noah hums in agreement, and wet heat pools between my thighs, my core clenching.

"Fuck, Caleb, I think our girl has a praise kink."

Before I can even process his words further, Caleb is devouring my mouth again as Noah feasts on my pussy, and I am lost to these two men. I let go of every thought as I slip into oblivion, trusting them with my body to know I am safe.

Chapter Thirty-One

Caleb

Noah made Jessica come twice more with his mouth and fingers as I fucked her mouth with my tongue. She responds so well to our every touch, and I know she'll be our undoing, because there is nothing I wouldn't do for her or Noah. Whether she realises it or not, there is no way we'll let her go.

"Ours," I say as she crests with her third and final orgasm with a silent scream.

Noah reaches for my erection, his eyes lifting to mine. I've already come twice tonight, same as him, but seeing Jessica in the height of pleasure is an aphrodisiac in itself, and we haven't even fucked her yet.

"What the fuck is she doing to us?" I ask as he sits up from between her thighs.

We need to clean her up, but I see the savage need reflected in Noah's eyes.

"I have no idea, but I need inside you," he says, his jaw clenching.

Jessica's passed out beside us, her chest rising and falling in a heavy staccato beat.

"Now."

I sit up and grab his hard length in my fist and tug. He throws his head back, closing his eyes with a deep guttural moan.

"Then fucking do something about it." I swipe my thumb over the head of his cock, wet with pre-cum.

The scent of our mixed arousal is heavy in the air.

He lets go of me and shoves my hand away, grabbing a pillow. I lift my pelvis for him to push it underneath me. He reaches into the bedside drawer for a bottle of lube. He coats his dick, moving between my legs.

I love powering him from the bottom and seeing him animalistic with all-consuming need.

I glance at Jessica. Is it wrong Noah is about to fuck me while she's passed out next to us? No, I don't think so. I saw the look on her face when she caught us fucking. I'm pretty sure she'd enjoy the show if she were awake.

Noah holds eye contact. I spread my thighs more as he circles my arsehole, pushing his finger through the first ring of muscle, prepping me before adding another, scissoring me open. His nostrils flare as he strokes his hard length, wet from his spit and pre-cum.

And then the head of his cock replaces his fingers, pushing through the barrier in one deep thrust. I grab his throat and squeeze as he thrusts. It fucking burns in the best possible way, his cock pressing against my prostate. He is the only man I will ever do this with. Only him. But doing it with Jessica in our bed, where she could wake up at any moment, turns me on more as I thrust up, taking him in as deep as possible.

A curse graces his lips, but it's silent as my fingers tighten around his throat just enough to cut off his airway. I reach for my dick and squeeze at the base, my arousal intensifying. I ease off my hold on his throat, loving how his dick swells inside me even more when he gasps for breath.

"Fuck," he croaks out, his eyes full of lust as he continues to fuck me with abandon.

"That's it, so fucking close," I say through my teeth and arch upwards. I swear he is touching me in places I have never felt before. How is that even possible?

"I know," he says, his jaw clenching, I can see it reflected in his eyes how close he is, how it's always been far beyond good between us, but this is on a whole other level entirely.

I squeeze his throat, cutting off his airway again. I need him to come, even with him fucking me. I need to watch him fall off the edge so I can follow.

"That's it, Noah," I growl. "Fucking fill me up. Give me everything you've got."

His entire body coils like a live wire as he bottoms out, pressing into my prostate as he explodes, his body dripping with sweat. I can barely keep my orgasm at bay as I let go of his throat and grip his hip, digging my fingers into his flesh as I fuck my other hand, my dick curving, my balls drawing up tight, and then I come like a fucking fountain, my cum hitting his abs, thick and hot. I swear I come harder than ever before.

"Oh fuck, fuck, fuck," he says as he gasps for air.

He is still spilling into me, his cum leaking out of me as I pulse around him; my orgasm continues to pump out of me in thick waves.

Grabbing the back of his neck, I sit up, pulling his mouth to mine and kiss him with reverence. When we pull apart, his eyes are blown wide, his nostrils flaring as he watches me watching him.

No words are spoken. The only sound is our laboured breathing as he lowers his forehead against my shoulder, his dick still twitching inside me. I'm overly sensitive, but I fucking love the way he begins to soften before slipping free. The sound is wet and filthy. I let out a deep growl of appreciation.

I glance over to Jessica; her breathing is heavy. How she didn't wake from us fucking is beyond me. Reaching over, I stroke her cheek, and she moves towards my touch like a magnet.

Noah's hands tremble as he pushes himself up and looks around, grabbing a discarded towel to wipe up our joint pleasure.

He gets off the bed and slips into the ensuite. I cover my face and lay back as I listen to the tap running before it's cut off, followed by footsteps as he returns.

"Here." He passes me a warm flannel. I sit up and wipe myself as he moves beside Jessica, gently cleaning her up. Apart from a slight shiver, she barely stirs. He pulls back the duvet covering her and slips in beside her, where she lets out a contented sigh.

"Let me go grab some more water." As I stand, he grabs my wrist, tugging me towards him. I lean over Jessica for a kiss.

"I love you," he says when he pulls back.

I nod. "Love you, too."

When I return to our room after checking the alarm and grabbing a couple of water bottles, I pause at the threshold. Noah is already lying down on his side facing Jessica, his eyes closed, his breathing already evened out as he succumbs to sleep, and I can't help but smile as I take a mental photograph.

I place a bottle on his bedside table and mine before joining them in our king-size bed.

Rolling onto my side, I pull Jessica into my body, her back flush with my chest. Noah moves closer and reaches over, his hand moving to my hip.

"Night," he mumbles.

"G'night," I reply and inhale Jessica's sweet scent, now a mixture of me and Noah. Something tightens in my chest. I never thought I could love anyone, and then I met Noah, and now with Jessica between us, I know I'm falling for her, too.

Chapter Thirty-Two

Noah

I leave Caleb with Jessica and slip out of bed. I woke up about an hour ago and haven't been able to get back to sleep. Watching Caleb spooning Jessica made my heart soar; it's the side of him only I ever get to witness, and the fact he feels like this towards her reiterates how I feel, too—she's ours.

Turning on the shower, I brush my teeth while I allow the water to heat up and look at my reflection, loving the marks Caleb's fingers have left on my body from our fucking last night. Even with me on top, he still tops from the bottom, and I fucking love it.

Stepping under the hot spray of the jets, I let the water cascade over my body and close my eyes, resting my arm on the wall and allowing my body to relax as steam fills the shower.

My mind wanders as I think of trying to find out about Jessica's brother and wondering what we're going to do about her ex. She needs closure one way or another, and we need to find a way to help her with that. But now there's this deep-seated need to make sure he's no longer a threat.

The shower door opening alerts me to Caleb's presence

before his arms wrap around me from behind. He kisses my shoulder.

"Morning," he grumbles.

"Morning." I turn my face towards him, and he kisses me.

"You all right?" he asks, moving me so he can get under the shower jets.

I nod, but it's a contradiction to my reply. "I think we should talk to Jessica about maybe making a statement about her ex."

He scoffs at that. "Or we can just take care of him ourselves."

The thing is, I know he's being serious. "Caleb, as tempting as that sounds, us behind bars isn't the answer."

He wipes the water from his eyes and slicks his wet hair back as he focuses on me.

"I never said anything about getting caught." He's not even joking. This man is ex-forces, trained in hand-to-hand combat. As much as I want to take the law into our own hands, that isn't how to do it.

Reaching for the shower gel and lathering it in the loofah, I nudge my chin for him to come closer as I work the suds over his torso.

"Caleb, I have no doubt you could take him out and make it look like an accident. But Jessica needs closure, a way for her to take her power back. Us going in with our fists isn't going to fix this. Turn."

He faces the wall, resting his forearm against the tiled wall as I wash his back.

"She's ours, Noah, and we protect what's ours."

I kiss his shoulder and wrap my arms around his waist, pulling him against my chest.

"I know. But we need to tread carefully. I don't want her to think we're anything like that arsehole. Don't you think she's already had enough violence?"

He turns his face towards mine, his eyes scanning my face.

"I hate it when you're right. Still doesn't stop me from wanting to gut the cunt like a fish, though," he admits.

I can't say I disagree with him there.

"I'll see how she is after the counselling, and maybe I'll try talking to her then."

The last thing I want to do is make her feel pressured.

He groans as I trail my fingers across his stomach. "Where are you going to take her shopping?"

I kiss his neck. "Selfridges, figure it'll have everything she might need."

Lowering my hand, I slowly work my fist up and down his dick.

"No expense spared. Get her whatever she wants."

"Of course."

He wraps his fist over mine, setting the pace. "Did you see how well she responds to us? She's fucking amazing, right?"

Caleb is big on communication, but his feelings he reserves for those he cares about.

"She is. Is it weird how well she fits in with us, a missing puzzle piece we didn't know we were missing until she arrived on our doorstep battered and bruised?"

I clench my jaw, the vivid image I don't think will ever disappear.

Caleb turns in my arms. "No, not weird at all. I just worry I might scare her away," he admits.

I let out a soft laugh. "She saw you fucking me. If that didn't scare her off, I don't think anything will."

He looks at me, lost in thought before he replies, "I don't know, I have this feeling like one wrong move, and she'll bolt. You know me, I like to push boundaries, but with her, I have to keep myself grounded, which is where you come in, but this doesn't change how I feel about you."

My throat feels tight as I try to swallow around the ball of emotion. "I know, and I love you, too."

Grabbing the back of my neck, he crashes his lips down on mine in a punishing kiss as he pushes me back against the wall, our hard lengths between us. It's not difficult when I'm around this man, but this isn't about sex, this is about emotional intimacy.

When we finally part with swollen lips, he smirks and then circles his finger in the air as he takes a step back. I turn around, and he reaches over my head for the shampoo and washes my hair and then moves on to my body.

But all it does is make me harder. It's like when we first met all over again.

He reaches around my hip and takes me in his fist, his head over my shoulder. "Is this for me or her?" he asks, tugging it hard.

"Fuck, I don't know."

His laugh vibrates down the length of his arm and to my dick as he stays pressed against my back, his cock hard between us as he wanks me off, and in less than a minute, I'm coming.

"Fuck." I brush my hair out of my eyes to look up at him, and there's a smirk across his face. I shove him backwards and then drop to my knees, my dick still pulsing as I reach for him and take his rock-solid dick into my mouth and to the back of my throat.

"I love your mouth," he says, gripping my hair as he thrusts into my throat, causing me to gag.

His hand goes to my throat, tilting my head just a fraction so I can take him even more.

"That's it, keep looking at me, just like that," he says, commanding as he begins to fuck my throat.

My hands wrap around his arse, my nails digging into his skin, my nose pressed against his groin as I give over to him and let him take what he needs. My eyes flutter closed, but his fingers pull against my scalp, causing me to look up.

"Eyes on me."

I reach between his legs to play with his ball sack the way I know he loves, and he thickens even more, cutting off my airway. This man fucking loves breath play, and I live for pleasing him.

His jaw tenses as his balls tighten, and he thickens, my eyes watering, and then with one last deep thrust, he comes down my throat, and I have no choice but to swallow until he eases off just enough for me to suck in a breath as he continues to pulse. I will never tire of this man. When his orgasm subsides, he reaches for my shoulders, pulls me to my feet, and kisses me.

Chapter Thirty-Three

Jessica

Waking, I roll onto my back and stretch, feeling sated in the best possible way as I blink up at the ceiling and notice the light is different. I glance around the room. Caleb and Noah's room is blanketed with their combined masculine scents, and I inhale deeply.

When I realise I am lying here naked, I pull the duvet with me as I sit up, recalling the events of last night. My core tightens as I remember what it felt like to have their mouths on me as they worshipped my body.

A shiver of pleasure rolls through me as my entire body heats from the memory. I look around and wonder where they both are, feeling a little discombobulated at waking up alone in their bed.

I hear the sound of the shower running from their ensuite and look around for something to throw on so I can go back to my room. The last thing I want is to be still sitting here like a hot mess.

Biting my lip, I look around, grateful when I see a discarded shirt on top of their chaise longue. It's better than running back to my room starkers or combing through their drawers. I stumble out of bed, my feet sinking into the plush, thick carpet, something I can't help but appreciate. Curtis has cold, hard flooring with only a couple of rugs. Shaking thoughts of him from my mind, I snatch up the shirt and slip it on, my fingers trembling as I do up a couple of the buttons. The shirt stops above my knees and smells like Caleb. I close my eyes and inhale deeply, my nipples pebbling beneath the cotton.

I startle from a noise behind me and spin around, my hand going to my chest. Caleb is standing in the doorway with a towel wrapped around his waist, his hair damp, as a cloud of steam surrounds him followed by the shower shutting off.

"Good morning, Jessica," he says, his eyes raking over my body.

I clear my throat. "Morning," I reply, my voice sounding a little too high even for me. I can hear movement as light filters into the room, and I'm vaguely aware of the curtains being drawn, almost casting a spotlight over Caleb. Seeing the tattoos covering his torso and arms like this in the light of day makes me want to go over and study each and every one of them.

I've never liked them before now; they were never really my cup of tea. But all I can think about is getting lost in the intricate designs for hours. Noah is the opposite, with only one over his heart and one on his ring finger.

"Going somewhere?" Caleb asks, prowling towards me like a lion.

I point over my shoulder. "To my room?" I reply, but it comes out more like a question.

He stops right in front of me, and I have to tilt my head back just to look at him as he towers over me. He smells clean and delicious.

"Hmm, looked as though you were sneaking out," he says, his hand going to my hip as if to hold me here. Not that it's necessary, as I'm currently frozen to the spot. I try to speak, but I'm suddenly feeling very tongue-tied.

"You look delectable wearing my shirt," he says. "Absolutely ravishing."

His warm breath skates across my face, fresh mint and all male, an intoxicating mixture, and then when Noah steps up beside him, his eyes sweeping over me before meeting mine, I feel like I might melt into a puddle on the floor.

"Hmm, I have to agree she looks edible wearing your shirt, Caleb."

My cheeks must be way beyond crimson, my entire body igniting at their intense perusal.

"How did you sleep, little one?" Caleb asks, his thumb circling my hip over the material of the shirt, but it might as well be non-existent the way his touch affects me.

I don't even have to think about my answer. "Good, thank you."

Once I woke from that nightmare, they coaxed me back to the present and sent me into oblivion.

"I'm glad," Noah says, his hand moving to my other hip. "So, the aim is to get you high on orgasms, is that it?"

I would be on fire now if I weren't already blushing profusely.

"Hmm, something tells me she wouldn't oppose the idea." Caleb leans down, and I tilt my face towards him. These men are like gravity. His mouth hovers over mine, brushing my lips with a soft stroke before I quickly turn my face to the side. But it's short-lived as he grips my chin, not enough to hurt, just enough to be firm as he directs my gaze back to his.

"What's wrong, little one? Too much too soon?" he asks, concern lacing his voice.

I try to shake my head but am unable to move, so instead, I cast my eyes down as I form a meek-sounding answer. "I haven't brushed my teeth," I say, self-conscious.

Noah chuckles as he steps into my side, his lips brushing the shell of my ear. "I've fucked your pretty pussy with my tongue."

The way these men talk is hot as hell. "Do you really think not brushing your teeth would put either of us off?"

I'm not given the opportunity to reply as he grabs the back of my neck and kisses me. I relent immediately, but all too soon, he's pulling away, and then Caleb is the one kissing me, and all coherent thought escapes me.

He slows the kiss and whispers, "Don't ever deny us again, little one, not over something like that." And then, as if to prove his statement, he nips my lip, not enough to hurt but more as a warning, before sucking it into his mouth and then letting go.

Noah's stomach grumbles, and I can't hide the giggle that works its way up my chest, breaking the tension.

"How about we let you get dressed, and we'll meet you downstairs for breakfast," Caleb says, kissing my forehead and stepping back.

I smile as Noah leans over to kiss my cheek before Caleb turns me towards the door and gives my arse a small slap, wet heat going straight to my core.

When I get to the door, I chance a quick look over my shoulder and wish I hadn't as they both stand in a towel each. I can't stop myself from looking them over one by one. Both of them are big guys. Caleb is all muscle, whereas Noah is lean. I know I saw them both last night, but something about seeing them now, in the light of day, is almost too much. How can they both be so uniquely beautiful?

"Keep looking at us like that, little one, and there'll be no going slow, even though your body probably still needs to recover. I'll bend you over that bed and fuck you raw until you're begging me to stop, and maybe not even then."

My eyes snap to his, and I swallow hard because right now, the thought of him doing just that has my entire stomach tightening with need, but I need space to think before giving myself over completely.

With that, I turn on my heels, and I swear I hear Noah's laugh follow me all the way to my bedroom.

Chapter Thirty-Four

Caleb

If her body were ready, there would have been no doubt in my mind she would have been complicit for me to do just that.

Noah looks at me, smirking, shaking his head with a soft laugh.

"Oh, fuck off, you were thinking it, too."

He doesn't deny it as he drops his towel and walks over to the chest of drawers, his arse begging me to take him.

"Fucking keep that up, and you'll be the one I fuck over the edge of the bed."

"Yeah, yeah, promises, promises," he says flippantly, purposely goading as he bends over and pulls something out of the drawer. By the time he straightens, I've crossed the room and am already behind him, my hand around his throat as I pull him into my chest, my erection pressed against his arse.

"Hmm, if I didn't know better, I'd say you were begging me to fuck you raw."

I love the way I can feel the roll of his throat as he swallows, the pulse in his neck beating against my thumb.

"I'm not going to reward you for being a dick, but if you behave the rest of today, I'll take you hard and fast." I reach down and swipe my thumb over his erect cock and bring it to my mouth and suck. "Delicious."

And then I run my nose along his throat before I bite down on his shoulder, not hard enough to break the skin but enough to leave a mark, a promise of what's to come.

I've always been insatiable for this man, but it's as though Jessica's presence has opened a door in Pandora's box, and it's ramped up my feelings tenfold.

He lets out a deep moan, grabbing the back of my neck and pulling me in for a kiss.

"No, behave," I say against his mouth before nipping at his lip, as I did with Jessica only moments ago.

I'm turning the bacon over on the grill when I feel her. "Tea?" I ask before turning to face her and I move beside the oven and lean back against the counter. She's wearing a simple pair of skinny jeans and a plain black vest top. No matter what she wears or doesn't, she is hypnotising.

Using my finger, I beckon her towards me and love how she complies without hesitation; how I'd love to introduce her to Formidable one day with Noah and me.

I tug on her wrist and pull her into my body. Her hands go to my hips as if to steady herself as I wrap my arms around her waist.

"You look lovely," I say honestly, but it's not just her looks. It's so much more than that. "Are you okay after last night?" I ask.

"Yeah, I am." Her cheeks flush the most beautiful shade of crimson.

"Good, because we have plenty more where that came from. You're ours now, little one."

She nibbles on her lower lip, a question shining in her eyes.

"What is it? Talk to me."

She looks over my chest before bringing her gaze to mine. "What do you mean by I'm yours now? You and Noah are together, so what does that make me exactly?"

I raise an eyebrow in understanding. "Ours. And we're yours. It means other than me and Noah, the three of us are exclusive to one another. We won't share you unless it's with each other." For now, this is just about the three of us.

Her eyes study my face for a moment. I've noticed it's a tell of hers. She's searching for a lie—an untruth.

Gripping the back of her neck loosely, I pull her toward me, needing her close, my other hand against her cheek.

"Jessica, you've been hurt physically and emotionally..." I cover her lips with my thumb before she can retort. "And as much as it pains me to see you at war with your head and heart, I also understand. So be patient with yourself while we earn your trust. I promise in time, you'll grow to trust us." And then I seal my words with a kiss. Even though expressing my feelings and voicing them doesn't come easy to me, I know she needs to hear them and for me to show her.

She deserves to see the truth in my words and my promise.

It's a claim as I devour her mouth with vigour. Lifting her onto the kitchen counter, I spread her legs and stand between her thighs, caging her in as she melts into the kiss.

A low whimper escapes her, causing my dick to twitch. This woman has no idea how much power she has over me already—over us. I slow the kiss before pulling back. Her eyes flutter open, pupils blown wide.

"Yeah, little one, you have the same effect on me, too," I say, nipping her bottom lip gently before gripping her hips and lifting her off the counter and back to her feet. "Come." I take her hand and guide her to the table, pulling out the chair with my free hand and ushering her to sit.

Such a simple act, and yet she seems entirely thrown by it. Once she's seated, I crouch down so we're at eye level.

"You'll need to get used to us taking care of you, in every meaning of the word, little one." It's a promise and declaration all rolled into one, and if I thought she was blushing before, it has nothing on her now.

"Noah is going to drive you to your appointment this afternoon. And then tomorrow, we thought we could take you out on an official first date."

She looks surprised. "You both want to take me on a date together—all three of us?"

I nod. "Yes, of course. Why wouldn't we?"

Jessica jerks her shoulders in a shrug, her eyes darting around the room, almost as though she's planning her escape.

Kneeling, I reach up and take her jaw in my hand. "Hey, if you're not ready, you can say that. We don't want you to feel uncomfortable. But we think it's time you got out of the house."

"I have nothing to wear," she blurts out nervously.

I'm unsure if she's clutching at straws, but just as I'm about to delve deeper, Noah chooses that moment to appear.

"And that, sweet girl, is why I thought we could stop off at Selfridges after your appointment."

He walks over and leans down, giving her a slow kiss, my hand still clasping her jaw. The display of affection sets my entire body alight with desire.

"Do you think you're up for that?" he asks against her lips.

She gives a subtle nod, it's not quite a yes, but it's not a no either.

"Then it's settled," I say, dropping my hand and rising as Noah straightens beside me. "Tomorrow, it's a date." And then I lean in and steal a kiss from Noah. He tastes like Jessica now, too, and nothing has ever tasted so damn sweet.

Chapter Thirty-Five

Noah

I worked from my laptop in the waiting room while Jessica had her appointment. She didn't speak on the way over, fiddling with her hands in her lap, eyes darting everywhere as I drove through London. But it wasn't to take in the busy streets or the tourists; she was on guard, checking her surroundings.

It's going to take time for her to feel at ease.

The sound of the door opening draws my attention away from my laptop, and I immediately close it and move to my feet as she walks towards me.

Her eyes are puffy, clearly from crying, and before I can think better of it, I open my arms and pull her into a tight embrace.

"You okay, sweet girl?"

Her fingers grip my shirt. "Yeah, just tired," she admits, her voice a little hoarse. I'm unsure if it's from talking or crying, but either way, it's better out than in. Even though she's been talking to Caleb and me and opening up, I'm sure there are still things she might not be ready, if ever, to speak with us about. As long as she knows we're here, if she wants to, that's what matters.

"If you're not up for going to Selfridges, we can sort something else out. You just say the word."

She pulls back, straightening her back, that resolve I love so much about her setting in. "No, I'm good, I promise."

I know she's anything but good, but if she's up to a little shopping excursion, I'm here for that.

"Come on, then, let's get out of here."

I let go of her and slide my laptop into its sleeve before zipping it into the laptop bag and then wrap my arm around her shoulder, nodding bye to the receptionist as I lead her over to the lift.

Once inside, I press the button for the ground floor.

She glances up into the reflection of the mirrored door and catches me staring. A smile pulls at her lips as her cheeks heat, and she looks down at the floor.

Nope, that's no good.

Unable to stop myself, I move behind her and pull her back against my chest, wrapping my arms around her waist and leaning my chin on her shoulder.

"Oi, you don't shy away from me. You're beautiful, can't blame me for staring."

Her eyes slowly rise until she's staring back at me in the mirror as the lift slowly descends.

Turning my head, I inhale, loving her unique scent—not perfume, a cocoa butter body lotion and all her. I kiss her cheek before peppering soft kisses along her collarbone, loving how she moves her head to give me better access, pressing closer to my chest as she releases a soft moan.

"You are the perfect temptress," I say, reaching for her chin and capturing her mouth with mine.

Teasing the seam of her lips until she opens up, the tip of my tongue strokes hers in a slow, sensual dance.

My stomach jolts as the lift stops, and I groan as I ease out of the kiss.

As much as I'm all for public displays of affection, devouring her in the lift of her therapist's building might not be the most appropriate.

I step back, leaving a cushion of air between us, but keep a hand on her hip as I guide her to the car.

She's more talkative on the drive to Selfridges.

I use the Oxford Street car park at the rear and stow my laptop in the boot before we make our way into Selfridges.

"First things first, how about a sugar hit?"

Since Jessica has been living with us, I've noticed she has a bit of a sweet tooth like mine, where Caleb can take it or leave it and is more savoury. My girl does love something sweet.

Taking her hand in mine, we approach the Foodhall, and I stop at a light blue counter. Behind is a pillar in the same colour and written in neon blue and pink 2D letters is Lola's Cupcakes.

I love the smile across her face as her eyes widen at all the cupcakes on display beneath the glass counter.

She opts for Red Velvet, and I get Cookies and Cream, and we each get a coffee, taking a small table in the corner. I also get half a dozen to go. It would be rude not to; Maggie loves something to go with a cup of tea before she takes care of the house, and even if Caleb doesn't fancy one later, I can have fun with him and some of the icing.

The thought draws my attention to Jessica as she brings her thumb to her mouth, but I lean over, grab her wrist, and take the liberty of licking the icing off.

My teeth graze the pad of her thumb. "Delicious," I say, holding eye contact, fascinated by how her pupils dilate.

I kiss the palm of her hand before releasing it, loving the blush that covers her cheeks that highlight her freckles, making them even more prominent.

When she's finished her coffee, we stay on the ground floor, and I lead her towards the makeup counters.

"I didn't know if you wanted to get any makeup or perfume."

Not that she needs either, but that doesn't mean she might not want it. It's about feeling good again in her skin.

She bites her lower lip, appearing uncertain, and I palm her lower back, pulling off to the side near the Tiffany jewellery counter where it's quiet.

"What is it?" I ask.

"It's been a hot minute since I last wore makeup. Curtis didn't like it, so I just stopped."

I grind my jaw before speaking and lower my face until I'm inches from hers. "Listen, this isn't about anyone else but you. If you want makeup, perfume, clothes, that's why we're here." My hand goes to the back of her neck, my thumb brushing her cheek. "You are free to be whoever you want to be. And that goes for wearing what you want to wear. Whatever that may be."

Her eyes glisten with emotion as she clears her throat. "Thank you."

I shake my head. "You don't have to thank me, sweet girl." Leaning in until my lips meet hers, I give her a chaste kiss and straighten to my full height.

"You ready?" I offer her my hand.

With a genuine smile, she takes it. "Yes, let's do this," she says, mirroring my words from earlier.

I can't wait to wine and dine her tomorrow night with Caleb. We have every intention of showing her how she should be treated.

Knowing how much she loves food, Caleb insisted on a Michelin-star restaurant, and of course, I had to agree. HIDE in Mayfair was a clear favourite, and we managed to book The Reading Room in the subterranean vaults in The Bar Below. So not only will she appreciate the food, she'll understand the sentiment of the décor, too. She loves to curl up with a book when she's not marathon-watching Marvel.

We did consider taking her to a hotel after, but honestly,

Saved by Two

although we played a little the other night, we don't want to be presumptuous or look as though we expect anything she's not ready for, besides we think the first time should be at home, where we think she feels the most comfortable.

Chapter Thirty-Six

Jessica

I stare at my reflection in the full-length mirror and have to double-take. It's been so long since I dressed up and put on a full face of makeup, even going as far as to curl my hair.

Noah was so patient with me yesterday. I saw his concern when I left my counselling session and found him waiting. Caleb is the same; he sits and waits for me in the reception area. It makes me feel guilty. They have lives, and yet lately, it's as though everything revolves around me, like I'm taking them away from more important things, and a tiny part of me can't help but feel like a burden.

Of course, neither has made me feel that way, and I know a lot of it is my own self-doubt. Greta, my therapist, has been incredible these past few weeks. Talking to her is helping. I'm sporadic at times. My thought process is all over the place; things surface out of the blue. It's emotionally draining, and my anxiety is rife right before a session, but I feel a little lighter each time I leave.

Shopping felt way out of my comfort zone. The saddest part is I used to love it, even if it was just to browse. Curtis played the role of a good boyfriend. He would come along and even hold some of my bags. Only later did his loathing become apparent to anything that didn't adhere to what he wanted to do. I only moved in with him because I was between student accommodations. Mason offered for me to stay with him, but Curtis was persuasive, it was only meant to be temporary.

I hadn't even considered makeup when Noah suggested we go shopping so I had something to wear tonight. I left Selfridges completely kitted out. I'd be lying if I didn't admit I felt like a child in a sweet shop. One of the makeup artists even helped me with a look for tonight with testers, so I knew which products to get.

Noah wouldn't let me pay, and when I tried to argue that fact, he shut me up with a searing kiss as he handed over his credit card. I can't even remember the last time I wore perfume. I was more indecisive about my perfume than I was over the dress. Noah helped as we smelt samples but refused to choose for me.

The dress was the one I was drawn to, but I kept finding excuses as to why it wouldn't be suitable, however, Noah was persistent and insisted I try it on.

I smooth my hands down the sleek black material of said dress—beautifully fitted, spaghetti straps, corseted bodice with lace trim, underwired cups, and a split hem which stops mid-thigh. As much as Noah tried to persuade me to go for a pair of Manolo Blahnik stilettos, I had his card marked. I knew there was no way he'd let me pay, just like with the makeup, so I opted for a gorgeous pair of Kurt Geiger black patent leather stiletto sandals with a side buckle fastening.

My nails are still battered from where I've been biting them, so I buffed them up as best I could with a coat of clear varnish and opted for a deep red lipstick and smoky eye makeup look.

I feel good for the first time in a long time—a bit more like me.

"Knock knock?"

My pulse races, and I suck in a deep breath as I look in the mirror. Noah is standing in the doorway, his gaze sweeping over me. Slowly, I turn around until I'm facing him.

"You look beautiful," he says, his arm behind his back.

He moves closer, and I can't help but admire how handsome he looks in a suit. I've seen Caleb in a suit for work, but this is the first time I've seen Noah dressed up.

"Wow, you look beautiful too… I mean, handsome." My skin flushes, but he doesn't seem phased as he rewards me with a dimpled smile.

"I'm flattered you think so," he says, moving closer and revealing his arm from behind his back, holding out a box of black roses.

"Oh, my God." I reach out and take the box, my hands trembling. "They're gorgeous."

"As are you," he says, kissing my cheek before stepping back.

I sniff back the urge to cry. "I can't believe you remembered," I say almost to myself.

Clearing of a throat draws my attention back to the doorway where Caleb now stands.

"Of course, we remembered. And those are Infinity roses. They should last a year."

I glance back to the gorgeous bouquet and then back to the man who commands the room as he stalks towards me, stopping beside Noah. Together, they're a force to be reckoned with. Caleb's eyes cast a leisurely perusal of me from head to toe and back up again. "Stunning," he says, moving into my space, his hand moving to the back of my neck. "May I kiss you?"

This man could take whatever he wants, but still asks, making my entire body tingle.

"Yes," I reply as he lowers his mouth to mine. It's over way too quickly, and I try to hide my disappointment.

"Later," he says, a one word promise as he uses his thumb to swipe over my top lip. "I'm almost disappointed it didn't smudge," he admits. And it takes a moment for my brain to play catch up as I bring my fingertips to my lips.

"It's a lip stain."

He smirks. "It's lovely, just a shame. I'd love to see that colour all over my cock."

I almost stop breathing and squeeze my thighs together as my lower stomach summersaults with a deep-rooted need.

These men are going to ruin me.

"We also got you a gift," he says, holding out a square Tiffany box tied in white ribbon in the palm of his hand.

My eyes dart to Noah and then back to Caleb.

"But you already got me a gift." I hold up the flowers for emphasis. Noah takes them from me and places them on the dresser.

"The roses were a token gift."

I shake my head. "But I don't understand. What about the other stuff, the dress, the makeup?"

Noah brings his fingertip to my lips. "We meant what we said about taking care of you. And we're celebrating, so let us have this—let us spoil you."

I mean, what am I even supposed to say to that?

Caleb keeps his palm extended until I take the box. I feel two sets of eyes on me as I unravel the white satin ribbon. I'm nervous, not because I think I won't like it, but because it's from them. I know I'll love it, but receiving so much attention from two ardent men has me weak at the knees.

Inside the box is the signature drawstring bag. I take a deep breath, thankful my ribs have almost healed to a dull ache.

Pulling the string, I peer inside and pull out a sleek gold bangle, turning it in my hand to see a striking centre motif and what I can presume are most definitely diamonds.

I cover my mouth, struggling to find the words.

"I don't know what to say. Thank you doesn't seem enough. I don't feel deserving of something so remarkable," I admit.

Caleb reaches out for the bangle as Noah takes the box and sets it next to the roses on the dresser.

Opening the bangle, he gently lifts my bare wrist (the other adorns my Rolex from Mason) and he wraps it around, clicking it closed.

"Perfect fit," he says, kissing the inside of my wrist. I reach out and touch his shoulder to steady myself.

Noah saddles beside me, takes my hand from Caleb, and kisses the palm of my hand.

"This bangle represents the connection we feel towards you, a reminder that even though you can't see it, you know it's there," Noah says.

Caleb's gaze lifts to mine. "We wanted you to have something tangible. If you want to change it, you can. We just wanted you to have a token from the two of us."

I can barely swallow past the ball of emotion deep in my throat; the last thing I want to do is cry, but these two men completely blow me away.

"No, I love it." *I love you, both of you.* The thought hits me out of nowhere, and before I can overanalyse it, Noah's lips are on mine, followed immediately by Caleb's.

They make me feel beyond anything I've ever felt before, and I care about them. Of course, I do. It's impossible not to, but...love? They've helped me in ways I could never have envisioned.

Do I love these two men?

The more I'm around them, the more I believe I could, but the thought of ruining this terrifies me to my core.

Chapter Thirty-Seven

Caleb

Jessica is radiant. But it's not the dress or the makeup—it's her. The way her eyes light up when she looks at Noah and me is enough to bring me to my knees.

I know she cares for us, it's as clear as the sky is blue, but I also can't deny that I see her hesitancy. It may not be conventional, but it does not make it any less. By giving herself to us, she's leaving herself vulnerable, but knowing she trusts us enough to try is more than we could have hoped. I'd never want her to feel pressured, not ever. And as much as we both want her, we want her to want us in equal measures.

Glancing in my rear-view mirror, I can't help but admire her profile as she looks out of the window at the passing traffic as we drive along Piccadilly. Noah gives me a knowing smile and winks as I reach over and squeeze his thigh.

When we arrive, Noah leads the way as we escort her into the restaurant set over three floors, the windows overlooking views of Green Park. HIDE has one of the best staircases in London. The laminated oak spirals through the restaurant's centre, creating a nature-inspired atmosphere that exudes sophistication and yet a comforting vibe. Her reaction alone proves this was the right choice as we descend the staircase to The Bar Below where we will be private dining for the evening in The Reading Room in the subterranean vaults.

The arch leading into the room is adorned with open books, and stacks of books line the semi-circle Chesterfield-style sofa surrounding a round table. It means we can both sit on either side of her as we wine and dine in private.

"Oh my God, this is amazing," she whispers as she glances around.

"Glad you like it." Noah holds out his hand. "After you, sweet girl." She lowers herself to the sofa and then scoots until she's sitting in the centre. Noah slides in on her right and me on her left. And when I see the split from her dress exposing her thigh, I'm unable to stop myself. I lower my hand and watch for her reaction as my thumb circles her satin soft skin.

Her cheeks heat, and she sucks in a deep breath as Noah stretches his arm over the back of the sofa, his fingers tracing her bare shoulder.

We make sure she gets a taste of anything her heart desires. The food is ten to none, the attention to detail sublime and paired with some fantastic wine.

When it comes time for dessert, the chef himself comes down, and we all commend him on the outstanding menu. Jessica is so open and lit up like Christmas as she talks to him about the food, and she gets animated as she begins to talk about ingredients. That's when she notices me and Noah watching her. She apologises for monopolising his time, but he's gracious and continues to talk a little longer before returning to the kitchen.

Jessica doesn't stop smiling the entire car drive home, filling me with pride. This was a big deal for all of us. I felt her nerves rippling through her, the tension so taut, but as soon as the starters arrived, she relaxed the same as at home, and everything felt natural.

She's still smiling when we step in through the front door as she lets out the most satisfied sigh.

"Thank you for tonight," she says, looking over her shoulder as I lock up behind us when we enter the hallway. Noah and I shrug out of our suit jackets, and I take them both and lay them on the small seat bench.

Noah reaches out for Jessica's hips, pulling her against his chest, and she giggles. "You're welcome, sweet girl." His lips skim the side of her neck before he takes her earlobe between his teeth, and she lets out a visible shiver.

"Do you want a nightcap?" I ask, but she shakes her head, and I'd be lying if I didn't admit I'm a little disappointed, not ready for the night to end.

"That's a shame. I'm not ready to say goodnight." Noah voices my thoughts.

She spins in his arms and drapes her arms over his shoulders. "Neither am I," she says demurely, sinking her teeth into her plump bottom lip.

"Hmm, so what did you have in mind?" he questions, his voice dipping an octave, walking until her back meets the wall.

"I'd like to spend the night with you, with both of you," she admits nervously.

I loosen my tie and undo the top button of my shirt.

"There's no rush, little one. We can wait."

She shakes her head as her eyes seek out mine, a determined expression on her face. "I don't want to wait."

Music to my ears. "Well, in that case," I say, stepping up behind Noah, my hands moving to his hips and squeezing as I lean in and kiss his neck. "Shall we take this to the bedroom?"

Noah guides Jessica up the stairs, unable to keep his hands to himself, and I enjoy watching them ascend the stairs and into our room. Noah flicks on the bedside lights above either side of our headboard.

Jessica is fiddling with her hands, and I can see them trembling slightly.

"Hey." I reach out for her, sit on the end of the bed, and pull her between my legs. "We can just sleep. There is no pressure to do anything you're not ready for." I know I've told her before, but it's important she believes me, that she trusts me.

"I just don't know how this will work," she whispers. Noah comes up behind her, wrapping his arms around her middle, his chin resting on her shoulder.

"We worship you. Make sure you are so consumed with pleasure you'll forget where you begin and we end."

Her eyes are cast down. "But how will it work when we all… you know?"

"Have sex?" Noah asks.

I love the way her cheeks blossom. "Yes."

"We won't do that until you're ready. We'll work you up to it."

She visibly swallows as Noah grips her chin, turning her face towards his. "It's okay, sweet girl. We know how to share, and we both love to watch." And then he seals his words with a kiss, causing her skin to break out in goosebumps. She's breathless when he pulls away.

His nimble fingers move to the zipper at the back of her dress as I slip my hand up between the slit and brush my fingers along the lace of her underwear before inching closer to the apex of her thighs.

She parts her legs subconsciously, and I brush my thumb over her sweet bud, my eyes trailing Noah's movements as he lowers the straps of her dress. Because of the bodice, it stays in place at the front but opens at the back. Noah kisses her collarbone.

My dick grows harder with each passing second, the tension in the room ready to snap.

"Hmm, did you know our girl was sitting next to us all evening without wearing a bra," he whispers against her ear.

She licks her lips before replying. "The padding meant I didn't need one, not with the straps."

"Do you know what would have made it better?" I question. Her eyes are cast down to look at me as I inch my hand toward the back of her calf, urging her to lift her leg. Noah steps back just a fraction, taking her with him in perfect sync with me until her foot is on my thigh.

"No."

The split in the dress gives me the access I crave as I slip my fingers under the lace of her underwear.

Her gasp is pure heaven.

"You not wearing these," I reply, my finger stroking over her swollen bud before slipping between her warm, wet folds, teasing her entrance.

Her mouth forms the perfect O, and all I can think about is her luscious lips wrapped around Noah's dick as I finger fuck her pretty little cunt, teasing her clit until she comes all over my fingers.

Pulling my hand away, I bring my finger to my mouth and suck. "Delicious."

I adore the reaction it evokes from her as Noah continues to stroke her spine and leave tender kisses over her flushed flesh.

Chapter Thirty-Eight

Noah

I watch as Caleb teases Jessica, the anticipation building of what's to come. We want her wet and ready when we show her exactly what she does to us.

Caleb unclasps the strap of her sandal, freeing her foot. Lowering his lips to her ankle, his eyes cast up, he swirls his tongue over the sensitive flesh. Her back arches, her arse presses against my hardening cock. Caleb has never failed to turn me on, but something about having Jessica between us only heightens my arousal.

I pull back as Caleb moves her foot back to the floor, and then in one swift move, he grips her hip and spins her until she falls into his lap, her back to his chest. He moves her hair over one shoulder, giving him access to her throat.

Kneeling, I raise her foot and remove her other sandal, kissing her ankle, and then I spread her legs just enough to give me access as I move between the apex of her thighs, my head covered by the satin material of her dress.

I inhale her fragrance, loving how sweet she is with the mixed masculine scent of Caleb. It's heady and invigorating.

My mouth moves to her swollen nub, and I lick over the lace, causing her to jerk towards me. Her gasp from above has me reaching down to unbuckle my belt as I pop the button and lower my zipper.

"What's he doing, little one?" asks Caleb, his voice deep, seductive.

I pull the material aside without any fanfare. She cries out as I spread her lips and spear her with my tongue. I love her tight channel—the way it pulses and clamps down—so fucking responsive.

"Tell me how he's making you feel?" Caleb asks again, only this time, it's more of a demand than a question.

"His tongue is…" I work my tongue into her faster, her breath catching as she continues telling Caleb. "His tongue is inside me."

His palm caresses my back. "And how does his tongue feel?"

I add a finger, still working her with my tongue, my thumbs circling her clit. She's a bundle of nerves, and it won't take long until she's coming.

"Good…" I add another finger. "Oh God, no better than good, it's ah, fuck."

Caleb whispers something I can't make out, but whatever he says causes her channel to contract around my fingers as she releases a rush of arousal.

I want her bare to me without her damn underwear in the way. Drawing back, I grab the waistband of her knickers and drag them down her thighs and legs, tossing them over my shoulder.

When I look up, Caleb has one hand down the front of her dress, and he's fucking her mouth with his tongue.

She moans as he pulls out of the kiss, and I duck back between her thighs, spreading her wide open as I impale her with my tongue.

A garbled curse escapes her as she begins to rock into me. I speed up.

"That's it, little one, let go."

I hear the sound of material ripping, followed by her surprised gasp as I flick my eyes up to find his filled with lust.

Her dress is bunched up in his fist, giving him the perfect view.

"Make her come, Noah."

His other hand squeezes her breast, her entire body coiling tight as her channel begins to contract around my tongue.

"More, I need more." Her words are like a moth to a flame; Caleb lowers his hand to play with her clit.

And I hook two fingers inside her, stroking her spongy, hot flesh.

She's riding my face now as Caleb circles her clit, and I know she's on the edge, her movements more erratic as she climbs higher and higher.

"That's it, little one. Come all over his face."

His words are like a trigger as her muscles contract, and she spasms as the force of her orgasm hits her, her release coating my face as she comes hard.

"Yes, just like that, good girl."

Her thighs grip my head harder, and I don't stop fucking her with my tongue and fingers until she's a writhing mess above me and her orgasm slows to sporadic aftershocks.

When I finally pull back and rise to my feet, Caleb grabs the back of my neck, pulling me in over Jessica's shoulder for a hard kiss; she lets out a whimper of arousal.

"Fuck, her juices taste so fucking good," he says breathlessly before releasing me.

I reach for Jessica's hands and pull her up. Caleb grips her hips to steady her as I tug what's left of the dress down until it falls to the floor, leaving her completely exposed.

Running my hands up and down her arms, I adore my touch's visceral effect on her.

Caleb moves off the bed, muscles rippling beneath his

shirt, his erection pressing against the crotch of his trousers as he removes the cufflinks one by one before unbuttoning his shirt.

I spin Jessica in my arms so she can watch as he drapes his shirt over the back of the chair.

He tilts his head, eyes glazing over as he takes her in, his gaze stopping at her wrist with the gold bangle before continuing his appraisal.

"Lay down on the bed, Jessica."

My dick hardens as she releases a whole body shiver, her breathing still heavy post-orgasm.

I let go and gently nudge her forward as she climbs onto the mattress. Caleb and I stand at the end of the bed as she turns around and scoots back, resting her head on the pillows. I don't think she realises how provocative her movements are until Caleb releases a groan from deep within his chest.

"Now, bring your knees up so your feet are flat on the mattress and spread those pretty thighs, let me see how worked up Noah's mouth has made you."

I'm happy to watch, loving how his words cause her entire body to flush. She takes a steadying breath, slowly doing as he requests. Something about the innocence of her unadulterated provocation has me pulling myself free from my trousers, fisting my cock.

"Good girl."

She swallows, licking her lips, her swollen pussy on display for us.

"Now, before we each make you ours, we want you soaking so you can take us."

He crawls up between her thighs, and I squeeze myself hard from base to tip as he darts out his tongue, licking the length of her slowly and causing her to arch her back.

Looking over his shoulder, his eyes zero in on my hand.

"Noah, come join us. Let's make her pretty little cunt wet."

She whimpers, her hands clutching the duvet on either side of her, the colour draining from her knuckles.

His hands spread her thighs wider, making room for me beside him. Jessica's chest rises and falls heavily, her nipples hard as she watches us, her teeth digging into her bottom lip.

Then, without preamble, I duck my head and lick over her wet folds. Caleb nudges my shoulder so he can gain access, too, and then together, we start eating her pussy. She tastes even sweeter now that she's already come once. I ease back, allowing Caleb to dictate the pace because I know he's getting off on it. Plus, I don't know how long I'll last before I need to be buried inside her.

"Please don't stop," she hisses, rotating her hips as her hand moves to my head, gripping my hair in a death grip as we take turns to impale her sweet-as-sin pussy with our tongues. "I'm going to come," she pants, and just like that, her muscles clench tight, and she explodes, crying out in gibberish, her fingers tightening their hold in my hair as she rides it out before she lets go, and then her body flops back onto the bed.

Caleb faces me, his chin soaked in her juices, before he kisses me.

And then I climb off the bed and strip out of the rest of my clothes. "How are you doing, sweet girl? You still with us?"

She nods lazily, her glistening arousal coating her thighs, those lips pink and swollen.

Caleb moves to his knees, grabs her ankles, and tugs her. She lets out a startled giggle as he gets off the bed and pulls her again until her legs hang off the bed.

"Jessica, we're both clean and checked regularly. And as you've seen, we don't use anything when it's just the two of us. But we will if you want us to use something with you."

Fuck me, his need for consent turns me the fuck on. Although it's a bit of a moot point, considering we both already came over her sweet pussy, yet I still love him for asking despite that.

She shakes her head. "No, I want to feel both of you," she says, her eyes moving between us.

Caleb unbuckles his belt, removing it in a whipping motion. The sound of him lowering his zipper follows as he pushes his trousers and boxers just low enough to pull himself free.

"Now, I'm going to let Noah take you first." He glances at me before his eyes focus back on Jessica. She's leaning up on her elbows, her body trembling. I don't know how much more she can take, but from how she's licking her lips and staring at Caleb as he tugs his hard length in a tight fist, she's ready for more. "But first, I need to feel your cunt wrapped around my dick."

I pass him a pillow, and he lifts her hips, shoving it underneath her. He leans over, his other hand moving to her throat as he kisses her and gently eases her back against the bed. I watch and suck in a breath as he lines himself up with her pussy, stroking his engorged head over her slick folds, her responding gasps an aphrodisiac.

And fuck me. I am so hard. I could come just from watching.

Chapter Thirty-Nine

Jessica

Something about how Caleb takes charge and talks to me has my insides burning like lava.

I glance down at his engorged head; his dick is so hard, almost angry, and I wonder how he's even going to fit. With trembling fingers, I lower my hand and trace the velvet veins along the length of his cock, unable to hold back my whimper.

"It'll be a tight fit, but you were made for us, don't worry," he says as my eyes spring back to his face.

I tense as he nudges against my folds and lowers his face until he's a breath away. "Relax."

I take a deep breath and try to do as he says as he slowly enters me. I gasp, and my hands move to grab his hips. And then his mouth is on mine. It's the perfect distraction as he continues pushing inside me, stretching me. He ends the kiss, trailing his lips to my ear. "You can take me, little one. That's it, just relax," he coaxes in a deep, soothing voice.

He raises himself enough for me to look down between us. I don't blink through the fear of missing this pivotal moment as he fills me to the hilt, my pussy snapping around his big, hard girth, filling me, owning me.

"Fuck," I hiss, biting down on his shoulder, my nails digging into his back, needing something to anchor me to this moment.

He groans and ruts inside me once before he goes still. I can see the tendons in his neck straining, but I also see it—the determination, the control to ease me into this gently. He pulls almost all the way out before sinking slowly back inside and rolling his hips once in the most delicious way.

I don't think I have ever felt so full, and then with a deep groan, he pulls out and stands to his full height, looming over me as he grabs the base of his dick hard, my arousal glistening along his shaft. I squeeze my thighs together and can't help the mewling sound that slips past my lips, my body craving more, so much more. I sit up on my elbows, licking my lips. There's this overwhelming urge to sit up and take Caleb in my mouth to please him.

And then he moves aside, and Noah is at the foot of the bed.

"Slide up the bed, sweet girl."

On shaky hands, I shuffle back until my head meets the pillow, my thighs parting of their own accord as he crawls between them in a predatory move until he's hovering above me.

"Do you see what you do to us?" Caleb says, climbing onto the edge of the bed, leaning against the headboard, his hand moving lazily up and down his shaft, his fingers skimming my cheek. I turn my face into his touch to look up at him.

"Are you sure you're ready?" Noah asks, pulling my focus back to him as Caleb caresses my face and jaw with his fingers. For such a powerful man, he has such a gentle touch.

"Yes, I'm sure." As scared as I am about everything that happens later or outside of this moment, right now, I want this. "I want you to help me forget. I want you to help erase him from me."

His jaw ticks as he tenses above me. Still, his eyes fill with understanding and with a look of concentration, he lines himself up with my entrance, his slick head stroking between my folds, before he begins to push inside. My core wraps around him like a vice until he's in, and we both groan. He's not as thick as Caleb, but he's longer, and he fills me deep.

"You feel so good," he groans.

Out of my peripheral, I see Caleb continuing to stroke himself as Noah begins to move slowly. Then their movements hit the same rhythm. With his other hand, Caleb alternates between stroking Noah's spine and touching my breast, his fingers skimming over my taut nipples before sliding over the globe of Noah's arse, and I hate that I can't see what made Noah thrust into me like that.

Noah might be the one inside me now, but Caleb is a part of this, and I realise it's not so much about sex as it is a joining.

When Caleb's hand returns to my breast, I slide my hands to Noah's arse, pulling him closer and driving him even deeper.

"Fuck, you keep doing that, and you're going to make me come," he admits on a ragged breath, sweat on his brow.

"Me too." I bite my lip, digging my nails into the flesh of his arse cheeks.

A deep groan emanates from Caleb. "Yes, that's it. Harder Noah, and faster, yes, fill our girl up." God, his words are like a battering ram as Noah begins to move with vigour. Each thrust becomes harder, deeper.

Caleb tweaks my nipple between his thumb and forefinger, and I cry out, clenching around Noah's dick, pulling closer to the edge. "Yes, Jessica, come all over his cock."

And just like that, everything is strung so tight, my stomach muscles clenching, Noah's pelvis rubbing against my clit, and I can't hold back. I begin to convulse my channel, contracting and squeezing around his dick.

Can someone die from pleasure?

If I thought he was moving before, I was mistaken. He just took it to the next level.

He thrusts deeper, hitting my cervix. I thrash my head back

and forth, my orgasm relentless as I scream out, my cries falling silent as his dick grows impossibly hard. I feel him tense right before he follows me over the edge with a guttural roar, shooting off as he fills me with his cum.

He tries to hold his weight off of me, but I dig my nails in, his seed continuing to spill into me, and I clench around him, taking every last drop.

"Fuck," he lowers his forehead to mine as we both try to catch our breath.

He stays buried inside me until his dick softens and slips free, my pussy still clenching, desperate to keep him there.

"Lucky there's two of us," he says softly, glancing over his shoulder to Caleb. I follow his line of sight, my breath stilling in my throat. Caleb's dick seems even larger, the tip leaking with pre-cum. "I think our girl is greedy for more," Noah says, my body heating as I lick the sweat from my top lip.

Noah rolls onto his side and then does something that causes me to cease breathing when his fingers move back to my pussy, pushing his cum back inside me. And fuck me if it isn't filthy and hot in equal measures. He smirks before pulling his hand back as Caleb moves between my legs. "Are you sore?" he asks, stroking the hair away from my forehead.

I bite my lip, tempted to say no, but I know he'll see a lie. "A little, but I want you," I reply honestly.

He hovers, his erection straining between us. "I can wait," he says.

And his words make me want to cry. I don't know if it's from the orgasms or how these men make me feel so damn special, but I swallow the emotion back down.

"Trust me, Caleb. I want this." I snake my hand between us and try to wrap my fist around his giant cock. He closes his eyes, throwing his head back in an agonised groan.

He studies my face, and whatever he sees is validation

enough. There's a pregnant pause right before he lines himself up and enters me in one deep thrust.

"Oh. My. God."

"Fuck, you feel tighter," he grunts, and then he begins to pump into me, my entire body moving from the force.

He stops suddenly, eyes so dark. "Hands above your head," he says. "Now grab onto the headboard, and don't let go."

I do as he asks, his dick hardening inside me, and I let out a moan as he begins to drive into me, and my fingers tighten around the metal frame of the headboard.

Everything inside me tightens, another orgasm ready to break free. "Shit, not again. I can't." I move my head side to side as his pelvis ruts against my clit, his thrusts all-consuming.

Noah chuckles, and I open my eyes to find him watching where Caleb and I join, his dick heavy against his thigh. "Yes, you can. You were made for us." His words hold so much conviction that I don't doubt him, but Caleb is almost carnal now, each thrust relentless. I'm sensitive and overstimulated, but it doesn't stop my entire body from bowing off the bed.

"That's it. Let me feel you strangle my cock as I fill you with my cum."

I'm gripping the headboard so tight, my fingers have gone numb.

"Yes," he chants as he continues with controlled dominant thrusts.

I cry, sobbing from the force of my climax—overwhelming and exhilarating—so many sensations attacking every cell of my body.

He speeds up, sweat coating his chest, his muscles bulging, and then he detonates with a deep-rooted roar as he fills me with his cum.

Barely coherent, I can hear them talking in soothing voices, but it feels distant, and I vaguely sense them cleaning me up and leading me to the bathroom, my legs almost giving out beneath me.

And then I'm floating on a cloud of hot skin and muscle when I stir in the middle of the night or morning. I don't know how much time has passed, and I don't care as I stretch, feeling an ache between my thighs, reminding me how they made me come apart only to put me back together again in the best possible way.

I inhale and smile as their unique and familiar scents surround me. Caleb's hand is on my thigh, Noah's arm across my stomach, a protective cocoon. With them, I feel safe. I feel cherished.

Chapter Forty

Noah

I wake up to soft snoring beside me, my arm still wrapped protectively around Jessica's waist. She's nestled between Caleb and me, her gentle breaths creating a rhythmic pattern. She stirs, and I immediately tense. It reminds me of the nightmares she's been having, the lingering trauma that still haunts her even in the safety of our embrace. I thought they'd stopped, but I've discovered otherwise this past week since she's spent every night sleeping with us. She may not wake screaming, but this is somehow worse—the sound of her frightened whimpers and rapid eye movement. It's usually before she wakes up or soon after falling asleep. Some episodes have only lasted a few seconds, whereas the most recent lasted minutes, even with me talking to her and trying to coax her awake by gently shaking her shoulder.

Caleb stirs beside her, his tousled hair a beautiful mess as he blinks awake. He holds my stare for a moment, and then, careful not to wake Jessica, he leans over and kisses my lips tenderly. It's a soft gesture, filled with the unspoken promise that we're in this together. I return the kiss, feeling a surge of warmth and affection radiate through my entire being.

As we pull away from the kiss, Caleb's eyes meet mine, and we exchange a wordless conversation. We both know that Jessica's healing process will take time. Our desire for her goes beyond mere physical gratification. We want to build something lasting on trust and mutual understanding.

Caleb strokes Jessica's cheek gently, his touch delicate as he tucks a strand of loose hair behind her ear. She stirs again, but this time it's with a soft sigh. It's been a week since that intimate night when we all came together physically and emotionally. But we've been taking it slow, adjusting to this new dynamic this past week, ensuring Jessica feels comfortable and safe in our arms. Our nights together have been peaceful, filled with whispered conversations and gentle caresses that speak volumes about the depth of our connection. But we still want to tread carefully, understanding the magnitude of her past trauma is still very present.

As dawn breaks through the window, casting a warm glow across the room, I trace my fingers gently along the lines of Jessica's face. Her eyes flutter open to meet mine, and I can't help but smile, grateful she didn't have a waking nightmare.

"Good morning," I whisper, my voice barely audible, not wanting to disturb the moment's tranquillity as I kiss her forehead tenderly.

"Morning," she replies, her voice laced with sleepiness and contentment. She stretches her body and then snuggles closer, seeking warmth and security.

"Good morning, beautiful," Caleb says, kissing her shoulder. He wraps his arm over her waist, his fingers intertwining with mine, completing the intricate puzzle of our newfound connection as we lay together, content in the moment.

As the morning sunlight bathes us in its warmth, all too soon, we know it's time to get up. We rise from the bed, carefully disentangling ourselves from one another. Caleb slips on a pair of boxers, still preferring to sleep naked where I've been sleeping in my boxers. I throw on a discarded t-shirt, exposing the rest of my body to the morning air as Jessica takes in the sight of us, her cheeks flushing with colour.

"Hmm, hold that thought, little one," Caleb says, leaning over her and stealing another kiss before straightening. "I'm going to jump in the shower," he says, heading towards our ensuite. The urge to join him is riding me hard; it's been a week since the two of us have been together.

"I'll go get breakfast started," I say, smiling as Caleb's arse disappears into the bathroom, the door clicking closed behind him.

Jessica slips out of bed, clad in one of my t-shirts, and I can't stop the sound of approval that vibrates my chest.

"No, please let me. You both have jobs to get to while I'm just…" She wraps her arms around her middle. Her vulnerability tugs at my heart, and I can't help but feel a sense of protectiveness toward her. I reach out and pull her into my arms.

"Hey, what's all this about?"

She bites her lip before lifting her chin to answer. "I don't know. I feel like a bit of a freeloader."

I frown, a retort on my lips, but she continues. "It's just I've always been independent, to a degree, anyway. And now, I don't know… I just feel like I'm taking advantage of your hospitality."

Lifting an eyebrow, I shake my head. "Hardly, granted circumstances have changed since you first arrived. You came here because you needed a safe place. And we never would have turned you away. But now things have changed. We don't have you with us out of loyalty or obligation because of Mason. We *want* you here with us." I smile, hoping she sees the truth in my words. I let out a deep breath when she returns it, though a trace of uncertainty still lingers in her eyes. The sound of the shower running is a distant echo as Caleb hums to himself in the shower.

"I just… I don't know. Sometimes my mind runs away with me. Neither of you has touched me since we slept together."

She lowers her face between us, and I use my index finger to tilt her chin.

"We've touched you." I stroke across her flushed cheekbone down to her lips, the pad of my thumb brushing over the satin soft flesh. "We've kissed you." I wrap my arm tighter around her waist, pulling her into me. "We've held you."

Her nostrils flare, and her pupils dilate, her breathing heavier.

"When you say touched you, do you mean because we've not had sex?" I love how the blush dips beneath the collar of my t-shirt, her nipples hard against the soft cotton.

She nods, tongue sweeping over her lips, urging me to lower my face to hers and kiss her deeply.

"We've been trying to take it slow. This thing between us isn't just about sex. But we'd never deny you. All you have to do is ask."

I lean in and seal my words with a kiss. I'd love nothing more than to spend the day worshipping her, but work is looming.

When I draw back, I tuck a lock of hair behind her ear. The red and blond strands frame her face, the splatter of freckles across her nose and cheekbones more prominent now since she's spent some time outside on the roof terrace.

"What time is your appointment again?" I ask.

"Not until two."

I hate the idea of her going alone. Caleb or I have gone with her all the other times, but we both have meetings that we can't put off and when she heard us talking about it, she said she'd get a cab. I could see it in Caleb's posture that he wanted to argue, to say no, but he knows she needs this—to take back her power.

"Don't forget to take your phone." Caleb got her a new phone, even though she insisted she had a phone in her bag—now in the bottom of the wardrobe instead of the end of her bed. It's a small step but one that makes me smile. Before, I always felt like she was on the verge of running, but now not so much.

He didn't care. He'd already purchased it and added her to our family plan and, of course, set up find my phone.

"I won't. Now, how about some pancakes?"

She knows the way to my heart is my sweet tooth, so I don't hesitate as I say yes.

My hands move to the underside of her arse cheeks before lifting her. I love how she wraps her legs around me like she's been doing it for years—her carefree giggle music to my ears, easing the tension that was there only moments ago.

I push her up against the wall and kiss her once more for good measure.

Chapter Forty-One

Jessica

I can't believe I did it. For the first time in almost two months, I went somewhere on my own. My anxiety was rife as I waited for my cab, and at one point, I felt a panic attack coming, but I used the 5-4-3-2-1 coping technique my therapist taught me. I look for five things I can see, four things I can touch, three things I can hear, two things I can smell, and one thing I can taste. I've always had Noah or Caleb coax me through it, but today was the first time I managed it alone.

Don't get me wrong, I was still a hot mess, but I feel proud of myself. There was a moment when I considered cancelling my appointment altogether, but I know I need to do this if I want to move forward.

I've not long been home—well, Caleb and Noah's—and yet nowhere has ever felt more like home to me, and I don't think it's the house so much as these two men. I opened up to Greta about my developing feelings towards them. I guess I expected her to tell me it's a trauma response, hell these men practically put me on a pedestal. Deep down, I question if, like with Curtis, I'm missing any red flags. But when I confided in her, she didn't think so, if anything, she reminded me that my feelings are valid and that communication is key. I can't deny we all have chemistry, even if it's not long-term; they already have one another, and it's not just a need where they're both concerned—it's deep-seated want.

I've never wanted anyone else the way I want these two men.

I took a nap in their bed when I returned after texting them that I was back and safe. I had this irrational fear I was being watched, which is impossible, no one knows I'm here, except maybe Mason, who I still haven't been able to reach. I know Noah is doing everything he can to help track him down. But I'm worrying more with each passing day.

To keep myself busy, I've prepared dinner for tonight, for when they both return home; it just needs to go in the oven. So now I'm sitting with a book in the small reading nook, and I feel a little lighter every day.

I know eventually, I'll have to face reality and decide what to do about Curtis. Caleb and Noah bagged the clothes I arrived in just in case I needed them for evidence later. A few days after, they also persuaded me to let them take some photographs of my injuries. I was conflicted, but they didn't push. I knew deep down they were right. As time passes, I consider standing up and pressing charges. I hate the thought of him treating another woman the way he treated me, and the guilt of knowing I could help prevent someone else from suffering at his hands pushes me towards making a statement.

I need to broach it with Caleb and Noah, but I just want to enjoy this bubble for a little longer.

A couple of hours later, they arrive home separately, and each greets me with a tender kiss, but seeing them embrace each other sets off fireworks in my stomach. Something about seeing them both together has my pulse racing, my breast heavy beneath my bra, my pussy aching.

It's more than just physical, it's emotional, too, and I want what they have... to be revered, worshipped, loved.

They give me hope that happily ever afters exist, even if theirs doesn't include me. I want to enjoy my time with them, no matter how sparse. We talked over dinner, and they asked how my counselling went, but they didn't push for any more information than I was willing to share. It's why, after we've all eaten, and everything has been cleaned away, I find the nerve to tell them what I want.

Noah's words come back to me. *"We'd never deny you. All you have to do is ask."*

Caleb lights the fire, casting the room in a soft glow as Noah flicks through the TV channels.

"What do you want to watch?" he asks me, not taking his eyes off the widescreen above the fireplace.

I take a deep breath and try to keep the tremble from my voice when I say, "You two—I want to watch you both together." There, I said it.

His eyes shoot to mine, and I can see Caleb moving towards me in my peripheral vision, but he stops a few feet away.

"And then what?" Caleb asks, his voice a deep rumble.

I swallow back my nerves. "And then I want to be with you, both of you again," I admit.

My eyes are still locked on Noah, and I'm unable to tear my gaze away. I shiver when Caleb's fingers stroke down the length of my arm and then back until his fingertips trace my collarbone. My body heats instantly.

"Are you sure?" he asks.

I nod. "Positive."

I love the way Noah looks at me with pride; me voicing what I want, what I need.

"Hmm, that's good. Noah told me you were feeling a little

insecure this morning. Worried we didn't want you like this again."

Of course, he did. "Since that night, we haven't... you know... been intimate again. And I wondered if you regretted it or if it was just a one-time thing." I don't know where I'm suddenly finding my courage, but there's something liberating about verbalising my feelings.

Caleb reaches out, his hand gently cupping my cheek. "Oh, little one, no. Never think that," he says earnestly. "We haven't slept with you like that again because we wanted to be sure it was what you wanted. We didn't want you to feel pressured or uncertain."

Relief washes over me, and I feel tears prickling at the corners of my eyes. Their words touch me deeply, banishing my insecurities. Caleb reaches down and intertwines his hand in mine, giving me a reassuring squeeze as he leads me over to the sofa to sit.

Noah leans in, his lips brushing against my temple—a tender gesture that fills me with a sense of safety and belonging. "I'm proud of you, sweet girl."

Caleb reaches out for Noah. "Come, let's give our girl a show."

I reach for the remote and find the radio station and lower the volume to set soft background music as they kiss before me. It's a sight to behold, watching these two men.

In no time, they've stripped down to their boxer briefs, and I watch their muscles contract as they rock against one another, their kisses turning hungrier with each passing moment. Heat pools between my legs, and I have to squeeze my thighs together to ease the ache, but if anything, it only intensifies my need that much more.

And when Caleb drops to his knees and lowers Noah's boxers, his erection springing free, so close to his face, I can't keep my whimper at bay.

Caleb turns his face towards me. "I've only ever got on my knees for one man," he says, reaching for Noah's dick, wrapping it in his big fist, causing Noah to moan as he looks down, his abs rippling across his stomach. "And I will do the same for you, Jessica. Because you both deserve to be worshipped." And then he turns, giving me the most glorious side profile as he wraps his lips around Noah's cock and takes him deep until his nose touches the soft patch of hair on his pubic bone, working Noah into a state of ecstasy.

Noah reaches for Caleb's head, his fingers digging into his short hair.

"You see, Jessica, Caleb loves to tease me, bring me right to the brink before he eases off and starts all over again."

I love how Noah talks to me while Caleb continues to give him pleasure.

Caleb pulls back, a string of saliva on his lips, which only turns me on more as another gush of wet heat pools in my knickers.

"Now, do I let him come or make him wait?"

Noah's dick strains towards Caleb's lips like a moth to a flame, his head leaking with pre-cum. The veins are prominent along his hard length.

"Jessica, you choose."

I don't need to think about my answer. "Let him come. Please let him come."

"Your wish is my command." Caleb holds his index and middle finger up in the air toward Noah. "Suck."

Noah lowers his face, grips Caleb's wrists, his lips closing around his fingers.

"Enough." The power Caleb exudes is electric. My nipples harden against my bra. I can no longer keep from fidgeting as I rub my legs together before lowering my hand between my thighs.

"Spread." Noah parts his legs, and Caleb slides his hand beneath his perineum to access his arsehole. *Fuck.*

Noah grabs Caleb's shoulder, fingers indenting his skin.

And then he takes Noah back in his mouth to the back of his throat.

My eyes flick between Caleb and Noah as I slip my hand inside my leggings and knickers, my folds wet as I rub against my clit. I watch, mesmerised, as Caleb drives Noah into pure euphoria.

He throws his head back, crying out with a resounding roar as he comes.

I dip my finger into my swollen centre, the palm of my hand brushing against my clit, and I contract, an orgasm hitting me hard and fast. I want to close my eyes, but I don't want to miss how Caleb stares up at Noah as he swallows every last drop.

I don't even have time to come down from my climax before they pounce, like predators, lifting me from the sofa until I'm standing before them and they're stripping me of my clothes.

Chapter Forty-Two

Caleb

I lean in and kiss Jessica. She moans, devouring my mouth as I brush her hard nipple with my knuckles.

When I withdraw, her eyes are full of desire.

"Did you enjoy that?" I ask, not that I need to—it's evident from the way we caught her fingering herself.

Noah is on her other side, stroking up and down the length of her arm, causing her to break out in goosebumps.

"Before we go any further, I need to ask if you've ever done anal?"

I don't mince my words, and it's impossible to miss the hitch of her breath before she answers, shaking her head. "No."

And the thought of being her first has my dick ready to explode, but only if she wants to. I would never force her.

"Do you want to try?"

She licks her lips and swallows. "Yes, but I'm scared."

I stroke the swell of her breasts. "We won't do anything you're not ready for. You can say stop at any time. Do you understand?"

A nervous smile graces her lips. "Yes."

Noah moves away to grab one of many bottles of lube

around the house and places it on top of the mantel above the fireplace.

We take turns kissing, stroking and teasing her soft, delicate skin, but without penetrating where she's aching for us the most. If I thought she enjoyed watching the two of us kiss, she's practically melting when I grab her and Noah by the back of their necks. Noah joins my mouth with hers as we kiss her together.

But I want more. I end the kiss.

"I need you to ride his face while I fuck your arse. It will help ease you into it. Do you think you can handle that, little one?"

She arches into my touch as my finger trails the length of her spine, her skin flushed, so fucking reactive.

"Yes," she sighs as Noah takes her pert nipple into his mouth and bites down.

I lower my hand between her legs and then cup her cunt.

"Oh, my God."

"Hmm, not God, but close." I bite down on her earlobe as I stroke through her slick folds with my middle finger, and then, without warning, I push it inside. Her hot channel pulses around the sudden intrusion, but her arousal makes it effortless.

"Get on all fours, straddle Noah, and arse in the air."

Noah lays back, his mouth still sampling her breast as she gets into position above him. Her perky arse rises as my finger moves in and out of her in fast, deliberate strokes, hitting her g-spot.

Flicking the cap of the lube, I unceremoniously squeeze it over her arse crack.

She shivers, the liquid no doubt cold, not that she needs to worry. She'll be burning up before she knows it, and in a good way.

"Noah, fancy joining me in her wet pussy."

He hums around her breast, his finger sliding inside her to join me as we alternate between thrusts.

We keep up a steady rhythm until she's dripping and panting.

"Do not fucking come until I say so."

She clenches around our fingers, and I look down at Noah's dick bobbing below as both Jess and I straddle him.

This gives me an idea for a position for another time, but for now, I need to take her arse.

Make it mine.

Claim her as ours.

I've never felt this possessive over anyone other than Noah, and when I catch his eyes on mine, blown out wide, I know he senses it, too. He licks his lips, and damn if I don't want his mouth wrapped around my dick.

Slipping my fingers free, I leave Noah to play as I pull her up by her hips, giving me access beneath her thighs as I lower my face and take him into the back of my throat.

"Fuck." He bucks at the contact, and I welcome the pressure.

My hand moves up Jess's spine until I reach the nape of her neck and push her down towards his chest.

I know he'll waste no time capturing her mouth as I fuck him with mine.

His taste is so fucking addictive, just like Jess, and with that, I move my mouth to her arse, spreading her cheeks as I begin to rim her rosebud arsehole, loving the strawberry-flavoured lube.

She moans into Noah's mouth as he continues to finger fuck her into a state of recklessness. She starts moving with abandon.

After I claim her arse, the next thing will be for Noah and me to take her cunt simultaneously. It will be a tight fit, but she can handle it. She was meant for us.

I pull away enough to speak while she's lost to the overriding sensations of us worshipping her.

"Noah, are you ready to let her fuck your face?"

His deep groan is all the answer I need as his hands move to her hips, tugging her down to his mouth.

She cries out, throwing her head back, and raises her hips.

I squeeze her hard. "Don't pull away from him, Jessica. Smother him, sit on his face."

Her hesitation is enough for Noah's head to fall back on the thick rug. "Sweet girl, I've got you. Now stop hovering and fucking sit on my damn face."

I love that he can let his dominant side out to play with her.

"Unless you don't want to?" I offer a challenge, hoping to spark the fire I know is heating below the surface.

Without a word, she sinks onto Noah's face, and he lets out a hum of satisfaction as he begins to lap her up like his favourite dessert.

She's writhing in ecstasy as she lets go, and I position myself behind her, spreading her arse cheeks.

Her rosebud arsehole calls me to fuck her with abandon, but I want her to enjoy it, too, so I have to restrain from being as aggressive with her as I would with Noah. Don't be mistaken. I make sure he's prepped and weeping to take my cock. And I always take care of him; aftercare is important to me.

But with Jessica, it's a more delicate dance. As much as I love pain with my pleasure, this isn't about hurting her but owning her. Showing her who she belongs to, that she is ours.

"Okay, are you going to take me like the good girl I know you are?"

Her body tenses as I push my engorged head against her puckered hole. A soft whimper echoes in the room.

"Relax. Prove that you're ours. Let me in, Jessica."

The fire cracks and hisses as some kindling snaps, the heat from the embers creating a warm reddish glow across her flushed, naked skin.

She lets out a deep breath, and her body relaxes under my

touch as I push past the first ring of muscle. She tenses. "Breathe, you're doing so well."

Noah lets out a deep moan, his hands cupping her arse and squeezing.

"Does she like that?" I ask him, and he grunts in response.

"Oh, fuck," she hisses as she pushes against me and allows me in further. How her ring of muscle snaps around me, holding me tight, is so fucking good.

I grit my jaw and edge forward until I bottom out.

"Fuck!" I hold still and grip her hips tightly as I allow her to get used to me, and when she pushes back again, I begin to move.

"Caleb, Noah," she says, her head bowing forward as Noah continues to work her with his mouth.

"Such a good fucking girl."

I go slow, as does Noah, a silent exchange of pleasure.

"Do you want Noah to fill your cunt with his cock, little one? Can you take us both?"

She stutters around her reply, Noah pulls her away from his face lifting her slightly. He peers around so he can see me, his mouth and chin glistening from her arousal. Fuck, that's hot.

"Oh, she's ready. So fucking wet," he says, his pupils blown wide.

Carefully, I crawl back on my knees and encourage Jessica to move with me as Noah changes position.

"Okay, sweet girl."

I reach around and stroke over her folds, and then slip two fingers inside her sweet pussy. She is dripping.

I pull out, and she lets out a small whimper.

"Usually, I wouldn't ask." This will happen, but I want to give her a choice, for the first time, anyway. "This is a first for the three of us, so do you want to ride his dick while I fuck your arse? Or let him ride your cunt while I fuck you from below?"

"I don't know, whatever you want," she says, peering over her shoulder. "I trust you."

Three magic words.

"Noah, you choose."

He raises his eyebrows, and I quirk one in response.

"In that case, I want to ride her pretty pussy while you fuck her from below."

I move and stretch out my legs, still sitting up.

"You heard the man, little one." I tug on her hips. "Get on," I say and position her legs on either side of me, so she's straddling my thighs, her wet cunt leaving a trail over my bare flesh. With her back to my chest, I lift her until she's right where I need her to be. And then, without a word, I push back into her arse. She's a little more prepared this time and eases into it so well—such a quick study.

"Okay?" No matter what, her comfort will always be important—yes, pain, but only when it's accompanied by pleasure.

She nods and watches as Noah gets onto his knees as I begin to lay back.

"Oh my god," Jessica says.

"That's it, lean back, and spread those legs," Noah says, his voice thick and gravelly, and I know this woman right here is about to ruin us in the best possible way.

Chapter Forty-Three

Jessica

To say my senses are on overload is an understatement. Every nerve ending is prying for attention as they use my body in the best possible way. I might die if I don't come soon. How they both intermittently manage to bring me to the brink and then stop as I'm about to come is beyond me. It's like my body will only play to their tune. I'm the instrument, and they are the musicians. It's a delicate dance, but I'm very invested in the outcome.

Noah slides his thick fingers through my folds, teasing my clit.

"Are you ready for me to fill you up with my cum?"

I nod quickly, and he laughs deeply as he curves two fingers inside me, my core tightening in anticipation with wet heat.

"You like being our dirty little slut, don't you?"

Oh my god.

"Yes," I say, my core clenching around his fingers as Caleb drives into my arse. "Fuck."

"Yes, that's what we're about to do. Are you ready?"

I don't think it's a question so much as a statement. I reach out for Noah, grabbing the back of his neck and pull him towards me.

Caleb grunts, thrusting up, his mouth clamping down on the column of my neck. As my lips meet Noah's, he kisses me to match the movement of his fingers, driving me higher and higher.

And then they're gone. I pull back from his mouth and glance down as he fists his cock working up and down his length, the head almost angry, all the veins prominent. I reach down and circle the tip leaking with pre-cum. I bring my finger to my mouth and lick the remanence of his desire.

"Such a good little slut. Do you want to taste yourself?"

My core pulses, my clit throbbing as he swipes his finger through my folds and brings it to my mouth.

"Suck, such a good girl."

Fucking hell, what is it about him saying both those things to me? It makes me whimper with want as I reach out and pull his finger into my mouth, hollowing my cheeks as I suck all traces of my arousal from his finger.

"That's it. Later you can do that with my cock—lick me clean after you come all over it."

Caleb thrusts up hard. And I groan as Noah pulls his finger free.

"Hmm, or maybe I'll be the one to lick it clean," Caleb says. "After I lick her cunt out and eat your cum."

Fuck me sideways, who even speaks like this? I bite my lip, needing to remind myself this is real, I am here, this is not an erotic dream. I repeat, this is not a dream.

"You like the sound of that, don't you? I can see you dripping," Noah says, as he positions himself between my spread legs.

"Fuck." He drives into me in one hard thrust.

I cry out from the intrusion, but it's sublime.

I'm so fucking full I can hardly catch my breath. No wonder they waited for my ribs to heal; there is no way I could have survived this.

"You both feel so fucking good," Caleb says as he and Noah find a rhythm—one in, one almost out.

I grab my breast, twisting my nipple as a hand slides between Noah and me, Caleb seeking out my clit as he sits forward slightly so we're in more of a sitting position.

Noah wipes tears from my cheeks. "Is it too much?" he asks through gritted teeth. He looks like he is barely holding himself together.

"No, it's…I can't explain it—" my words are cut off as Caleb tightens his grip on one of my hips, thrusting up. "God, please don't stop. I'm so close," I say as tears roll down my cheeks.

"Don't worry, little one, we've got you," Caleb says before Noah leans over and kisses him. I tilt my neck back to watch them fuck each other with their mouths as they continue to fuck me, and I whimper.

A profound sensation builds as I bear down, and I brace myself. "Oh my God," I croak out. "It's too much. I need to stop. I feel like I'm going to…" I try to pull back from the impending sensation, but they are relentless, pulling me back in again.

"Going to what, sweet girl?" Noah asks, a quirk on his lips.

"Wet myself," I reply in a breathless whisper.

Noah shakes his head. "No, you won't, little one." He looks at Caleb, and they share a smile.

"That sensation is going to lead you to the best release you've ever had." Caleb's lips skim along my collarbone before reaching the shell of my ear. "Keep chasing it. Ride it out and let it happen. Do not fucking fight it, Jessica." He bites down on my earlobe as he pinches my nipple, and Noah rubs my clit.

And whatever this is has overridden my body. Even if I wanted to, I am powerless to stop it as it takes me under and over.

So intense.

My channel pulses as I come. It's explosive as I reject Noah's cock, coating him in a wet release as I scream out, confused as I convulse in pleasure. And then Noah is back inside me, pumping into my very wet core, the sound of his balls slapping me as both he and Caleb fuck me with wild abandon.

I scream something incoherent, my body no longer my own. It's theirs.

They ride harder and faster, and I wish I were more coherent in appreciating them as they both come undone. And then I'm coming again as it hits me out of nowhere. I have no idea what that was before, but my body convulses as my orgasm slams into me. Stars light behind my eyes, and everything goes dark as I struggle to breathe.

"Fuck, that's it." Caleb grunts.

Noah moans. "Yes, just like that."

Vaguely, I feel them both slipping out of me, causing me to shiver and feel a little empty until I'm suddenly sandwiched between two damp and muscled bodies.

I can feel the rapid heartbeat of Caleb against my back as I rest my head on Noah's pec, the rise and fall of his chest from his heavy breathing.

It takes me a moment before I have enough of my wits about me to find my voice again; it's hoarse when I finally do speak.

"What was that?" I ask.

Caleb's chuckle vibrates behind me, and I glance up to see Noah's lips form the most devilish smile.

If I thought my face was hot before, it has nothing on the burning of my cheeks now. I try to look away, but Noah grabs my chin, holding me prisoner.

"You squirted, sweet girl, and it's nothing to be ashamed or embarrassed about. Just you at the height of pleasure."

I clear my throat. "Oh, I thought I was going to wet myself."

Caleb rubs his calloused palm up and down my bare arm, causing me to shiver. "And if you had, that would have been perfectly okay, too, little one. Pleasure is pleasure."

He kisses my shoulder, and I smile up at Noah.

"It was intense. I have never experienced anything like it."

Noah lowers his face and kisses my forehead. "Then we're honoured to be your firsts *again,*" he says with a wink.

Caleb presses against me, his hard, heavy length resting on my lower back.

Goosebumps skate across my skin as he wraps his arm around my waist, brushing Noah's cock in the process, which twitches in delight.

We should probably move and clean up, but I need a minute or maybe five as I let out a yawn and close my eyes.

Chapter Forty-Four

Noah

We lay there in a slick, sweaty cuddle as Jessica's breathing evens out, her lips parting on a deep exhale.

"She's not as conditioned for this as we are," Caleb says, sitting up and leaning over her shoulder, moving her hair off her cheek. "But I think we'll have fun building up her stamina." He kisses her temple before reaching out, kissing me, and then getting to his feet.

I stare down at Jessica until Caleb returns with lukewarm washcloths, passing one to me.

"Hmm, as much as I want to lick her cunt clean of your cum, I think she needs her rest."

The image of him doing just that has my dick twitching with excitement.

Carefully, he cleans between Jessica's legs.

"She can shower in the morning. Let's get her to bed, and maybe I'll lick you instead."

I grab the back of his neck and pull him towards me for a deep kiss, a guttural moan leaving my chest.

"Don't tease me," I say, pulling away and resting my forehead against his, breathing him in. I love that he not only smells of him now but of Jessica and sex, too, fuck. My dick bobs. It's like an aphrodisiac. "You know how much I love your mouth." And it's true; he's already had me in his mouth, but it's never enough where he's concerned. He makes me ravenous for more.

Caleb pulls away slightly, reaches up and wraps his hand around my throat and squeezes the perfect amount that has my breath stalling. Staring down at my now fully erect dick, he lets out a deep, chest-filled groan. "You're fucking insatiable. I love it and you."

He lets go and scoops Jessica into his arms. She wraps an arm around his neck, burrowing into his chest.

"Grab a couple of bottles of water." He starts walking towards the stairs. "I'll take her to our bedroom while she lays there blissed out on sex-induced sleep. I am going to show you exactly what my mouth can do. So, hurry the fuck up."

Caleb doesn't need to tell me twice. I make my way into the kitchen where a cold breeze brushes against my naked body, and I shudder. Looking for the source, I notice the back door cracked open. *Strange.*

Maybe Caleb didn't close it properly when he took the rubbish out.

I pull it closed, flipping the lock and setting the alarm before grabbing a couple of bottles of water and turning off the lights. I make my way upstairs and to our room.

Caleb has the duvet pulled back, Jessica in the middle of the bed. Caleb has always insisted on being closest to the door. I think it's to do with his protective nature and, to be fair, I can fall asleep anywhere, so it's never been an issue.

"You'll be busy underneath me." And with that, he grabs my wrist and tugs me towards him, snatching one of the bottles from my hand. His eyes hold me captive as he twists the cap and downs it all in one gulp. I watch, mesmerised, as the veins along the length of his throat flex as he swallows.

My dick throbs, knowing soon he'll be doing the same with my cum.

I place the other bottles on the bedside table and then spit into my palm before taking my stiff shaft in my fist, working it up and down in long, smooth motions. Caleb's eyes are dark as he levels his gaze on the action, his nostrils flaring, chest rising and falling with heavy breaths.

"Do you like the idea of Jessica being beside us while I work you into ecstasy?"

I let out a gruff laugh. "You know I do. But I think I enjoyed her watching even more."

We both look over her nestled beneath the cover. One of her breasts is showing, a leg hooked over the outside of the cover. Her hair is a tousled mess, her breath evened out, and she slips into a deeper sleep.

My dick grows harder in answer to his question.

"Come shower with me."

I grab his hand and trail him towards our ensuite. He takes another look over his shoulder at Jessica, content with what he sees, and follows me inside. We leave the door ajar in case she wakes, and I wish I could make her nightmares disappear.

Caleb starts the shower, and I follow him inside. He stares at me with renewed vigour.

"My feelings for you have increased with her being here. I can't explain it," he admits as he lathers up his hands and circles his finger in the air for me to turn.

"I know what you mean. She's special."

He begins to wash my back, massaging my shoulders. For all his provocative words, I know he loves this part, taking care of me afterwards; it's what he did before he was able to use his words.

The room steams up. "Head back." I do as he says, loving the feel of his hands against my scalp. I swear this man has magic fucking fingers.

Once I rinse and turn back to face him, I give him the same care and attention.

"Do you feel any jealousy when we're all together?" I ask as I rinse his back.

He shakes his head, wiping excess water from his face as he smooths his hair. "No. There have been times when we've been to the club, it would rear its ugly head, but it only made me harder for you. I knew it was illogical, as there were no feelings involved. But it's different with her. Do you?"

"No, I don't."

He turns to face me and reaches out, pulling my wet body against his. "I'm okay if you ever want to be with her, and I'm not here. I don't want you feeling like you can't let go without me."

I smile, leaning in and nipping at his jaw. "Same goes for me."

He grips the back of my neck, his eyes so serious. "I think I'm falling for her."

I nod in understanding. "Me too."

"But that doesn't mean I love you any less."

Kissing him, I murmur against his lips. "I know, and ditto."

We dry off quickly, not wanting to leave Jessica any longer than we have to before we both climb in on either side of her. I lay on my back, and instinctively she rolls onto her side, her arm moving across my chest as Noah spoons her from behind with his arm over her waist. His hand entwines with mine.

She's like a piece of us we never knew was missing.

Chapter Forty-Five

Jessica

I wake with a start, sweat coating my skin, my heart racing. It takes me a moment before I can move from the sleep paralysis. Who knew it was even a thing? It takes me a moment to find my bearings, surrounded by the smell of Caleb and Noah. I'm safe with the two of them, yet the nightmares are back in full force. It's dark except for the light from the hallway creeping in through the crack in the door. An arm tightens around me and pulls me into their chest—Caleb.

Noah is lying on his back, my leg hung over his thigh, and my bladder protests the reason why I woke.

As carefully as possible, I untangle myself from the limbs surrounding me and slip out from beneath the thin duvet, crawling down to the end of the bed before climbing out and making my way to the door. I pause, pushing the door open more, which casts more light across the room, and I glance back.

Laying before me are two naked men, the light duvet barely covering them. Men like them should be illegal.

It's a sight to behold, and if it weren't for my bladder screaming at me, I would happily stay here admiring them both while they sleep. It's so surreal, seeing them both so relaxed, and I realise it's the first time I've been able to admire them openly.

My bladder is becoming increasingly painful as I smile and rush to the bathroom in my room. They have an ensuite I could use, but I don't know why I still use mine. It seems ridiculous to be self-conscious about using their toilet, even more so after last night.

My cheeks heat as the memories come flooding back, and I switch on the light as I gently close the bathroom door behind me.

It stings as I pee, but in a good and truly fucked way. I already know I want to do it as often as they allow.

Because as much as it pains me to say this, they already have a relationship, and whatever this is between the three of us, I feel as though my part is temporary, and that thought isn't one I want to give purchase to; it hurts so much more than I care to admit. It leaves an ache in my chest. I have never felt like this before.

I stare at my reflection. I look the same and yet different.

It was barely two months ago that I arrived here, bloody and bruised. They've given me refuge, a safe haven, and I will never be able to repay them. They've quite literally given me a new lease on life.

After I wash my hands and face, I quickly brush my teeth. Shivering, I step back into my room and go to my chest of drawers to pull out a t-shirt when I notice all the drawers are open haphazardly. I frown at first, confused about what I'm seeing.

I cover my mouth. "Oh my God," I mumble into my palm as I spin to take in the room. My hand does nothing to stifle my scream.

I begin to back away from the sight before me when a hand lands on my shoulder. I go to scream again when his deep voice stills me.

"What the fuck?" Caleb's voice booms into the room.

The light is suddenly switched on, and I blink at the brightness, shaking as Caleb steps around me and pushes me behind him, where I'm met with Noah's bare chest. He pulls me to his side as he tries to see around Caleb.

I swallow, trying to process everything my eyes see, but my brain is having trouble deciphering.

My once white bed linen is smothered in claret, the sheets cut up and ripped into pieces. My underwear drawer has been tipped out on top, shredded into pieces.

It's him. He's found me.

I can barely get oxygen into my lungs as I struggle for breath.

"Easy, sweet girl," Noah says as he wraps me in his arms, my back facing the room. I bury my face into the crook of his neck as I breathe him in, using his scent as an anchor.

"Someone broke into the fucking house," Caleb roars, and I flinch.

"Fuck," Noah says, carefully pulling me away from his chest. "Earlier, the back door was ajar, and I thought maybe it was when you put the bins out. *Shit.*"

He rubs his hand over his face, and I step out of his hold, wrapping my arms around my body, my eyes darting all over the room into every corner, expecting Curtis to jump out at any moment. My stomach bottoms out. I feel the telltale rise of bile as I rush back into the bathroom and barely make it to the sink in time to expel the contents of my stomach.

A calloused palm rubs up and down my spine as the other holds my hair away from my face.

When my stomach is empty, and it turns to dry heaving, it finally subsides, and I run my mouth under the tap to rinse it out, then wipe the back of my hand over my lips.

I'm shaking when soft cotton touches my skin as Noah pulls my arms into my dressing gown from the back of the door. He pulls the robe tie tight, and I'm grateful to be somewhat covered up.

And then I follow him back into the room, where Caleb is on his phone, no doubt pulling up the camera footage from outside the house.

"Is that blood?" I ask, nodding my head towards the bedspread, which is ruined.

Caleb glances up, his eyes the colour of steel. "No, it's some sort of dye."

And that's when I notice two Polaroids on the bedside table. I step closer and reach out, but Noah stops me.

"Don't touch it. We'll want to dust for prints."

I pull my hand back.

"Sorry," I whisper, my eyes raking over the pictures until I realise what I'm looking at. It's us three, all naked in the height of pleasure. The second is me asleep alone in their bed. I want to vomit all over again, knowing we were being watched, and I know in my gut it was Curtis.

"Shit." I can barely keep the tremble from my voice.

Noah hands Caleb a pair of joggers and a t-shirt. I didn't even notice him leave the room.

"Come on, let's go wait downstairs."

I begin to panic and pull away from Noah.

"Wait, what? Wait for who?" My voice is high pitched. I'm hyperventilating now, but I can't help it.

Caleb is the one who takes hold of my face between his strong, calloused palms. "Little one, I need you to calm down for me. Can you do that?"

His question sounds surprisingly soft, which gives me a moment of pause. I watch as he exaggerates, taking a deep breath and then exhales, urging me to do the same.

"That's it, deep breath in, deep breath out." And then, when I gulp enough air into my lungs, he walks us back into the hallway, Noah closing the door behind us.

"Sorry," I say in a whisper. "I panicked for a moment. I thought that was blood. He was here, watching us. I'm so sorry," I say, taking a step back. My thoughts are becoming sporadic, all rambling into one heated mess.

"I should go. This is…" I wave my hand towards the door and begin to pace, muttering under my breath and trying to get my thoughts in order. "He found me. This is bad, shit."

Noah steps in front of me, causing me to stop pacing. "Jessica," he says, my name slowly. "Let's just go downstairs." His voice is calm but laced with concern—for me.

He's concerned for me, yet I brought trouble into their home.

"But this is all my fault." My voice cracks as my emotions bubble to the surface. The urge to run is front and centre.

"We should all go, get away, go somewhere he can't find us." I'm babbling as Noah grips my elbow loosely and walks me downstairs and into the living room.

I peer over my shoulder, looking for Caleb.

"He's checking the rest of the house," he says.

My body tenses. Did he already tell me that? I have no idea because all I can hear is the rapid beat of my heart thumping in my ears like a brass drum. He directs me to the sofa and urges me to sit. I pull my legs up underneath me and try to make myself as small as possible, squeezing my eyes closed. Noah says something else, but everything is a blur.

Chapter Forty-Six

Caleb

That son of a bitch was in our fucking house.

I was so consumed by Noah and Jessica, I let my guard down, and in doing so, I failed to notice as he waltzed right in like he had the fucking right to do so.

I swear he will rue the day I was born.

Jessica is a pile of shaking limbs, her sentences incoherent as Noah leads her downstairs. From the outdoor CCTV footage, I could see that he came and left within fifteen minutes. That's all it took to rip all her bed linen and destroy all her underwear.

But how the fuck did he find her?

Once I am confident the house is clear, I head back downstairs; Noah is kneeling in front of Jessica, holding out a glass of whiskey as he tries to coax her back from the vacant expression lining her face. A few hours ago, she was flushed and thoroughly fucked—content, happy and safe. Now she's reverting to the girl who arrived less than a few months ago.

"Damn it." Noah moves as I step up beside him, towering over Jessica. She doesn't even look up. "Hell, no." I lean down, wrap my fingers around her throat, and squeeze just enough to draw her attention to me when she gasps for breath.

"Fuck, Caleb." Noah grabs my arm, but I shrug him off.

"Jessica." I squeeze again, and her eyes begin to focus. "You with us, Jessica?"

She licks her lips and swallows. I keep my fingers where they are to keep her grounded.

"Yes," she says, but her voice sounds broken.

I let out a breath. "I am so fucking sorry. This is my fault."

She tries to shake her head, but I tighten my hold.

"No, don't you dare. I left the door unlocked—left us vulnerable."

I glance at Noah, who clenches his jaw, but he says nothing as I continue.

"But he's fucking delusional if he thinks he can walk into our house and threaten the people I love."

Shit, that's something I need to talk to Noah about, just the two of us, not just blurt it out in the heat of the moment, even if I mean it.

"Fuck," I say under my breath.

Noah's hand lands on my shoulder, telling me silently it's okay.

Swallowing, I focus my attention back on Jessica.

"I need the Jessica who implicitly gave herself over to me last night. Can you do that, Jessica? Can you still trust me?"

Her eyes go wide. "I never stopped trusting you," she replies, sounding hurt that I would even insinuate as much.

"Good." I lean in and give her a chaste kiss on the lips and then rest my forehead against hers before pulling back and holding my hand out. Without me needing to ask, Noah passes me the whiskey.

"Drink this."

She takes it from me and takes a long sip, coughing once she's swallowed. "That's it and the rest."

She finishes it as instructed and hands me back an empty

glass. Noah is already back with the bottle, pouring me two fingers worth, and I down it in one go.

And then he pours himself one, doing the same.

"Who's coming?" Jessica asks, hugging the robe around her small frame. She looks so fragile, yet she's one of the strongest people I know.

Noah clears his throat and steps past me, sitting beside her and pulling her to his side.

"Some friends of ours—they're skilled in things like this."

She frowns. "Like this?"

"Yeah, security breaches, stalkers."

I sit on the edge of the solid oak coffee table, knowing any other circumstances, Noah would be riding my arse for doing so, but he refrains.

"What I don't get is how he found you."

Pulling up the feed, I zoom in as he looks up at the camera and then points to his eyes and back to the camera before making a slicing motion with a knife along his throat, smirking.

"Are we sure it's him?" Jessica asks, eyes darting between me and Noah.

"You tell me."

I rewind it a few frames and turn it to face them both.

She watches, her lips parting.

"Yeah, it's him." Her lip trembles as she blinks back unshed tears, but it's useless as they roll down her cheeks.

She quickly swats them away.

"Did you ever tell him about us?" Noah questions as he takes the tablet to look over the footage.

We don't have any cameras in the house, but now I'm contemplating remedying that.

"No, never. He was always really jealous."

She bites her thumbnail, lost deep in thought, and then lurches forward.

"Oh, my god." Her eyes go wide. "My phone, could it have been when I switched on my phone the other day?"

Noah looks at me and then back to Jessica. "Possibly. I didn't think you were using it."

She shakes her head. "It was just to check in case Mason had reached out. But it was just threatening messages from Curtis."

Noah cups her cheek. "Why didn't you say anything about the messages?"

"They were sent weeks ago, so I guess I was being naïve thinking he'd lost interest. Do you think that's how he found me?"

Noah drops his hand from her face and moves to his feet. "There's only one way to find out. Where's your phone?"

She glances at him and back at me. "In my rucksack in the bottom of my wardrobe, but it's switched off now."

Noah is already on his way up to her room.

"Shit, Caleb, I didn't even think."

I reach out for her hand and squeeze it gently. "It's okay. We should have checked with you."

I run my hand through my hair, desperate for a haircut, but I know how much Noah likes it when I grow it out.

"He's not going to get away with this," I say more to myself than Jessica, who is worrying her bottom lip. Noah returns, her phone in hand, laptop under his arm and some connector cables.

I move so he can set it up on the coffee table.

"Passcode, please?"

She holds it to her face, unlocking the screen.

"Thank you." I know he could have easily accessed it, but I'm sure he doesn't want to waste more time than necessary.

A knock at the door causes Jessica to jump and cover her chest with her palm.

"I'll get it. Are you comfortable wearing your robe, or did you want to put something on quickly?"

She's about to be surrounded by men, so I at least want to give her the option.

"Noah will go with you as I see the guys in."

He holds out his hand and pulls her to her feet, and I wait until they disappear upstairs.

Taking a deep breath, I go to the front door, checking the cam before turning off the alarm and pulling the door open.

"Caleb," Elliot says in greeting with a nod.

Usually, his presence alone would bother me. He's a good guy, but he'll always be Noah's ex, and what can I say? I can be a jealous bastard. The crazy thing is, I knew him before I even met Noah, and there was a time we were even friends. But I need to push my ego aside. If anyone can help, it's these guys.

"Hi, man, thanks for coming." I hold out my hand, and he doesn't hesitate to take it and give it a firm shake.

Letting go, I step aside.

"Hey, Jax," I shake his hand and then River's before closing the door behind them.

"Noah will be down in a sec. He's just with Jessica."

Elliot tilts his head as if he's about to speak, but footsteps draw our attention as they both come downstairs.

"Well, I'll be damned, Jessica Harper. When he said Jessica, I did wonder."

She smiles as he approaches her, and he pulls her into a quick hug before stepping back.

Okay, yeah, I'm still a jealous bastard.

I walk up and pull her to my side. I can't hide my smile as Elliot glances at her attire. She's in one of my t-shirts, and a pair of Noah's jogging bottoms rolled at the waist.

Chapter Forty-Seven

Noah

I know having Elliot here isn't easy for him—I know he tolerates him for me. I loved Elliot, but the way I love Caleb is so much more profound. When Caleb and I first met, I was still grieving my relationship with Elliot. Even though it was a mutual decision, I had hoped things would be different when he returned from his last mission, but I couldn't have been more wrong. I can't even pretend to understand what he went through on that last mission; they lost a friend, a brother in arms, and he ended up having half his leg blown off.

I was his friend before we were lovers, and his injury didn't change how I felt about him, but he wouldn't see reason. The man who left and returned was not the same.

But even then, I could still read Elliot. I knew I wasn't what he needed. And that was when I met Caleb. He was already friends with Jax.

We follow Jessica and Caleb into the living room.

When Elliot is wearing trousers, apart from the limp and the flat foot, you wouldn't know that he wears a prosthetic.

But I notice how River places his palm on Elliot's lower back as we enter the living room. *Interesting.*

He might think it's a subtle move, but it's clear something is going on there—good for them.

As long as he's happy, that's all that matters. I glance at Caleb; his expression is harsh. I smile and see the slight curve of his lips. His eyes quickly peruse my body before his stoic expression returns.

His arm is still wrapped around Jessica's shoulder, and I love how she leans into him for comfort and support. I don't know if they're even aware they're doing it.

Elliot clears his throat.

"Okay, you good if the guys check out the room while I get started on the phone?"

He glances between Caleb and me.

"Yeah, of course, the room is this way."

I leave Caleb and Jessica with Elliot while River and Jax follow me upstairs.

"Did you touch anything?" Jax asks as I open the door to the room.

I shake my head.

River lets out a whistle and walks over as he assesses the mess on the bed.

"Well, it's clear this was personal." He looks over his shoulder. "Ex, by any chance?"

"We very much don't think it's anyone else."

I grind my jaw, angry the fucker even got in our house in the first place. We're meant to be keeping her safe, for fuck's sake.

Jax walks over and studies the Polaroids without picking them up. It wouldn't see the light of day if it were anyone else and under any other circumstances. Unless it was taken by one of us and we had consent to do so.

It feels surreal standing here, watching them go through the room, studying it. I feel violated for Jessica. The longer we stand here, the angrier I'm becoming, my blood boiling as I take in her destroyed underwear.

"Is that?"

I can't even finish my sentence.

"Yeah, it looks like semen," Jax says, his jaw tight.

Pinching the bridge of my nose, I take a deep breath, feeling sick to my stomach. This was a personal attack, and he needs to be stopped if he's capable of this after what he did to her. I dread what he would have done if we hadn't taken her back to our room. The fact he took a photo of her while she was asleep in our bed angers me more than the one he took of us having sex. A fucked up part of me hopes he saw what we did to her, how she loved everything about it, how much pleasure we elicited from her.

"Please, whatever you do, don't tell her. She doesn't need to know that."

When I look up, he nods in understanding. He moves over to the wall, kicks his foot up and leans back.

"How long have the three of you…you know?"

If it were anyone else asking, I'd probably tell them to fuck off, but this is Jax.

"We admitted our feelings to her last week, so not long," I admit. "We've never taken advantage of her, but we couldn't deny our attraction to her either."

His lips curve into a smile. "Mason is going to kill you when he finds out, though. You know that, right?"

I raise an eyebrow. "I think someone else will be at the top of this list if we don't find him first."

He runs his hand through his hair. "That's true. I think once he calms down, he'll be okay. It's obvious how much you care about her."

River looks up, his eyes flicking between the two of us. "Nah, I'd still rip you a new one. Sisters are off limits."

Jax rolls his eyes. "Better the devil you know than the devil you don't."

River shrugs. "Yeah, okay, I guess when you put it like that."

"Besides, it's a bit of a moot point," I say, moving towards the door. "He's still unobtainable."

Jax pushes off the wall with his foot and reaches out to grip my shoulder. "We'll track him down. In the meantime, we need to find out what this arsehole thinks he's playing at."

I look back to River. "Do you have what you need?"

"Yeah, man."

I leave the room with a curt nod, not wanting to be here longer than needed. "Do you know anyone who can get out here on short notice and gut that room?" I ask Jax as I make my way towards the stairs.

"Yeah, I'll link you up with our contact."

The sooner any trace of him is gone, the better.

Chapter Forty-Eight
Caleb

I wrap my arm around Jessica as we stand in front of the fireplace, my thumb working circles over her hip. I'm unsure if it's to soothe her or keep myself in check.

To think, only a few hours ago, we were fucking right here on this very rug, and now we're checking her phone to see if the prick has access to her location.

I watch Elliot as he connects his computer to the phone and gets to work. It's not hard to see how attractive he is, even more so with his hair swept back, and his glasses add the sexy computer whiz vibes perfectly.

But when I look at him, I'm reminded of how much he meant to Noah. I don't know why I'm such a jealous bastard when it comes to him. All I know is, until Jessica, no one other than Noah has ever gotten under my skin like this, carved into my very soul.

It's why, no matter what, I will do what needs to be done to protect them both. I might be a civilian now, but my trigger finger works just fine.

"Yeah, he tracked your phone to here," Elliot says, peering up from underneath his glasses.

She moves closer to my side. "Does it work both ways? Can you track him?" I ask, already formulating a plan of attack.

He's been in our home, defiled her clothes, her bed.

"Yeah, I can track him without even using her phone."

His fingers work over the keyboard so fast that he doesn't need to look at the keys. His eyes are trained on the screen in front of him.

It's deathly quiet sans his fingers attacking the keys. "Can I get you guys a drink?" I ask, my arm dropping from around Jessica's waist.

"I can do it," she says, her voice small, the polar opposite to how vocal she was this morning, her new air of confidence buried, yet again.

Elliot looks up. "I'd love a coffee, and so will River. Jax takes tea if it's not too much trouble." He smiles softly as Jessica nods and looks up at me expectantly with a silent question.

"No, little one, I'm good. Are you sure you're okay to make it?"

She gives a firm nod, and I lean down and give her a slow kiss. I feel her tense, but just as quickly, she relaxes and kisses me back before pulling away, her cheeks heating.

Elliot clears his throat, and I sit on the opposite sofa. His eyes dart to Jessica's retreating form before coming back to meet mine.

"It's new, and before you start, we haven't taken advantage of her, if that's what you're thinking."

He holds up his hands. "I never said you did." Tilting his head, he studies me for a beat.

"You care about her, don't you?"

I'm unsure if it's rhetorical or if he's looking for a response, but I find myself giving him one anyway.

"Of course, I do. I don't make a habit of public displays of affection with someone I don't."

His smile is a little lopsided, endearing. "I can see that. You look at her the same way you look at Noah."

With that, I raise an eyebrow. "Which is?"

"Like you would burn the world to the ground and anyone who gets in your way to protect her."

My heart skips a beat because, yeah, he's not wrong.

"It's what we do for the ones we love, right?"

His focus returns to his laptop. "It sure is."

I sense Noah before I see him rounding the banister of the stairs, the other guys on his heels. He walks over to me and squeezes my shoulder. I peer up as he lowers his face to mine, giving me a quick kiss before straightening and focusing on Elliot.

River moves to the empty seat beside him, their thighs touching as he looks at the laptop.

Jessica walks back in and pauses when she sees everyone back in the living room. Her shoulders pull inwards, and I fucking hate it.

She clears her throat. "Do you take sugar in your coffee and tea?" she asks, her eyes darting to the guys.

They all shake their head, say no thank you, and then she hurries back into the kitchen.

"She looks spooked," Jax comments, taking one of the free armchairs. "Not that I can blame her."

"It's why I plan on taking the cunt out," I say, moving to my feet and pacing.

Noah grabs my wrist. "Don't you think I want to kill the bastard, too? But what about Jessica? Have you thought of how it will affect her—"

"How will *what* affect me?" she asks, returning on the tail end of the conversation with a tray in her hands, the cups clinking as her arms tremble, probably still from the adrenaline of everything that's happened.

Noah is in front of her in three long strides where he takes the tray from her hands and puts it on the small coffee table.

She rolls her eyes and moves past him to hand out the mugs. Pride fills me. That's our girl.

Noah takes his coffee and kisses her temple as she wraps her hands around her mug, and I hold out my hand for her to come to me. She moves without missing a beat, and I pull her close. She leans into me. Noah stands on her other side. The need to protect her and guard her is our sole priority. The fact he was in our home while I let my guard down fills me with guilt and shame.

"You didn't answer me," she says, eyes rimmed red.

I let out a sigh and run my fingers through my hair.

"That I want to take the bastard out."

She doesn't know much about my time in the armed forces, and maybe one day I'll tell her, but not yet. It's hard, though, seeing her face fall from my confession.

"You'd do that. You'd what, beat him up, teach him a lesson—kill him?"

Jessica steps back. It's such an unconscious move. I don't think she even realises she's done it until Noah wraps his arm around her shoulder.

"If I had to, yes. All of the above."

Her mouth opens and closes as she tries and fails to respond.

It's my job to protect her, yet the man who assaulted, beat and raped her managed to get into the one place she should have been safe.

Her eyes glisten as she leans into Noah. Does she not understand what I would do for the ones I love? Not that it matters. She probably thinks I'm no better than the cunt who hurt her. Without another word, I turn and walk towards the kitchen.

My heart constricts. Shit, it hits me out of nowhere. I'm no longer falling—I've fucking fallen.

"Caleb, wait," Noah says, reaching out to stop me as I pass him.

I shrug him off. "No, I just need a minute."

And with that, I walk away, feeling all eyes on me.

Chapter Forty-Nine

Noah

I stare after Caleb as he walks away, his shoulders tense. Control is something he prides himself on. The fact he admitted to her what he would do in a room full of people, friends or not, is a show of his control slipping. It's a side of him I have no doubt he never wanted her to see, but nobody is flawless.

Jessica looks up at me, her brow furrowed. "Should I go and talk to him?" she asks.

As much as we all need to discuss this, I don't think now is the time.

"No, just give him a second, okay?"

I kiss her temple as she leans into me.

Someone clears their throat, and I glance over to Elliot, who's looking over the top of his laptop. His eyes slide back to the screen.

"What is it?" I release Jessica's shoulder and walk towards him and around the chair to see the screen as I read what's in front of me.

"What is it?" Jessica asks, her voice almost inaudible.

I look up as Caleb returns to the living room, his eyes going straight to Jessica and me as he stops beside her but keeps a cushion of air between them. My heart sinks until she reaches for his hand, entwining their fingers. A look of surprise crosses his face, but it only lasts a few seconds before he squeezes her hand, and I breathe.

"Your ex-boyfriend has been suspended," Elliot says, turning the screen to face Caleb.

Caleb softly tugs on Jessica's hand, coming over to see what's on the screen.

I watch as Jessica reads it. Her complexion turns ashen.

"It's my fault," she says, her eyes wide as she looks up at me.

Caleb reaches for her shoulder, turning her to face him, her hand still in his.

"How is this your fault" he questions, his jaw ticking.

"I was thinking yesterday how I should report him. And look, he hurt someone else."

Her eyes turn glassy. "You're not the reason he's been suspended for poor misconduct, sexual assault, or any of the other things listed. He's the only one who is responsible—no one else."

She shakes her head as if to argue; I agree with Caleb. The allegations show this isn't something new, and if anything, the police force has failed by not pursuing the ones raised in the past.

"Sweet girl, he's right. This is not your fault. But if you still want to report him and make a statement, we'll support your decision."

She's blaming herself for actions outside of her control. Jessica wears her heart on her sleeve. She's pure and selfless, the way she'll give you the last biscuit and see to your needs before her own. She feels so deeply, and I'm in awe of her empathy, even more so after how she's been treated.

"Yes, I have to report him. I need to do this."

Caleb pulls her into his chest. "Then we'll take you," he says, holding her tightly.

"We can keep a track of him as long as he's using this phone," Elliot says, looking towards me.

"Thanks, man."

It's another forty minutes before the guys all leave, and it's just the three of us left in the living room. It's almost six in the morning, and I know I won't have a chance in hell at getting back to sleep. I'm still way too wired.

Jessica is curled up on the end of the sofa, a vacant expression on her face.

"Jax knows someone who can come do a cleanup and gut the room, but they'll need two days." I glance back to Jessica before focusing on Caleb. "I don't think it's a good idea to be here while that's happening," I admit.

He rubs the stubble of his jaw, a frown on his face. "The new surveillance will take a couple of hours. Elliot called in a favour, so they're coming here at nine." I notice it's the first time he's ever mentioned Elliot without a hint of hostility.

"I was thinking we get her down to the station, let her make her statement, and then we could take her to Camber Sands for a couple of days, at least until everything is sorted out here."

He nods. "Yeah, I think that's a good idea. I'll have my meetings rescheduled."

"Okay, I'll get a hold of Bishop and ask him to get in some essentials."

He's the guy who maintains and looks after our property there. It sits in between Viking Bay and Louisa Bay—a stone's throw away from the beach—with a sea view from the master bedroom. I think some sea air is just what Jessica needs. What Caleb and I love about it the most, other than it being right by the beach, is that everything local is within walking distance, so there is no need for a car.

Jessica showers while Caleb and I get dressed and pack a weekend bag.

"Shit, what about clothes for Jessica?" I ask as Caleb ties the laces of his trainers. "I don't think she will want to touch anything he had his hands on. She has a clean pair of leggings and knickers on the airer."

Caleb straightens, pulling his phone from his pocket. "Give her one of your T-shirts. And I'll see if Wendy can grab her some essentials, and then we can swing by the office on our way out of the city and grab them."

I reach for the back of his neck and pull him towards me. "I love you."

"I love you, too." And then he kisses me, letting go when we hear the water from the shower shut off.

It's after two in the afternoon when we finally finish at the police station. After discussing it with Caleb, we also decided to report the break-in. The more evidence against that cunt, the better.

Caleb left about an hour ago to run some errands while I sat in with Jessica as she gave her statement and gave them the clothing we had bagged from that night she first came to us.

She looks exhausted by the time we step through the automatic doors onto the pavement. I wrap my arm over her shoulder and kiss her temple. Squinting up at the cloudless blue sky, the sun shining, I know it will be gorgeous weather in Camber Sands. I just wish we were taking her there under better circumstances.

It feels like this is a huge relapse from all the self-healing over the last few weeks, and the one place she found solace in has now been tainted. Caleb admitting he would take Curtis out was said in anger, even though I know if he had to, he would do it in a heartbeat.

And that's a conversation maybe we need to have with Jessica. The thought of her feeling at odds with Caleb scares me because I don't want to lose this, lose her.

Caleb pulls up outside, I open the door for Jessica to climb into the back, and then I take the front passenger side.

"I got you both one of those iced coffees you like," Caleb says as he pulls away. "And there are some snacks in the bag. We can stop if you're hungry or eat when we get there."

"Thank you." I pick up my coffee, grateful for the caffeine fix, and take a huge mouthful.

"Get where?" Jessica asks after it registers what he just said.

I look over my shoulder to see her sitting behind Caleb, sipping on her coffee.

"We're taking you to Camber Sands for a couple of days while we sort out the security at the house." I don't add about fixing up the room.

"Oh, I've never been." She says, staring out of the window.

"You'll love it. It's right by the beach." I know she loves the seaside. It's one of the many things we've talked about. Instead of replying, she smiles, but it's forced, like the ones she mustered when she first came to us.

I glance at Caleb, who looks to the rear-view mirror and then back to me. His lips form a straight line as he reaches out to squeeze my thigh, and our eyes meet in a shared moment of affection and uncertainty.

Chapter Fifty

Jessica

Camber Sands was beautiful, a nice escape from the chaos that follows me everywhere. Caleb and Noah still somehow managed to make our time there special, even under the circumstances, and they are memories I will cherish.

They held me through the night, even though I tried to fight it. Sleep came eventually, and when I woke soaked in sweat and frozen with fear, they were there to coax me back. They've been tactile and afforded me kisses, but nothing else beyond that, and honestly, I'm grateful. I love being with these men any way they'll have me, but the thought of being with them again so soon is overwhelming. They make me feel more than I ever thought possible. And I think they can sense that I need a few days. Their patience with me, as always, is unwavering.

As we return to what feels like home, there's this foreboding presence, a heavy weight I can't seem to lift no matter how much I try.

Curtis has already taken so much from me; his intentions were as wicked as ever when he invaded my sanctuary. Caleb arranged a security upgrade, and Camber Sands provided a temporary refuge. But now it's back to reality.

It's time for my next counselling session—a crucial step in my journey to reclaim my life—and I know deep down that I need to face this challenge alone. It's an opportunity to prove that I am no longer a victim.

"Come." Noah holds his hand out once we enter the house and kick off our shoes, leading me upstairs as Caleb does something to the alarm panel.

I almost crash into him when he stops outside my room, wondering why we're standing here and not heading straight for their room. And there it is—self-doubt creeping in, and I'm wondering if I've been on the wrong page with them all along.

A firm hand caresses my lower back, and Caleb joins us as Noah pushes the door open and switches on the light.

He grips my hand as he steps inside, and I enter behind him, Caleb a welcome presence at my back as I take in the room.

"What did you do?" I ask as my eyes sweep the room, the smell of fresh paint assailing my senses as I take in the new furniture and decor. "It's completely different."

"We didn't want you to come back and feel uncomfortable, not when this is meant to be a safe place." Noah reaches up and cups my cheek.

"Of course, we still want you in our bed, but if you need a moment, we want you to know you can still find tranquillity here, between these walls," Caleb says, resting his chin above my shoulder.

"If you don't like it, we can change it." Noah's voice is uncertain.

"No, it's perfectly fine, but it's too much." I hold my hand out to the expanse of the room. "I hate that I've turned your lives upside down. It makes me feel selfish for wanting you."

Caleb's arms wrap around my waist. "Jessica, you haven't turned our lives upside down. You've turned us inside out. We're the selfish ones for wanting you."

I have to hold back the overwhelming urge to tell them I'm in love with them, the words heavy on my tongue.

"Then we're all selfish," I reply instead. "Thank you, I'll find a way to repay you."

Noah furrows his brow as though my last sentence was offensive.

"Your happiness is the only thing we want," Caleb whispers into my ear, sending a shiver down my spine. It's so easy to let myself get swept away and caught up in how they make my body tingle and my pulse race. I never knew my body could react like this.

I want to tell them to take me to bed, to consume me, ravish me, make me scream, but I also know sex isn't going to fix this; it's not going to make the situation with Curtis just disappear. I'm done hiding, I want my life back.

Stepping out of the wall of muscle that is all Caleb, I turn to face the two of them.

I take a deep breath and release it as my words rush out. "I have a session with Greta tomorrow afternoon, and I'm going —alone."

Noah's eyes go to Caleb and then back to me.

"No. One of us will come with you," Caleb says, staring at me in disbelief.

I shake my head and cross my arms. "No. I want to do this on my own—I need to do this on my own."

Noah opens his mouth to speak, but Caleb beats him to it, his eyes filled with concern. "It's not safe."

"Is *anywhere* safe?" I blurt out and immediately regret it when I see the wounded look on his face as he steps back. "I didn't mean it like that. I know I'm safe with you."

Caleb purses his lips together as he shakes his head. "You're not going alone."

Noah intervenes, reaching for Caleb's wrist as if to ground

him. "Caleb, as much as I know where this is coming from, it's not your call to make."

If I thought I had wounded him before, by his expression now, I was sorely mistaken.

"I don't want to come between you," I say.

"You're not." They both say simultaneously, their gazes now fixed on me.

I shake my head. "That's not what it feels like."

Caleb's entire posture is tense as he clenches his fist at his side, his protective instincts raging. "Please, Jessica. Just think about this." His concern for my safety is palpable, and the affection in his eyes is impossible to ignore.

I throw my hand up into the air. "I have thought about this. I spent the entire drive home thinking about nothing else."

Moving from one foot to the other, I try to get my thoughts in order, needing them to understand.

"Well, at least let one of us drive you and pick you up."

I shake my head. "But that defeats the purpose of me going alone, Caleb." I don't know how to explain this to him, *fucking hell*.

Noah interjects gently, placing a comforting hand on Caleb's arm. "Caleb, I think Jessica needs to do this for herself. It's a chance for her to reclaim her independence."

His words strike a chord within me, soothing the apprehension that threatened to overpower my resolve. The old me would have given in to Caleb, just like I used to give in to Curtis, and I won't be that person again, even if I love Caleb. Curtis is hiding in plain sight, but soon karma will catch up to him. In the meantime, I need to confront the demons that still haunt me—to stand tall in the face of fear.

I nod, grateful to Noah. "I just need to do this, to prove to myself I'm not a victim, that Curtis no longer controls me."

Caleb sighs, rubbing the bridge of his nose. "I won't lie, Jessica. I don't like it. But I don't want to suffocate your independence either. I never want you to see me as someone no better than Curtis."

I step forward and reach up to cup his face between my palms. He's let his beard grow out the last few days, and the hairs tickle my skin. "I don't, Caleb. You're nothing like him." I hope he sees the sincerity in my eyes and hears the truth in my words. I might be young, naive even, but I'm learning to listen to my instincts and trust myself again, just like Greta's been encouraging me to. And every fibre of my being tells me that Caleb and Noah are good men. I trust them. My feelings for them might be new, but my love for them outweighs any feelings I ever had for Curtis.

He covers my hands with his and leans his forehead against mine. "I know you're a grown woman. It's in my nature to want to protect you."

He takes a deep breath, and when he exhales, it skates across my skin.

"All right, Jessica. But promise me you'll call or text the moment you're done. You'll get an Uber there and straight back."

"I know, Caleb and I will, I promise."

Noah presses up behind me, cushioning me between them. His presence provides an extra layer of comfort. His calm demeanour and unwavering support give me the added strength to face this hurdle.

"Thank you," I say, my voice filled with gratitude, but I wish I had the courage to tell them the three words that convey how I truly feel.

Chapter Fifty-One

Caleb

It went against every fibre of my being when Jessica said she wanted to attend counselling alone, but she and Noah were right. She needed to do this for her, and it wasn't about what I wanted or needed.

She needed that space to reclaim some control over her life, to find her inner strength again. Even though I see it in everything she does, she needs to be the one who believes it.

I didn't want her to leave our embrace. I wanted it to linger, draw it out for as long as possible before her Uber arrived. Of course, Noah was a pillar of strength, forcing me to come to our gym and work out.

She texted on her way and then again when she arrived. And in that moment, I couldn't be more proud. She's a fucking warrior. I realise how easy it would have been for her to cave and allow me to dictate her decisions. And honestly, it's fucking endearing watching her stand her ground. I never want to break that spirit I love so much about her.

Finishing my set, I grab a towel and wipe the sweat from my face before reaching for my water and drinking it down greedily.

I watch Noah as he slows his run down to a walk, his spine glistening from the exertion.

"Noah."

He looks over his shoulder as he turns off the running machine and steps off as I toss him a towel. I watch as he wipes it over his abs; the muscles contracting with the movement.

I sit forward on the bench, resting my elbows on my knees, the sound of the air con ticking loudly. The air is thick with the smell of salt and sweat from our combined workout.

"I told you I was falling for Jessica."

Slowly, he walks until he's standing before me, and I look up.

"But the truth is I've fucking fallen." My voice wobbles. I love Noah. I would choose him above all else, except that now extends to Jessica, too, and I'm left feeling exposed and more vulnerable than I ever have.

"I know." I glance up, and he smirks. "I think I knew it before you did."

I shake my head and grab his wrist, pulling him down onto the bench beside me and angling my body towards his, our knees touching.

"It's okay." His calloused palm rests against my jaw. "I'm in love with her, too."

"I wanted to say it before we watched her walk away—before she got in that fucking Uber." I let out a humourless laugh. "There she is, brave enough to step out into the world on her own as she goes to get help for her trauma. A *fuck you* to the cunt who abused and tried to intimidate her when he stepped into our home. And I don't even have the courage to tell her I fucking love her. What kind of man does that make me?"

Noah's hand moves to the back of my neck so fast, the air rushes from my lungs. He tugs me towards his face, his breath warm against mine as he speaks. "Shut up. You're one of the bravest men I know, Caleb. Did you hear me declaring how fucking in love with her I am?" he asks, his eyebrows curving. "No, because deep down, we both knew it wasn't the right moment. Besides, I always want to be open with you. I never want to tarnish what we have by not being transparent. We're in this together or not at all." I could melt under the intensity of his gaze.

I close the distance. My lips brush against his as I claim his mouth. Our teeth clash as we kiss with abandon, and my entire body tightens as we fight for control. I bite down on his lower lip, and he groans as I lave it with my tongue, my hand moving to his shorts, needing to touch him, needing the skin-on-skin connection, and his hand fumbles with mine.

Like magnets, we move at the same time and stand as we free one another. I pull out of the kiss and spit into my palm before wrapping my thumb and index finger around the base of his shaft, and then I stroke up and down before closing the rest of my fingers around him in my fist.

He groans before spitting into his palm, reaching for me, and tugging me forward until our erections are pressed together. The sounds of us grunting as we climb higher—it's pure, carnal need. There's no edging, teasing, or prolonged gratification as we gyrate against one another, craving the ecstasy of our impending release. Everything evaporates around us as we get lost in the moment.

In seconds, our climax is building, and we both come hard and fast, our combined cum pumping in hot spurts over our hands and stomachs.

"Fuck," I hiss as his dick bows and pulses, and mine spasms until we're spent.

Breathing him in, I rest my forehead against his and close my eyes. Neither of us moves as we catch our breath.

My phone pings as we part, and Noah reaches for a towel so we can wipe ourselves up. Snatching up my phone, I read the text.

Saved by Two

> Jax: No movement from her ex. He's quiet, too quiet. There's been no movement from his property. I'm sending one of my guys to check it out. I'll update you once I know more.

> Me: Okay, thanks, man.

Noah reads the message over my shoulder.

"Let's quickly shower." Jessica still has another thirty minutes until her session finishes, and I want to be ready, waiting for her when she comes home.

I stare at my phone, waiting for it to ring or a message to appear. "Anything?" I ask Noah as he pulls out his phone.

He shakes his head. "No, nothing, but it's only been two minutes since her session ended."

I want to say he's right. Not everyone is as compulsive as I am about their timekeeping, but still, worry creeps in, a knot tightening in my stomach.

"Do you feel it, too?" I ask after a couple more tension-filled minutes.

He walks over to the window and looks outside. "Yeah, something doesn't feel right."

My phone pings, a vibration working up to my elbow, my arm. My pulse races with each passing second as I swipe the screen.

> Jax: No sign of him, and the house is empty.

Noah swipes his screen and brings his phone to his ear.

"Fuck, it's going straight to automated voicemail."

Trying to ignore the ever-growing sinking feeling in the pit of my stomach, I say, "Check location services to see if you can bring up her location."

I bring up the GPS tracker app installed on my phone.

"Shit, I've got nothing, you?"

Using the tracker app, I get a hit on a location.

"Fuck, she's moving away from the city." Noah twists my hand to look at the screen.

Unbeknownst to Jessica, we surreptitiously placed a tracker on her bangle, the meaning behind it representing the connection we feel towards her and that even though she might not be able to see it, it's there.

Panic surges through me like a tidal wave, threatening to drown any rational thoughts. The worst scenarios flash through my mind—Jessica is in danger.

Noah and I exchange a glance, our eyes reflecting the same fear. Without hesitation, we take immediate action.

"Jax, Jessica's been taken," Noah says as we both rush towards the front door, and I grab a set of keys and make a beeline for Noah's car.

"I'll send you the link, yeah, okay, yeah."

Jax said he would track her location and meet us since she's heading more towards his direction. Noah's just clipping on his seatbelt as the engine roars to life.

I gun the engine, the urgency punching the weight of my foot on the accelerator. City traffic makes it impossible to race through the streets. Instead, I navigate the maze of roads as Noah puts the location into the Sat Nav. I try to keep my mind focused on the task, but worry gnaws at my thoughts, threatening to consume me.

The weight of uncertainty becomes almost suffocating.

As we approach the city's outskirts, our surroundings transform from the familiar hustle and bustle into country lanes and winding roads where shadows stretch longer. A sense of foreboding settles over me.

My grip on the steering wheel tightens, my knuckles turning white. The pulsating urgency drowns out all other sounds, the beat of my heart in sync with the rhythm of the road. With every mile we cover, the need to protect Jessica burns, a flame that won't be extinguished until she's in our arms again.

Soon, we're approaching a clearing that leads into Epping Forest. Fury ignites in me. We see a Land Rover up ahead, and then Jax jumping out, followed by the other guys as we pull up beside them.

"Her location has pinned to within a mile radius," he says before I've even cut the engine and climbed out of the car. "We need to split up."

Jax tosses both Noah and me an earpiece headset. "We'll split into three groups."

"Elliot is going to stay on point here while we spread out."

River passes us each a torch; it's already dusk, and the surrounding woodland will disappear into darkness within minutes.

I've never been more grateful for someone else taking point. I know I'm not thinking rationally.

"Noah, you're with River. Caleb with me. Tommy, you're with Luke."

And with that, we break apart.

Chapter Fifty-Two

Jessica

I wake up in a haze, disoriented and frightened. Everything is a blur, and I struggle to remember how I ended up in this unfamiliar place. As my mind begins to clear, the memories flood back, filling me with dread.

The last thing I recall is leaving Greta's office after I insisted I had to go alone. Because I needed to do it for myself, refusing to be a victim.

I step outside, checking the app on my phone for my Uber, when a body steps into my line of sight, crowding me on the pavement. Before I can react, silver glistens, followed by a sharp needle jab to my arm. As I look up into the soulless eyes of Curtis, a sinister smirk plays on his lips.

"Let go," I stammer. "What did you do to me?"

The grip on my phone loosens, and I watch helplessly as it clatters to the ground in slow motion, the screen shattering into a spiderweb of cracks. I try to call out for help, but my voice is weak, and my words are slurred gibberish as my head begins to spin.

Curtis tugs me hard into his side, wrapping his arm around my waist like a snake. "You didn't really think you could escape me, did you, Jessica?" His voice sends shivers down my spine. "I warned you never to leave me."

My heart races as he drags me down a nearby alley towards a car, my legs barely able to keep up. I feel weak, disoriented, and trapped. Panic sets in, and I desperately search for a way out, but my thoughts are clouded by the effects of whatever he injected me with. Every step feels like an eternity as we reach the car, and he forces me inside.

The world fades away as the drugs take hold. My last thought is of Caleb and Noah as my consciousness slips away and darkness consumes me.

I find myself in a clearing, surrounded by a forest. The air is heavy with silence, and the realisation of my predicament hits me like a tidal wave.

Curtis looms over me, his eyes burning with a dangerous intensity. He grabs me roughly by the throat, his grip tight and painful. "Listen carefully, Jessica," he hisses, his voice dripping with malice. "Your life depends on your obedience."

I reach up, clawing at his hand around my throat as I struggle to breathe. He squeezes hard once before shoving me and letting go. I just about catch myself before face-planting on the muddy earth beneath me.

Fear clenches my heart, and I know I am in grave danger. Curtis is capable of anything, and I struggle to get my thoughts in order. All I know is I feel utterly helpless.

And at this moment, I wish with all my being that I had listened to Caleb and Noah. They'll never know how much they mean to me. I long for their presence, even though I'm unaware of how much time has passed. It's dusk, so maybe a few hours.

"Where are we?" I croak out, my eyes scanning all around me. If I could get the keys off of him somehow, maybe I could make a run for it.

"A forest. Miles from anywhere. So don't even think about trying anything. No one is going to save you."

I lick my dry lips, my throat raw as I swallow. I watch him pacing up and down. His eyes keep going to his phone, the backlight lighting up his face creepily. How did I ever find this man attractive?

"They'll be here soon."

I don't want to know who they are, but unable to stop myself, I ask who?

"Some people I owe a lot of money to. I'm using you to pay off my debt."

I must have misheard him, the drugs making my hearing fuzzy.

"What?"

He looks over, his smile pure evil as he trails his eyes over my body, and I shiver, wrapping my arms around my middle.

It's eerily quiet out here, and I realise how truly alone I am.

"I owe some nasty people a substantial amount of money." He moves, lowering himself in front of me. His breath is heavy with the repugnant smell of alcohol. "So, when they get here, I'm giving you over to them as payment." He reaches out and strokes my hair. I don't move, frozen with fear at such close proximity.

He sneers at me. "I saw you with those two men while they fucked you." His fingers wrap around the loose hair, and he pulls, my head snapping forward, my scalp stinging, forcing water to my eyes. "You're disgusting. I would have taken you back, but not after witnessing that."

Reaching for my top, he tugs it down, exposing my bra and shoving his hand inside the cup, squeezing my breast hard. "But that being said, maybe I will take you for one more ride before they take you and offer you out for money."

I can barely breathe. Is he saying what I think he's saying?

"People are trafficked all the time. Did you know the government reports close to thirteen thousand victims a year when it's closer to one hundred thousand?"

He leans over me, flicking his tongue out and licking my

cheek. I'm unable to suppress my gag. His eyes grow dark, and before I see what's coming, he backhands me across the face, my body slamming to the ground from sheer force.

And then he's on top of me, his erection pressing into my lower stomach as I try to shove him off, but he's too heavy.

"I love it when you fight back. It makes me so hard."

I slap at him mindlessly, crying out, desperate to be free, when he shackles my hands in one of his, shoving them above my head, my bare arms digging into the ground.

"If you keep on like that, I'll fuck your arse raw. Show you what a real man can do. Prepare you for what awaits you when I hand you over."

His words are suffocating, and I struggle to keep my fear at bay. I cling to a glimmer of hope that someone, somehow, will rescue me from this nightmare. I pray that Caleb and Noah are searching for me, which is pathetic. I don't even know if I believe in God. But without the phone they gave me, I have no other lifeline.

He rips at the waistband of my leggings, his nails scratching my skin as the elastic protests.

Ringing causes him to freeze. "Fuck," he curses, his knee moving to my stomach as he uses that hand to pull his phone from his back pocket and accepts the call.

"Hello."

I can't hear who is on the other end of the phone as he digs his knee into me hard before releasing my hands, but the sinister smile he gives me, the lewd way he's sneering at me now, has my entire body freezing again.

"I'll send you my location now."

He taps at his phone and then looks down. "You're lucky we were interrupted. We're about to have company."

I need to fight back against the darkness that threatens to consume me. I won't let Curtis break my spirit.

"I have money. If it's money you need, I can get you the money." It's a last-ditch attempt to win him over.

He laughs, the sound both bitter and hollow. "You seem to forget I've seen your bank statements."

"Yes, but Caleb and Noah have money. They'll pay you. I know they will." I try to hold back my tears, but it's impossible. If I don't try and make a run for it, this is over.

Pushing myself into a sitting position, I move to my knees, digging my hands into the mud beneath my fingers. I stagger to my feet, bumping against the car's bonnet.

"I'll do anything you want me to, but please, don't do this."

His phone pings with a message, he looks down, and I know it's now or never.

With every ounce of strength I can muster, I lunge forward, smashing the heel of my hands into his eye sockets and smearing them with mud. With a guttural scream, he lashes out, punching me in the face, dropping his phone in the process. I raise my knee and slam into his junk as hard as I can and then punch my arms and legs as fast as they will go, him hollering out and swearing behind me. My body is heavy, my movements sluggish, as though I'm running in quicksand.

I trip, slipping into a ditch, a broken branch cracking loudly as it snaps, a jagged edge impaling my palm. I cry out, unable to stop myself, my pulse racing in my ears, bile rising in my throat. I choke to swallow it back down.

"You cunt, I'm going to make sure you pay for that."

I push myself to my feet, but one of my ankles gives out beneath me, almost dragging me back down. I force myself to keep moving as he continues to call out, his voice coming from every direction as he tells me all the vile things he's going to do to me when he catches me.

I can barely see in front of me as I move into the shadows of the trees.

My breath whooshes from my lungs when suddenly I'm

sliding, wet mud beneath my feet, unable to keep myself upright. The side of my head bashes against a tree trunk—hard. Something damp and cold drips down my temple, everything growing darker as my body finally fails me.

And then I fall.

Chapter Fifty-Three

Noah

My heart pounds in my chest as I step into the eerie silence of Epping Forest. The sun disappeared on the horizon, a pale glow through the dense canopy of trees, creating twisted patterns on the forest floor. A shiver runs down my spine, partly from the chill in the air but mainly from the tension and fear that grips my entire being.

Caleb's usually confident demeanour was replaced by a look of determination. As we separated, neither of us spoke. A silent exchange between us said everything we needed. *I love you, and we will find her.*

River is quiet beside me. His sharp gaze scans the surroundings, his senses on high alert. The low light enough to make out his strong jawline, emphasising the small scars from the battles he's fought.

As we delve deeper into the forest, the silence becomes suffocating. The rustling of leaves beneath our feet amplifies the tension that hangs in the air. Every shadow seems to hold secrets, every crack of a twig a potential threat. The sun is now long gone. We've been moving deeper into the woodland. It's almost twenty-five minutes since we split up. We switch on our torches, and my grip on mine tightens, the beam of light trembling slightly as I sweep it across the path ahead.

And then there's the unmistakable sound of a gun firing in quick succession.

"What the fuck," I hiss as we come to a stop until the echoes of the gunshots disappear.

Jax's voice speaks clearly into my earpiece, and River and Thomas quickly respond, confirming everyone is okay. I let out a strangled breath. The thought of Jessica and Caleb being anywhere near those shots is like someone stepping over my grave.

"We're close to where the shots were fired. Be on alert," Jax says before going silent.

I can't think past the fear that threatens to consume me, and I stagger, falling to my knees. River is there, a hand firm on my shoulder, giving me the few seconds I need as his eyes scan our location.

Taking a few deep breaths, I straighten, and he drops his hand as I push back to my feet. "Fuck, sorry."

"It's fine. You good?"

I nod even though I am anything but—knowing there's a possibility those gunshots could have been for Jessica, though something in my gut tells me it wasn't her and that she's okay.

"We've found a body. Male, execution style. It's Curtis. Area clear."

I let out a staggered breath… wait if he's dead, where the fuck is Jessica?

"Keep looking," I say to River.

I force myself to focus solely on the task, shutting out the doubts and what-ifs that threaten to consume me.

Suddenly, a distant sound reaches my ears, a faint cry carried on the wind. And I know it's Jessica.

Hope surges through me, overpowering the fear and doubt.

Without hesitation, we quicken our pace, pushing deeper into the depths of the forest.

The undergrowth becomes thicker, and the trees crowd in all around us as if trying to block our path. Branches reach out like skeletal fingers, grasping at our clothes, clawing at our skin. We press on, battling against nature's obstacles, refusing to be deterred.

Finally, we reach a small clearing bathed in the light from the moon. And there, in the centre, is a figure limping haphazardly.

River aims the torch's light towards the figure who tries to run, but it's more of a hobble.

"Jessica!" I lurch forward and start running. "Jessica!" I repeat. Closing in on her, I grab her around the waist and pull her against me. She thrashes out, arms flailing.

"Fuck." I spin her in my arms. Her eyes are wild, unfocused, River holding light upon us like a halo.

Tears streak down her face. "It's me, Noah." Voices sound in my ear, but I don't have time to acknowledge them as I try in vain to calm Jessica down enough to notice it's me.

I don't think she can hear me past her fear, so I grab her hands and bring them to my face, hoping my touch will calm her down enough to bring her back to the moment.

"Jessica," I repeat her name. "I've got you."

And then her arms are around my neck as she plasters herself to my body. I stagger but hold her just as fiercely as she sobs into my chest.

"You're safe, sweet girl. I've got you."

River comes up beside me. "The area is clear, but we need to head back to the other guys. It's been called in," he says, relaying some of what I missed.

Jessica is full-on shaking now, and I step back, pushing her away from my body as she whimpers.

"I just want to help warm you up," I say as I shrug out of my hoodie and pull it on over her head and pull her arms through

Saved by Two

carefully. I don't know if she's hurt, but we need to move right now.

I bend my knees and cup her behind her thighs and lower back, lifting her into my arms.

"Do you want me to carry her?" River asks.

I shake my head. "No, you just lead the way."

Almost twenty minutes later, we find ourselves in a clearing. Jessica looks up at the car and begins to panic in my arms.

"Hey, you're okay. You're safe."

She shakes her head. "No, you don't understand. Curtis wants to use me to pay off his debt."

Caleb is on us before I can reply, and he pulls her into his arms, his face burying in her hair.

"Fuck, are you okay? Are you hurt?"

He looks up at me and reaches out for my face, kissing me hard before focusing back on Jessica.

"Did he hurt you?"

Jessica is sobbing, her words garbled. By the time we've calmed her down, we're surrounded by numerous police vehicles.

They manage to get a statement out of Jessica as a paramedic checks her over in the back of an ambulance. Caleb and I refuse to leave her side, not even when our blood was on fire as she recounted what happened—how he threatened to give her away so she could be used in degrading ways.

"I want to see his body," she says once the officer tells her they have everything they need for the witness statement.

The officer looks uncomfortable, glances at Caleb and me.

"Please, I need to know he's gone."

"I'll have to check with my sergeant." The officer leaves the confines of the ambulance.

I crouch down, cupping Jessica's bruised cheek. "Are you sure, sweet girl?"

She nods. "I need this."

Caleb reaches over and takes her hand in his. "I'm so fucking proud of you, Jessica. What you did to get away—you know how much courage that took?"

Jessica doesn't answer, just waits until the officer returns, nodding her permission.

I help her down the ramp, and Caleb hooks his arm around her waist to keep her off her sprained ankle, and I take her hand in mine, her nails caked in dried mud.

The body is surrounded by tape with markers in several places as we move closer.

Curtis's lifeless body faces up, his eyes wide open—a bullet to the head, one to the chest and one to each kneecap.

Jessica makes no sound as she surveys his body, and then when she's done, she looks at me and Caleb and says, "Can we go home now?"

The officer nods, and we approach the open clearing where our car waits. Jax moved it when they went back for their Land Rover.

Caleb helps her into the back and clips on her seatbelt, sitting beside her.

I spend the entire drive glancing in the rear-view mirror as proof she's back with us and safe.

Chapter Fifty-Four

Caleb

Jessica fell asleep on the way home and was groggy when she woke, which turned into a full-on panic attack. It took us over ten minutes to calm her down enough to get her in the house.

I carry her through the threshold and straight upstairs to our bedroom as she clings to my jumper. Carefully, I sit on the dark blue chaise longue with her cradled in my lap.

Noah rushes into our bathroom and starts running her a bath, then leaves to go back downstairs. She raises her head to look up at me, her face dirty, tear-stained, bruised, and her hair matted to her head.

"I'm so sorry." Fresh tears spring to her eyes, and I wipe them away with the pads of my thumbs. "I should have listened to you," she says with a hiccup. "It's all my fault."

"Jessica, it's not your fault. And you have nothing to apologise for. You're safe now. That's all that matters." I lean down and kiss her forehead.

"You're not mad at me?" she asks, sitting up in my lap.

"No, Jessica. I'm not mad at you." And it's the truth. She wouldn't be the woman I fell in love with if she were anyone else. Am I livid that the cunt took her? Yes. Do I blame her? No.

"I'm mad I wasn't able to protect you."

Her brows furrow. "But you found me. How did you find me?"

I lift her wrist. Her palm scratched and muddy.

"With this." I tap one of the diamonds encrusted on the gold bangle. "One of these is a tracker."

She twists her wrist and studies the diamonds. "I don't understand."

Noah walks in with a tray of mugs and some biscuits, and I carefully lift her off my lap until she's sitting at my side.

He hands her a mug. "Careful, it's hot."

Her hands tremble as she blows softly, taking a tentative sip. Noah hands me mine, holding it by the rim so I can take the handle, and then rushes back into the bathroom to check the bath. When he returns, he sits on her other side.

"What did you mean about a tracker?" she asks, staring at me over the rim of her mug.

I lick my lips, trading a glance with Noah before lowering my eyes back to her.

"When we got you the bangle, we added a special tracker just in case of an emergency. It means we can track your location so long as you're wearing it."

She swallows hard, and I go still, ready for her to tear it off her wrist. Or tell us how wrong it was to do that without her knowledge.

"I hate to think what would have happened if you hadn't." Her eyes dim as she stares ahead, gaze unfocused.

Noah reaches out for her wrist and turns the bangle, his expression contemplative. "We never wanted you to feel violated, and in hindsight, we should have told you."

"So, when you said about not being able to see it—the connection always being there, is that what you meant?"

I nod. "Partly, yes, but as we said, we wanted you to have something tangible from us."

Noah holds out a plate with an array of all her favourite biscuits, and she takes one. Bringing it to her mouth, she nibbles around the edges.

Noah stands, and she startles, almost spilling her tea. I quickly reach out to take it from her trembling hands.

"Shit, sorry." Her voice wobbles.

I place the mug on the floor as Noah gently guides her to her feet. I stand.

"Come on, sweet girl, let's get you in the bath. You'll feel better after."

She limps slightly, keeping the weight off her foot. As he guides her past me, her hand shoots out, and she grabs my hand, entwining our fingers, and I follow them into the bathroom.

Noah turns off the taps, and I let go of her hand and ease her out of Noah's hoodie. She shivers, wrapping her arms around her middle. Under the spotlights of the bathroom, all the marks marring her skin are highlighted. Her top is ripped, and there are marks leading down to her breastbone.

"Do you want to talk about it?" I ask, as vivid memories of her arriving here beaten and bruised swirl through my mind.

Noah steps around to her side and waits for her to answer.

"No, I'm not ready to," she admits, her eyes cast down.

He reaches for her hand and tugs gently for her to drop her hands. "Would you prefer it if we gave you some privacy?"

I hold my breath, my jaw clenching—the thought of leaving her to deal with this on her own eats at my soul.

She looks up, eyes connecting with him, and replies, "No, I don't want to be alone." And as selfish as it sounds, I'm glad because I need to be near her, to prove to myself she's here and that she's safe.

Noah helps her step out of her leggings, and then she removes her top and bra. Her hand moves to her wrist, where she spins the bangle.

"You'll need to keep your hand out of the water," I say, nodding towards her bandaged palm as I help her into the bath.

Scratches on her waist lead lower, and I have to bite back my anger. Her eyes follow mine, and she squirms, trying to turn away from me, but I grip her hip gently to still her.

"Hey, you never have to hide—not from me, not from us."

Her lip trembles as Noah guides her to sit down until she's submerged in the water. He keeps her hand over the edge of the bath.

I reach for a loofah and squeeze body wash into it before gently guiding it over her arm and shoulders. Noah sits on the edge of the other side and starts untangling her hair. Between us, we quickly take care of her until her hair is washed and her skin is free from dirt and grime.

I lay awake, watching Jessica nestled between us and finding comfort in the rise and fall of her chest. It took her hours to drift off, but she's been restless, with small whimpers and bad memories that followed her into her dreams.

"She's going to be okay," Noah whispers, reaching out to my hand that's resting on her stomach. "It's raw, everything that's happened. She just needs time to feel safe again."

I wrap his hand in mine. "How long have you been awake?"

"Not long."

A small smile tugs on my lips. "Were you watching me?" I ask with mock chagrin.

"No more than you watching our girl."

I glance back at her face. "Touché."

Our girl.

He squeezes my hand, and we both fall silent as we watch Jessica.

All I wanted to do today was tell her I love her. It consumed me. But that was before she was taken. And then, when we finally got her home, the words were there on the tip of my tongue, but I couldn't get them out and not because I didn't want to. But because I didn't want the first time to be in the embers of a traumatic event.

I want her to see the truth in my words as I worship her and show how much she means to us.

Chapter Fifty-Five
Noah

Jessica has been going through the motions this past week—eat, sleep, repeat.

As each day passes, she withdraws more and more into herself.

"I fucking hate this." Caleb tugs at his hair, his hands on his head as he paces in front of me in the kitchen.

"Me too, but we need to be patient."

His eyes cut to mine, the blue surrounded by flecks of green and yellow so stark in colour, his lips forming a straight line. "You don't think I know that?"

I refuse to answer him when he's riding himself so hard. Instead, I walk over, grip the back of his neck and squeeze.

"Shit, I'm sorry," he says, his shoulders deflating as he squeezes his eyes closed.

Resting my forehead against his, I take a deep breath. "You don't have to apologise. I get it, believe me, I do."

Pulling back, he kisses me before turning to the coffee machine.

"Morning."

I spin and do a double take. Standing in front of me is Jessica, dressed and freshly showered.

Smiling, I walk over to greet her with a kiss. "Morning, you look nice."

She blushes and gives me a shy smile as Caleb comes over, handing me my coffee before he grips the back of her neck and steals a kiss. "Morning, beautiful. Breakfast?" he asks.

Moving around him, she replies, "I can do it."

I raise my eyebrows and look back to Caleb, who shrugs.

Pulling the loaf of bread from the bread bin, she peers over her shoulder. "Do you want some toast?"

We both shake our heads. "We've already eaten. Thank you, though," Caleb replies.

Leaving her in bed wasn't easy by any means, but working out is also a release, so Caleb and I got a session in this morning while she still slept.

Popping the bread into the toaster, she flicks the kettle on and then turns to face us. We're both standing there staring, and she flushes at the attention.

She takes a deep breath and stills herself before speaking. "So, I have a session with Greta this afternoon at five," she says, fiddling with her hands, eyes flicking between Caleb and me.

I nod and see Caleb do the same out of my peripheral vision. It will be the first time she's left the house.

"That's great?" I say, but it comes out more like a question.

Licking her lips, I can tell she's nervous, and as much as I want to pull her into my arms, I also feel as though she needs the space.

Squaring her shoulders, and on a rushed breath, she says, "And I'm going to go alone." It's impossible not to hear the worry in her voice as she speaks and then quickly averts her eyes. Then surprisingly, Caleb is in front of her in three quick strides, placing his coffee cup behind her on the counter. She squeezes her eyes closed.

He nudges her chin with his index finger until her eyes flutter open, and she stares at him.

"Then we'll support you," he says firmly.

She blinks, taken back, her hazel eyes soft. "You will?"

"Of course, we will," I say as I move up beside him until she is caged in by the two of us.

I reach for her hand and squeeze it gently. Her palm is scabbed over now and healing well.

"Really? You're not going to tell me how selfish I am, especially after what happened last time?"

"Hell no," Caleb replies. "Your strength fucking slays me." I couldn't agree more.

This is a huge milestone for her, and it makes me proud to know that Caleb and I are on the same page.

"I just... I don't know. I thought you might be cross with me because of last time." Her teeth dig into her bottom lip.

I shake my head. "No, sweet girl, not at all. We've been worried about you. What happened was traumatic. We know you need this."

Caleb cups the back of her head. "It's hard to see you suffering in silence, Jessica."

Because that's what she's been doing.

"I'm sorry," she says, her eyes filling with tears.

He lowers his mouth inches from hers. "I know I can be overbearing, and the last thing I want to do is ever make you feel trapped."

She shakes her head. "You don't—" The toaster makes a thwack sound. She startles with a nervous laugh, which somewhat helps defuse some of the tension.

"Noah or I are happy to drop you off or pick you up. Or if you want to get an Uber—whatever you need to feel in control again."

Jessica studies him. It makes me sad when I know she's

searching for an untruth, but I also can't blame her, not after everything she's been through.

"Thank you," she says, and just like that, they move simultaneously, sealing her soft words with a kiss.

He pulls back, and she looks at me shyly as I lean in and kiss her too.

Jessica got an Uber in the end, but that didn't mean Caleb wasn't pacing like a lion in a cage the entire time. Regardless of our feelings, we know this wasn't about us, it was about her.

To keep myself occupied, I decided a celebratory dinner was in order. She might not even be hungry when she gets home, but I wanted to do something anyway, just in case.

I even set the dining table with candles.

I'm in the living room, straightening up the coffee table when I see a book Jessica has been reading. She's dog-eared the pages. I can't help my chuckle, knowing how much that will grate on Caleb's nerves.

Caleb's phone rings, and I glance up to see him frown before he swipes the screen to answer. "Mason?"

Dropping the book, I stand before him as he turns on speaker phone.

"Fuck, sorry, man. I've been out of the country—undercover babysitting gig. What the fuck is going on? Is Jessica okay?"

Before either of us can respond, footsteps alert us to another presence. I didn't even hear the front door.

"Hello, fucking answer me. Is she okay?"

Jessica's eyes shoot to the phone in his hand, her mouth falling open as she rushes forward.

"Mason?"

"Jessica?"

Tears fill her eyes as Caleb presses a button and hands her the phone, her hand trembling when she brings it to her ear.

"Yes, it's me," she says with a choked sob.

She's nodding at something he says. "No, I'm okay, I promise. Caleb and Noah have been taking care of me."

I can't help but smile. How she stares at us as though we're her heroes blows my mind. This woman saved herself not once, but twice. The only hero here is her.

She sits down on the sofa, listening to Mason speak, tears rolling down her cheeks freely, but they're not tears of sadness, they're tears of joy.

Taking Caleb's hand in mine, I tug it gently, nudging my head towards the living room door, and we back away.

Jessica shoots to her feet. "Wait, where are you going?" she asks, pulling the phone away slightly from her ear.

"Just giving you some privacy to speak to your brother," I reply. "If you need us, we'll just be in the kitchen."

Her eyes soften, and she nods. "Okay, thank you," she says as she pulls the phone back to her ear as she sits down.

As soon as we're in the kitchen, Caleb grabs me and embraces me tightly.

"Thank fuck for that," he says, and it's only now I feel some of the tension that's been building finally start to dissipate.

We have no idea where Mason has been or what happened, but seeing Jessica light up and the joy on her face is all that matters.

Chapter Fifty-Six

Jessica

I can't believe Mason will be here tomorrow. It seems like forever since I saw him last, and it's been just under two weeks since I found out he was okay. Hearing his voice and speaking to him was exactly what I needed. He couldn't tell me much, only that he was undercover and out of the country. We've talked since then; he's called me every chance he gets. Yesterday, he told me he'd be back tomorrow to come and get me.

My eyes roam across my bedroom. Even though the guys gutted and refurnished it, I only come here to dress and use the bathroom.

They've shown me what true pleasure is—worshipping me in a way I never thought possible. They know my body better than I do. The truth is, they've ruined me for anyone else. My nights are spent between them, safe in their arms. They're like my own personal weighted blankets. I can't imagine what would have happened if they hadn't opened their home to me. They've been patient and kind, helping me heal, and the thought of losing them makes me feel sick. But these two remarkable men had a life before me. This was never meant to be long-term. I worry it's my selfish need, wanting them both the way I do, using them as emotional crutches.

I pull all my clothes from the dresser, pile them onto the bed, and then pull out the small suitcase from when they took me to Camber Sands. I flip it open and carefully begin to add my clothes.

They've seen to my every need and bought me everything I could want, and even if I could repay them for that, I could never find a way to repay them for their kindness.

I glance at the few shirts I've accumulated from Caleb and Noah, grabbing them off the back of the chair and bringing them to my nose. I close my eyes as I savour their familiar scents. But it's not just them. They smell of me, too. I open my eyes and add them before going into the bathroom and collecting some of my toiletries. The rest I can pack in the morning.

Walking back into the bedroom in a daze, I'm startled by Caleb, and I drop what's in my hands. I scramble to pick them up, my heart jackhammering in my chest.

He's leaning against the doorjamb, his arms over his broad chest, his ankles crossed, with a deep-set frown as he studies me and then the suitcase.

"Going somewhere, little one?"

I swallow and push to my feet, dropping my lotions and bottles on the duvet.

"I was going to tell you and Noah tonight at dinner. Mason is coming to get me tomorrow." But I've been putting it off, not knowing how to broach the subject. Unable to look at him, I add the shampoo and conditioner bottles to the inner partition of the case. Out of my peripheral, I see Caleb push away from the doorway until he's beside me.

His index finger reaches my chin as he lifts my face until I stare at him. I'm trapped in the depths of his stern, intense gaze, his eyes dark, swirling with a mixture of emotions I can't quite decipher.

"And why is Mason coming to get you, exactly?"

I swallow and try to keep my voice level. "He said I could stay with him for a while. Until I find somewhere permanent to live."

"Hmm, I thought that was what you were doing here—with Noah and me."

My heart lurches in my chest; we never discussed this being permanent, but then we never really discussed it at all.

"This was temporary," I reply, and instantly regret it. He appears almost *hurt*. "I just mean, it's time I let you both get back to your lives."

He drops his finger, taking any warmth away as he steps back, his gaze accessing, calculating.

"So, you were just going to pack up your stuff, eat dinner with us, and then drop the bombshell that you were leaving us?" He waves his hand towards the suitcase and then back to me. "Just like that, you were going to leave. Do you not want to be here? Is that it?"

"No, not at all… it's complicated." A word I fucking detest.

He crosses his arms over his chest and raises an eyebrow.

"Oh really, well, how about you enlighten me."

I shake my head, his smell intoxicating, his close proximity confusing my senses. "I don't even know how to explain it…"

His tongue pokes at the inside of his cheek, his entire body tense. "Well, how about you fucking try." I've heard him angry before, but not directly at me. It's intimidating.

"I can't keep doing this thing with you and Noah."

He rears his head back as though I've slapped him. "What?"

I shake my head. *Fuck.*

"I mean that you and Noah are together, and I don't want to be between you."

His brow creases, shooting up to his hairline. "Hmm, and yet if I do recall, one of your favourite places is between us. Us both buried deep inside you, just like last night."

The heat that infuses my skin is almost instant. "That's not what I meant. Physically, we're great together, but I can't keep doing it."

I see the way he clenches his jaw, his eyes probing as he stares me down, and unable to handle the scrutiny any longer, I look away and grab whatever is on the duvet and begin to haphazardly add it to the case to give myself something to do with my trembling hands.

"And why exactly is that? Do you not care about us, is that it?"

Now I feel as though I've taken a physical blow. I glance up from the clothes. "What, no, of course, I care about you, I care about you both a lot, but…"

Expelling a deep breath, his nostrils flare. "But what?"

I lick my lips, swallow, my throat dry, and I pretend to focus on the case. "I care about you both, but you love each other."

Out of my peripheral vision, I see him drop his crossed arms and take a measured step towards me.

"Have we ever made you feel like a third wheel in this dynamic?"

I don't need to think before answering and giving him my attention as I turn to face him. "No, of course not." I've always felt very much included.

He's staring at me now. His gaze is hard and steady, unwavering, the way his face gives nothing away. It's like steel, and yet his eyes are full of emotion. I have to swallow past the lump that forms in my throat.

"Have we ever made you feel less than you deserve, that we only wanted you for sexual pleasure?"

That question stings. "No, of course not."

Flexing his fists, he reaches out and grips my hips, his fingertips pressing into my flesh, not enough to hurt, just enough to keep me still.

"Did we coerce you into doing anything with us you didn't want to do?"

Okay, now his questions are beginning to piss me off.

I cover his hands and try to push them away, unable to think while he's touching me.

"You're making this sound sordid somehow. Everything we did and shared was consensual. Please, don't cheapen what we had."

He moves so fast, the breath leaves me as he backs me against the wall. His face is so close to mine, I can see the speckles of colour around his pupils. And yet he's not touching me. There's a cushion of air between us, letting me know I can move if I want to—I'm not trapped.

"But isn't that what you're doing by implying what we all shared was just purely physical? A chemical reaction to our mutual attraction?"

I turn my face away from him. "No."

"You're lying, Jessica."

Somehow, him calling me out and using my name to do it claws at my chest.

"You want the truth?" I ask, anger lacing my words.

He nods. "Yes."

If he wants to know the truth, I'll tell him.

"Because Caleb, who will be there to catch me when I fall?" The words get stuck in my throat, and my eyes well with tears.

He moves his hands beside my face. "We will, Jessica, because we already fell. We've just been waiting for you to catch up."

I squeeze my eyes closed, the impact of his words like a branding iron searing into my soul.

"Little one, look at me." I can hear the anguish in his voice. "Please don't shy away from this. Please don't close yourself off to me."

He caresses my cheeks with his thumbs, a coaxing touch so

gentle, I open my eyes, failing to blink back the tears he catches with his thumbs.

"You say that now, but I'm still fucked up, Caleb. I still have issues, stuff I need to work through. And nothing about any of this with us is conventional. It won't be easy."

Caleb's expression softens, his eyes roaming over my face. "I know that, and Noah knows that. Nothing worth having will ever be easy. But we're willing to try and face those challenges together. Find a way to make this work between all three of us."

He drops his hands and slowly steps back. He hardly moves, and yet the distance is too much. "Believe me, we want that. We want you. We want you to stay. But if you don't, and you want to leave, I won't stop you."

And with that, he turns and walks away.

I already know I don't want to leave because when given a choice, I realise there no longer is one, not where these two men are concerned. Because I've already lost my heart to them. Nothing about this is going to be linear, but if I can't fight for them, for myself, how can I expect anyone else to?

Chapter Fifty-Seven

Caleb

My entire body is tense as I turn and walk away, leaving Jessica stunned. I won't force her, not ever. I want her to want us the way we want her. I head into the dining room and straight to the small bar in the corner. Grabbing a crystal tumbler, I pour two fingers of whiskey and take a huge gulp.

"Caleb."

I pause the glass to my lips as her hand grips my shoulder, and she tugs. Placing the glass down, I relent and turn to face her.

"I'm sorry. I know I'm a mess, but I also want that. I want the two of you."

I grip the back of her neck. "Are you sure?"

She nods, determination in her gaze, and I cave, my lips crashing against hers in a searing kiss. It's a frenzy as we each strip each other of our clothing until we're left in our underwear.

Gripping her arse, I lift her until she wraps her legs around my hips and then I pin her against the wall.

"Wait," she says breathlessly, turning her face away. I panic, almost dropping her, thinking I've hurt her.

"What about Noah?" she asks, rolling her hips, causing friction between us.

Gripping her chin, probably a little too hard, I make her look at me. "What about him?" I ask.

"He's not here, and we're about to..." She looks down between us, the bulge of my erection heavy in my boxers. "Have sex."

I'm stunned momentarily, lost for words, until she grinds her hips against me, and I groan.

"He won't mind, I promise."

Her eyes study me. "Are you sure?"

I nod. "Would it bother you if I were fucking Noah without you being there?"

She pushes her head back against the wall. "What, no, of course not."

I smile. "Exactly, and neither will he. Now, are you going to get on your knees and take my dick like a good girl?"

My hold on her releases, and she slides down until she kneels before me and pulls down my boxers. I kick them off at my ankles.

There's no teasing as she takes me into her mouth, eyes on me. I watch as she hollows her cheeks and takes my dick like a good girl. I could get lost in her mouth as she pleasures me. But I don't want to come down her throat. I grab her by the shoulders, and she releases me with a pop before I have her standing back against the wall as I drop to my knees, tear her knickers off and pull her hips towards my face.

"Lose the bra and touch your tits while I tongue fuck your cunt."

Her entire body flushes as she does as she's told. I pull her to my mouth and start fucking her with my tongue slowly. She whimpers, and I know how close she is, but I don't give it to her; instead, I force myself to pull away. Tugging her by the wrist, I spin her to the dining room table until her back is to my chest.

I bend her over until her bare breasts are flush against the table and kick her legs apart, keeping one hand on the top of her spine as I line myself up with her wet cunt and drive into her in a deep, hard thrust. She lets out a muffled curse as her nails dig into the polished wood with every hard thrust. She moves over the surface, entirely at my mercy.

"You'll never talk of leaving us again, will you?"

I pull out to the tip and wait for her to answer.

"No, I'm sorry."

Leaning over, I lick a trail over her back as I slam into her again.

"Are you sorry, or are you so desperate to come you'd say anything in this moment?"

I stay rooted inside her, filling her to the hilt, her channel clenching around me, desperate for me to move.

"I'm desperate to come, but it's true I don't want to leave you or Noah," she says, her voice muffled, her cheek pressed against the table.

"So why did you threaten to do it?"

I roll my hip, and she groans, trying to push back against me, but I keep all my weight on her, making it near on impossible. She groans out in frustration.

"Because I don't want this to end. But when you and Noah decide you're done with me? I won't come back from that."

Her words slice my heart.

"Is that what you thought? That we would ever be done with you?"

She tries to shake her head. "No, I don't know. I'm scared."

I almost pull out of her completely. "Scared of us—scared of me?"

"No, the power you have over me, the way you make me feel."

I thrust back deep, and her walls flutter around me, prepping her for an orgasm, one I've been holding at bay. Her wet channel is so primed and ready, desperate for a relief only I can give.

"And how do we make you feel?"

A tear leaks from the corner of her eye, and I lean over her, licking up the sweet and salty trail.

"Like anything is possible, and this is what it could be like to be truly loved."

I freeze at her admission. "And?" I press, needing her to say the words.

There's a long pause of silence, just our heavy breathing. "That I love you both more than I ever thought possible."

Wrapping her hair around my fist, I pull her head up as I lean over, my lips a breath away from hers.

"Fuck, Jessica, we love you, too." I could hold the words back, prolong the torture, but she's already been tortured enough.

"You do?" Her voice is so quiet, I almost don't hear it over the heavy beating of my heart.

I wrap an arm around her waist and pull her up enough to slip a hand between her and the table, seeking out her clit. She groans, arching into me.

"Yes, both of us. You're the piece we never knew was missing."

Working her clit between my index and middle fingers, I roll my hips, hitting the spot deep inside her that drives her absolutely wild.

"You're ours, now and always, if you'll have us."

"Yes," she says, her voice breaking as I continue to thrust into her, bringing her closer and closer to her release.

"Please, Caleb, let me come."

Instead of answering her, I continue to drive into her the way she craves as her tight, soaking-wet channel pulses around me, and I near my own release. Letting go of her hair, I grab her hip to guide each thrust, hitting her in the exact right spot.

"That's it, little one. Let go and come for me."

I pinch her clit just as her walls clench around me, and she lets out a deep sound of pure ecstasy as she tries to reject my cock, but I'm too deep. Instead, she strangles it like a fucking viper suffocating its prey, and I realise she is topping me from the bottom, and I am entirely at her mercy. My release comes so suddenly, I roar out with unbridled pleasure.

"Fuck!" I know she'll likely be left with bruises from the edge of the table and the way I'm gripping her hip, but I can't fucking help it. I feel fucking feral.

I unload everything I have to give into her, filling her to the brim. The sounds are fucking erotic as fuck, and I swear I even black out for a moment. Is she nirvana?

After resting over her spent body, I ease my weight off of her. "Fuck, did I hurt you?" I ask, my voice sounding hoarse.

"No," she replies, trying to catch her breath as I slip free from her, our shared arousal coating her inner thighs, making me want to drop to my knees and lick her clean. Spinning her to face me, I do just that, and there is something savage about my need for her, the way she drives me to the edge of oblivion and beyond.

One of her hands goes to my hair, the other to my shoulder as I hook one of her legs in the crook of my arm.

"Oh. My. God."

I nip at her clit, causing her to cry out as I continue to eat out her pussy, and I know before I'm finished, she will come again.

"Caleb, I'm, shit, it's too much. Stop… no keep, oh fuck, fuck, fu…" The words die on her lips as she lets out a ragged scream, one I swear the neighbours will hear, but I don't give a flying shit. As long as she's satisfied, that's all that matters.

Her orgasm crashes through her, and I keep her pinned where she is as she pulses and convulses tiny tremors before her leg gives out, and I pull her into my lap. I wipe her damp hair away from her face. Her eyes flutter open, and her lips slip into the most content smile I've ever seen.

"Fuck, you're beautiful."

With a trembling hand, she reaches up to my face, wipes some of the residue from my lips, and then cups my cheek. "You are, too," she says, looking at me with unadulterated love and affection—the same way Noah looks at me—and something inside me fuses, and I know it's her soul joining mine. She's a part of me now, just like Noah.

"I love you," I say, brushing the sweat from her temple.

"I love you too," she says, her eyes drifting closed.

Not that I can blame her, we need to work on her stamina, and that was a workout even for me. Smiling, I lift her into my arms and carry her to bed.

Chapter Fifty-Eight

Noah

Walking into the house, I'm met with random items of clothing strewn across the living room, and the smell of sex hangs heavy in the air.

    Caleb texted about an hour ago and told me he caught Jessica packing up her clothes to leave. I almost up and left a very important deal that would have cost my company hundreds of thousands.

    He followed it with a picture of her lying asleep on his chest and told her we loved her.

    I kick off my shoes and make my way upstairs. My belt and tie are already off when I enter our bedroom.

    Both of them are a naked tangle of limbs.

    Dropping my shirt to the floor, I slip out of my trousers and boxers, my dick already hard from the sight before me as I slip into bed beside Jessica.

    I run my fingers up and down her arm. She groans as I wrap an arm around her waist and pull her back against my chest. I just need her skin against mine.

    "Noah," she says sleepily.

    "Yes, sweet girl."

She turns her face to the side until she's looking up at me and gives me the most beautiful smile as her hand reaches up to the back of my head, pulling me down for the sweetest kiss. The taste of both her and Caleb has my erection pressing against her arse.

"Hmm, you taste amazing," I say, pulling back, her lips swollen from kissing Caleb. "So, Caleb says you were going to leave us."

Her face sobers, her contentment slipping. "I was scared about how you both make me feel," she admits.

"And how do we make you feel?" I ask as I lift her leg by the back of the knee, hooking it over my thigh as I rest my erection between the apex of her thighs and then begin to move back and forth slowly.

"Oh, God."

I kiss her cheek. "Jessica, concentrate. How do we make you feel?"

She groans. "You make me feel wanted. You make me feel loved."

I turn her head, capturing her lips with mine, and kiss her hard before pulling away. "Because we do want you, and we do love you."

Her eyes glisten with tears. "I love you, Noah."

"I love you, too."

She squeezes her thighs; my dick grows harder, and I moan.

"Are you sore?" I ask. I can see the marks marring her skin from whatever she and Caleb have been up to, and as much as I want her, it will never be at the expense of causing her unpleasurable pain.

"Only a little, not enough to not want you."

Without waiting any longer, I lift her leg as I line myself up with her slick, waiting entrance and ease in slowly. It's a tighter fit from behind, and the accompanying moan she releases as I slowly thrust inside until I bottom out is sinfully erotic.

And then I begin to move.

Her breaths come out in short pants as I reach around to stroke her clit.

I can already feel her fluttering around me, but I want to look into her eyes when she comes. I pull out, and she whimpers.

"Ride my cock; I want to look into your eyes when you come." I roll onto my back, and when she turns, she straddles me, already reaching between us for my cock as she guides it to her entrance and slowly sinks until I'm deep inside her.

I grab her hips, loving the marks from her and Caleb fucking. "That's it, fuck."

She reaches for my hands and laces our fingers together as she guides them up either side of my head, her body pressed entirely against me in this position.

She moves on my cock so slowly, it's almost agonising. Fuck me, this woman is a temptress. As our pleasure builds, the soft sounds of our breathing are heavy as she rides my cock. She lets go of my hands and sits up, arching her back, her hands resting on my thighs, and I can't look away as I watch how well she takes my cock.

I look up at her hair, a beautiful curtain of loose tendrils around her face and shoulders, and I reach up to play with her breast and give some attention to her nipples.

Her teeth dig in to her lower lip as she throws her head back. I pinch hard, her gaze shooting to mine as I start fucking her hard from below, each thrust deeper.

"That's it, sweet girl, eyes on me."

Sweat coats our skin, and I know she must be exhausted as her limbs tremble. I sit up, and she groans as I slow down before rolling her onto her back. With a satisfied moan, I press deeper, hitting her cervix.

"Fuck," she cries out, lost to the sensations as she grips my arse, her legs hooking behind my back.

"You were made for me—for us," I say as I pull out to the tip before thrusting so deep, she cries out.

And then her hot channel clamps around my cock as she comes, her eyes rolling into the back of her head, her mouth forming an O as she spasms all around me, forcing my release to follow her over the edge. I love the feeling of my cum filling her, and the thought of one day me and Caleb putting a baby in her causes my orgasm to keep going in short, hot tremors.

I collapse on top of her, and she holds me tighter. I know I must be crushing her, so I roll onto my side but refuse to pull out, loving the small aftershock of her channel as it pulses.

Wiping the hair away from her face, I smile when she looks up at me, her eyes sated.

"I love you, Jessica," I say, my mouth moving to hers, a mutual confession leaving her lips.

"I love you too, Noah."

And then I kiss her until my dick grows hard again, and I make slow sweet love to her until she's writhing in my arms and coming all over again.

Looking over her shoulder, I watch Caleb, his tongue poking the inside of his cheek as he leisurely fists his cock up and down. "Did you enjoy the show?" I ask with a wink.

He laughs. "Very much so."

Jessica reaches out behind her, silently asking for his hand, so we're all joined.

I know I'll need to move soon so we can clean up, but just for a little longer, I want to savour this moment.

Jessica

Epilogue

"So let me get this straight," he says, pointing between Caleb and Noah. "You're both fucking my sister?"

I cringe, my cheeks burning. The way Mason says it like that makes it sound so vulgar.

"Watch your damn mouth," Caleb says, his voice hard but otherwise calm as he moves to his feet, fists clenched. "We're in love with your sister. There's a huge difference."

I don't know how this escalated so quickly.

Mason arrived to pick me up. Of course, I forgot to tell him I was staying. After finally admitting my feelings and all the lovemaking last night, I was practically comatose until late morning. Thankfully, I was already showered and dressed, and the guys had cleared the living room of all underwear traces before he arrived.

Suddenly, Mason charges towards Caleb, and I shoot to my feet and jump between them, Mason barely pulling his fist back in time not to make contact.

"Fucking hell, Jess. I could have hurt you."

I'm shaking with adrenaline as Noah pulls me into his side, checking I'm okay.

"You need to calm down, man, or leave." Noah's voice holds no room for argument, and I'd be lying if I said his assertiveness wasn't a turn-on. I glance at my brother and quickly shake the thought away, so not the time.

"So, you're telling me that both of you, who were already in an established relationship, are in love with my sister? You expect me to believe that?"

He's breathing heavily, and if humans could have steam coming out of their ears, he would.

"Yes, why would I fucking lie?" Caleb's calm demeanour is slipping.

"Oh, I don't know, because you're both *fucking my sister*!"

Caleb is the one who lunges forward, grabbing Mason by the throat. "Don't ever talk about her like that again," he grits out.

I gasp, trying to pull away from Noah, but he has me pinned to his side, and I realise he's barely containing his rage. There is way too much testosterone floating around in this house, and I am severely outnumbered.

Enough is enough.

"I am standing right here, in case you hadn't noticed. And I don't appreciate being spoken about like I wasn't."

Caleb glances over, some of his anger dissipating when he looks at me with something akin to pride in his eyes.

"I love them, Mason."

He covers his face with his palm and scrubs it over his short beard.

"Listen, we never took advantage of her. All we've done is try to protect her in your absence. You were the one who said you trusted us implicitly," Noah says.

Mason's shoulders drop. "But she's my sister," he replies, hurt evident in his voice.

Noah looks down at me and smiles, showing off those damn dimples. "Yes, but we have a connection, and I sure as hell won't pretend otherwise. What we have isn't going to be hidden like some kind of sordid little secret. Jessica deserves better than that." Noah cups my cheek affectionately, and my cheeks heat. "Especially after everything she's been through."

Mason groans. "How would you feel if you were in my shoes, man?"

Noah looks at Caleb. It still blows my mind how they can have a conversation without words. Caleb gives Noah a curt nod and replies. "Honestly, initially, I'd be pissed off, protective as shit… but once I thought about it, I'd be glad she found someone like you."

Mason shakes his head.

"Fucking hell, man, tell me how you really feel." I see his lips twitch. "But I swear if either of you so much as makes her cry, even once, I will ruin you, friends or not. There will be no coming back from it."

Noah smiles, letting me go as he steps forward.

"Her happiness is and always will be our priority," he says, offering his hand towards Mason. I think he will ignore it, but to my relief, he clasps it and shakes it before pulling him into a quick hug.

Caleb takes Noah's place as he lowers his voice, but I still hear him. "I'd burn the world to the ground for her if she asked me to."

Resigned, Mason grunts, pulling him into a hug. "So romantic. And on that note, can we at least keep the public displays of affection to a minimum? At least until I have time to wrap my head around this," he says as he releases Caleb with a slap to the back.

I roll my eyes. "As long as you're all in agreement," I say, crossing my arms.

Mason steps forward, opens his arms, and I go willingly as he holds me against his chest.

"I'm so fucking sorry I wasn't here to protect you and didn't vet the bastard properly."

I pull back and look up. "It's not your fault, Mason. But I'm going to be okay, I promise." And when I look at Caleb as he stands beside Noah, I know it's true.

Love has a remarkable ability to mend even the deepest wounds. And with these two men by my side, keeping me balanced, I know we can conquer whatever life throws at us.

Together, we'll create a new definition of love—one that transcends traditional boundaries and embraces the beauty of the unconventional. Our love story is just beginning, and I can't wait to see where it takes us.

Letter to Reader

If you made it this far, thank you so much for reading. I really hope you enjoyed Jessica, Caleb and Noah's love story and these characters resonated with you in some way.

I'd be extremely grateful if you'd consider leaving a review, it doesn't have to be anything wordy, just an honest review or a simple rating, they all mean the world to me.
Amazon
Thank you again for reading.

L SPULLEN
writing dreams into reality

Acknowledgments

I'm going to keep these short and sweet…

Mum, thank you for being my biggest supporter and best friend. I love you.

To those who have stood by me through all the highs and the lows, especially the lows, thank you from the bottom of my heart, I love you.

Special thanks to Crystal, Cassie, Julie, Dusti, Lynz, Ash, Kelly, Willow, Ruth, Kirsten, and Kayleigh, I love you all.

To my small but mighty permanent ARC team, Aelicia, Jessica, Jo, Jenn, Katja & Dorothy, thank you and I love you all. To the new to me ARC readers thank you so much for taking a chance on me and this book.

To all my friends, family and author friends, I love you and thank you.

Harley, my most loyal companion, gone but never forgotten.

To you the readers whether you've been here from the start or are new to me, thank you. I appreciate your support more than you know.

I hope you'll stick around as I continue to write dreams into reality.

Also by L.S. Pullen

Where the Heart Is

Dysfunctional Hearts

Hearts of War

Burning Embers

Midnight Embers

Forever Embers

Cruel Embers

Unforeseen Love

Unpredicted Love

Unexpected Love

Saved by Two

About the Author

L.S.Pullen, aka Leila, was born and raised in North London, but now resides in Peterborough, England. When she's not walking her adopted pooch Luna, you'll likely find her squirrel spotting or taking care of her bunnies, Bucky & Beatrix.

She is passionate about everything books, lover of photography and art. And in true English cliche fashion, loves afternoon tea. No longer working the corporate life, she is currently writing full time and managing a small craft business Cosy Book Stop.

For more books and updates:
lspullen.co.uk

Printed in Great Britain
by Amazon